The Maker of Men
and his Formula

The Maker of Men
and his Formula

by
Jules Hoche

translated, annotated and introduced by
Brian Stableford

A Black Coat Press Book

ISBN 978-1-61227-426-3. First Printing. August 2015. Published by Black Coat Press, an imprint of Hollywood Comics.com, LLC, P.O. Box 17270, Encino, CA 91416. All rights reserved. Except for review purposes, no part of this book may be reproduced or transmitted in any form or by any means, electronic or mechanical, including photocopying, recording, or by any information storage and retrieval system, without permission in writing from the publisher. The stories and characters depicted in this novel are entirely fictional. Printed in the United States of America.

TABLE OF CONTENTS

Introduction 7
THE MAKER OF MEN 15
DOCTOR QUID...192
MEISTER FULT 203
A MECHANICAL COUPLE 238

Introduction

Le Faiseur d'hommes et sa formule by Jules Hoche, here translated as *The Maker of Men and his Formula*, was originally published by Félix Juven in 1906. Jules Hoche was a relatively prolific author with more than twenty books to his name—it is difficult to be sure of the exact number as the Bibliothèque Nationale does not seem to have copies of them all—but no biographical information seems to have been collated in his regard; he has no entry in Wikipedia or any other encyclopedia accessible on line. Nor is Hoche mentioned in Pierre Versins' *Encyclopédie de l'utopie, des voyages extraordinaire et de la science-fiction* (1972), even though he wrote at least three novels that fall within that encyclopedia's purview, one of which—the one translated herein—is one of the most remarkable works of the unusually fecund period that followed the introduction to French readers of the works of H.G. Wells. Presumably, his fiction is so hard to find that Versins never ran across any of the three during his long years as an assiduous collector.

Thanks to the vast multiplicity of documents on the world wide web, however, it is now possible to piece together at least a sketchy biography of an author who appears to be far more interesting than his virtual absence from recorded literary history suggests. He was born in 1858 in Alsace and spent most of not all of his early life in Strasbourg, where he completed his education. Although his name was then spelled Hosch and he spoke German as well as French, he definitely thought of himself as French, and disapproved very strongly of the annexation of Alsace by Germany following the Franco-Prussian War of 1870. In 1917 he published a long nostalgic account of the province and its people, looking forward avidly to the possibility that it might be returned to France when the Great War ended, entitled *En Alsace reconquise*.

Although the Bibliothèque Nationale catalogue does not identify Jules Hoche as Jules Hosch, several recent specialist bibliographies filling in the gap left by Versins and acknowledging his contributions to speculative fiction do; oddly enough, however, none of them note that his contributions to that genre began in the only full-length book he published under his original name, the collection of five stories *Folles amours* [Crazy Amours] (1878). The highly idiosyncratic stories in that collection—gathered under the general rubric of *contes pathologiques*, although two of them also have variant subtitles—not only demonstrate his fervent but somewhat skeptical interest in the scientific perspective, but also his wry and jaundiced attitude to the subject of amour, which he characterizes here, and in many of his later books, as a species of mental aberration in itself, as well as a rich source of neuroses. There is a certain temptation to regard the longest story in the book, "Mathilde"—an account of a passionate but doomed love affair analyzed as a case study in mental pathology—as an autobiographical transfiguration; if so, it might go some way to explaining the ambivalence and perversity of his lifelong fascination, but such inferences are always hazardous, and the suggestion can only be made, as Hoche himself would put it "with all reservations."

At any rate, the author Frenchified his name when his student days concluded and he went to Paris to obtain work as a journalist—a career he followed throughout his working life. His first book under the Hoche signature, *Parisiens chez eux* [Parisians at Home] (1883) was based on interviews he did with various notable individuals—including Jules Verne—in which he paid special attention to their domestic surroundings, attempting to use décor as a guide to character. His first novel was *Le Vice sentimental* [The Sentimental Vice] (1885), a study of amour that is more anthropological than psychopathological, but no less ambivalent than the stories in his earlier collection. From then on he published both fiction and nonfiction on a regular basis. *Parisiens chez eux* was successful, reprinted several times, and his next non-fiction book, a travelogue-cum-anthropological study of Palestine and Syria, *Le Pays des croisades* [The Land of Crusades] (1885) also seems to have done well, but his fiction never seems to have caught on. The most successful of all his books was *Bismarck intime* (1898; tr. as *Bismarck at Home*) which offered a distinctly irreverent account of the great man. The similarly light-hearted *L'Empereur Guillaume II intime* [The Emperor Wilhelm II in Private] (1906) might have done as well had its long-term prospects not suffered somewhat, understandably, from the effects of the Great War.

Hoche tried his hand at feuilleton fiction in the 1880s, but the extent of his dabbling is difficult to ascertain; the one serial of which mention survives, "La Faubourguienne" [approximately, The Slum Girl] (*L'Événement*, 1887), was not reprinted under that title, and perhaps not at all, although there is a possibility that it is the same work as *La Fiancée du trapèze* [presumably The Bride of the Trapeze] (1887). He maintained his ambition to produce more reputable work, however, in the moderately pretentious *Confessions d'un homme de lettres* [Confessions of a Man of Letters] (1890). There was a gap in his production after *La Vie romanesque, Féfée* [The Romantic Life, Féfée] (1892), however, and it was not until after the turn of the century that he suddenly became prolific as a writer of fiction, his preoccupation with the perversities of amorous attraction being elaborately displayed in a cluster of novels, some of which he grouped under the collective rubric *Moeurs d'exception* [Exceptional Mores].

The sequence began with *Saint Lazare, roman social* (1901), a study of the prison to which the prostitutes of Paris were sent when they violated the regulations then imposed on their profession, and the anthropologically-inclined *Chez les îlotes, amours extra-sociales* [Among the Helots; Extrasocial Amours] (1902); it continued with *Le Vice mortel* [The Mortal Vice] (1903), *La Carrière de Lucette* [Lucette's Career] (1903), *La Corruptrice* [The Corruptress] (1904) and *Le Mauvais baiser* [The Evil Kiss] (1905). The photographic essay *Mes 5 femmes, essai de polygamie* [My Five Wives; an

Essay in Polygamy] (1905) might be regarded as an eccentric extension of the set.

Following on directly from that cluster—which might have been written over a longer period but had initial difficulty finding a publisher, *Le Faiseur d'hommes et sa formule* must have seemed a radical departure for Hoche, although it appeared at a time when several other notable novels wholly or partly inspired by Henri Davray's translations of H.G. Wells were published in Paris, including André Couvreur's *Caresco surhomme* (1904)[1], Arnould Galopin's *Le Docteur Oméga* (1906)[2], Charles Derennes' *Le Peuple du pôle* (1907)[3] and Maurice Renard's *Le Docteur Lerne, sous-dieu* (1907)[4], all of which were similarly penned by writers who had no significant track record in *roman scientifique*. Hoche, at least, was returning to territory he had began to explore thirty years before, although it is probable that nobody knew that except him. *Le Faiseur d'hommes et sa formule* is one of the most striking works in the set, and it is difficult to understand why it fell into a greater obscurity than the others.

Like Couvreur, Galopin and Renard, once he had started experimenting with what Renard called "scientific marvel fiction"—a term invented to distinguish "Wellsian" scientific fiction from the previously-dominant "Vernian" species—Hoche was keen to continue, and the list of books by the author included in the preliminary matter of *Le Faiseur d'hommes et sa formule* lists as "sous presse" *Les Bouleverseurs du monde* [The Disruptors of the World], although that work was not, in fact, published by Juven and pre-

---

[1] tr. as *Caresco, Superman*, Black Coat Press, ISBN 978-1-61227-254-2.

[2] tr. as *Doctor Omega*, Black Coat Press, ISBN 978-1-0-9740711-1-4.

[3] tr. as *The People of the Pole*, Black Coat Press, ISBN 978-1-934543-39-9.

[4] tr. as *Doctor Lerne, Subgod*, Black Coat Press, ISBN 978-1-935558-15-6.

sumably was not really "in press." No such title ever appeared, but it seems likely that the intended book is the narrative that appeared from Ferenczi in 1908 as a twenty-episode part-work under the collective title *Gil Dax, Empereur des Airs* [Gil Dax, Emperor of the Air], in a format aimed at younger readers, far more downmarket than the earlier work. His third novel in that vein, published by Albert Méricant, *Le Secret des Paterson* [The Paterson Secret] (1911) is a greatly elaborated and geographically-transplanted version of the basic theme of the comedy "Meister Fult" from *Folles Amours*, which, although recast as a thriller, retains the farcical adaptation of the balcony scene from Romeo and Juliet featured in the original. The novel that followed it up from the same publisher, *Le Mort volant* (1913), is a crime novel with no speculative content.

The Great War inevitably provided Hoche with abundant journalistic work, while putting a damper on his publications in book form, but he seems to have continued to write fiction, and when circumstances eased, he succeeded in publishing the novels *Premier Amour* [First Love] (1917) and *Le Mannequin de cire* [The Wax Doll] (1918) as well as the celebration of Alsace, and he published *Filles d'Alsace* [Daughters of Alsace] (1919), *Fédora* (1919) and *Il faut aimer* [Love is Necessary] (1919) in a rush thereafter. He published a further handful of novels before his death in 1926, including *Le Maquis sentimental* [presumably Sentiment in Hiding] (1922); a thriller involving hypnosis, *L'Effarante aventure* [The Frightening Adventure] (1923); *L'Étrange imposture* [The Strange Imposture] (1923) and *Floria, orpheline de guerre* [Floria, War Orphan] (1925). Little information is available is available about these novels, but that very obscurity, and the fact that the one traceable review of *L'Effarante aventure* describes it as "dangerous for weak imaginations and utterly vain for others" suggests that the author's slide downmarket had continued. It is entirely possible, therefore, that *Le Faiseur d'hommes et sa formule* marked the peak of his achievement, so far as fiction was concerned.

Le Faiseur d'hommes et sa formule is obviously inspired by H.G. Wells' *The Island of Doctor Moreau*, and reproduces the basic structure of Wells' plot, but it is clearly an attempt to go further than Wells in imaginative terms, featuring a much bolder project in the manufacture of human beings, with more complicated results. Whereas Dr. Moreau confined himself to surgical methods of adaptation, Hoche's Dr. Brillat-Dessaigne borrows a project from another notable work of *roman scientifique*, Louis Boussenard's *Les Secrets de Monsieur Synthèse* (1888)[5], which involved starting from scratch—with Ernst Haeckel's hypothetical *urschleim* [primordial slime]—and subjecting it to a process of accelerated evolution. The ultimate success of Monsieur Synthèse's experiment had, however, been momentary and dubious, while Hoche grasped the nettle very firmly, and only begins his story long after the initial experiment has succeeded—but has, perhaps inevitably, run into difficulties in its aftermath.

Indeed, Brillat-Dessaigne goes further than either Moreau or Synthèse aspired to do in trying to elevate lower life-forms to the human level in the great chain of being; he is convinced that his Pure Ones are not merely human, but anticipations of the ultimate humankind, the true culmination of the progressive evolutionary scale. The most interesting feature of the novel, viewed as a *conte philosophique*—it is also a melodrama, with a startlingly extravagant climax—is the fact that the Pure Ones disagree forcefully with their creator's opinion of their superiority. The hypothetical narrator, caught between the two, is not the kind of person who is capable of deciding the dispute, which is thus left wide open for the reader's contemplation, but numerous hints are provided to assist in its pondering. Although tempted to abridge the title of the translation for reasons of economy, I decided against it because the true subject of the story is Brillat-Dessaigne's "formula," not in the sense of the recipe by which he has cooked up his artifi-

---

[5] tr. in *Monsieur Synthesis*, Black Coat Press, ISBN 978-1-61227-161-3.

cial men, but in the sense of his essentially-contentious formula of human perfection.

There is a sense in which Hoche's fascination with the difficulties and perversities of amour lies at the very heart of this story, as it did so many of his works, but it is addressed here in two very distinct ways, whose juxtaposition is only confronted directly in passing, and is effectively left to speak for itself, with an inevitable ambiguity and irony. That might not have assisted the work's popularity—many readers prefer much clearer statements of what an author wants them to think, whether they are prepared to agree or not—but it is certainly arguable that it is a virtue rather than a flaw. Some readers might also have found the novel uncongenial for the same reason that many people found *The Island of Doctor Moreau* uncongenial, in that it is a remarkably violent work featuring death and destruction on a massive scale. To some extent that is forced by the sheer scope of its invention, given that it is the kind of story that requires a "normalizing ending" to obliterate all its innovations, but it has to be admitted that the addition to the schema of the Unclean Ones, in contrast to the Pure Ones, as well opening numerous interesting biological and philosophical questions, adds an element of horrific bizarrerie to the violence of the climax, which some readers might consider excessively garish. After more than a century of melodramatic inflation in the genres of popular imaginative fiction, however, modern readers cannot possibly react with the same shock that some of the original readers might have felt in 1906.

Whatever the novel might have sacrificed in terms of shock value, however, it has lost nothing in terms of its capacity to stimulate and challenge thought and imagination, and it remains one of the outstanding items of the "scientific marvel fiction" of its era. As an interesting addendum, I have appended three of the five stories from *Folles Amours*, all of which have some relevance to the evolution of *roman scientifique*, although only one of them qualifies as "scientific marvel fiction." That one is "Meister Fult," a rather slapdash story, doubtless written by the author in his student days, but fascinating nevertheless, not simply for its imaginative reach but also because its very lack of coherency gives it a surreal absurdist texture far ahead of its time; it is an authentic precursor of Alfred Jarry's endeavors in *roman scientifique*. "Le Docteur Quid," here translated as "Doctor Quid," and "Un Couple mécanique," here translated as "A Mechanical Couple," are equally unusual and ground-breaking in their narrative uses of science, and the latter, in particular, is highly idiosyncratic in its combination of the literal and the metaphorical, not merely in its terminology but in its quasi-allegorical plot. Although they might be regarded as only one step removed from juvenilia, the three short stories are as striking in their own fashion as the novel, and help to round out the reader's perception of a writer who had a truly remarkable way of looking at the world and representing it in fiction.

The translation of *Le Faiseur d'hommes et sa formule* was made from a photocopy of the Juven edition made by Jean-Marc Lofficier from a copy provided by Marc Madouraud. I am very grateful to both of them for enabling me to translate a title of particular interest to me, by virtue of its theme. The translations of the three short stories were made from the copy of the 1878 Dentu edition of *Folles Amours* reproduced on the Bibliothèque Nationale's *gallica* website.

Brian Stableford

THE MAKER OF MEN

I

First, the décor:

The immensity, which is to say, nothing but the sky and the sea, a very blue sea, apparently freed from the primordial physical laws, for, in spite of the universal conflagration, it does not manifest the slightest sign of boiling. And doubtless these things are in that order, in this place—the middle of the Indian Ocean, in the vicinity of Sumatra—for all eternity. That which is not for all eternity, even though participating in the bleak immutability of its frame, and which is merely an entirely transitory accident of the picture, is the frail white boat simulating, at a distance, a smudge on the prestigious canvas, and in which two individuals are sitting face to face, ferociously impassive in appearance: my wife and me.

You know that I am incapable of lying, my dear Jules Hoche; I swear to you that it was at that moment—which is to say, the moment when the mutinous crew of the *Samarang* disembarked us in the middle of the Sunda archipelago—that the very simple plot of our fantastic story had its commencement.[6]

---

[6] Author's note: "In my turn, I feel the need to declare that my stenography reproduces adequately faithfully the story of my friend Maurice d'Autremont; I have even tried hard to conserve the form dear to the narrator, a kind of continuous pedal-note of humor that transforms the words, superbly spanning sentiment and irony, outlining in the same delicate and precise stroke the enormous and the infinitesimally small, the most

Take note also that a tract of sea, in the region of the equator, exactly resembles a tract of sea off Marseille, and that it is necessary, in no matter what latitude, not to expect any new effect from the Ocean unless one has decided firmly, to extract it oneself. For it is only the changing of our environment that magnifies or degrades things, and décor only has the value that we put into it. Personally, I did not put anything into it, deliberately, and my state of mind closely resembled that of an amateur sailor tacking between Nice and Beaulieu.

It was not the same for my wife, whose delightful face, harsh and firm for me alone, had always given me, since our marriage, the sensation of a lovely park with tender pasture, fresh green waves, from which I was separated by a wall bristling with shards of broken bottles—the wall of her almost hateful indifference—but which was allowing, for the moment, an intense curiosity to filter through those shards, as to what I might be thinking about her, and of everything that had happened to us, by her fault.

Because it was her fault, as you can imagine. At forty, a globetrotter like me, who has been around the world three times, no longer dreams of anything but peace and repose in the permanence of a setting that does not vary, and not moving therefrom. And it was certainly with that thought in mind that I had offered myself, in marriage, the delightful jewel that, between the four walls of some small country house, might continue to evoke all the scattered magic in the world.

But think now about all the little girls who, five or six years before the time at which this story begins, were bouncing balls off the walls almost everywhere that there were agglomerations of humanity to contain; imagine that one of those little girls—the prettiest, certainly, and the most mischievous—might perhaps still be playing that insipid game had my afterthought not abruptly could the trajectory of her puerile

---

unusual and the most banal appearances, all the while doing himself the favor of conserving, in the bosom of veritably hallucinatory situations, a relative impassivity."

destiny to make her a wife—my wife—and picture the anger of that little girl, whose ball I confiscated, giving her a million in exchange: a million that I assured her in the form of a dowry, to obtain forgiveness for my age and hers.

What do you expect? I had become so used to paying for everything in gold that the idea had come to me quite naturally of buying the person who would embellish my retreat, rather than searching, perhaps for years, for the improbable chance of finding someone capable of loving me for myself. My wife was only eighteen. But it is not with impunity that one is, in the life of a young woman, the man who brings her prematurely, and perhaps a trifle despotically, out of the era of innocent games. She made me understand that on the very night of our wedding by saying to me, in the calmest fashion in the world: "I shall be your wife, since it is my duty to be, and since I've been obliged to consent to the bargain to which you have, in a way, constrained my parents, but on one sole condition, which is that you will always do my bidding, and never ask me to love you."

I acquiesced, letting her suppose that my way of comprehending our reciprocal duties was not too far removed from her ideal of a heartless doll. She was, moreover, able to put me to the proof. As you can imagine, she did not have to be begged. And that is why she imposed upon me, without hesitation or remorse—on me, whom she knew to be obsessed by a dream of definitive repose in carpet slippers—the insipid chore of a nuptial voyage to the Far East.

I admired her then because, things having turned out badly, and our situation having become almost critical, she was able to remain indifferent, stoical, less preoccupied with the fear that she most certainly have been feeling than those she thought she was inflicting on me, without yielding to the desire, natural among women who have someone to tyrannize, to throw back on me the responsibility for her personal faults.

Take note my dear friend, that I share your opinion; I consider that certain women are exquisite creatures, that it is necessary to love them as much as one can, while being careful not to allow them to become excessively aware of it. You will agree, however, that their sex, viewed as a whole, presents the same inequalities as ours. Save for a rare elite who merit our admiration and our most elevated suffrage, the greater number can only legitimately lay claim to a certain number of kicks up the backside, in order to prevent them from becoming intolerable, not to say dangerous.

I don't say that mine merited being classed in the latter category, but it's certain that she had taken charge of me, with the sole entitlement of my prior tenderness—which is to say, the very reason that confirmed her congenital inferiority.

In any case, our nuptial voyage had just entered a phase so alarming that it seemed to me to be logically bound to end in a denouement ignominious for both of us. A mutiny had, in fact, broken out aboard the small Portuguese ship on which we had taken passage in Malacca. I had intervened, taking the side of the captain, on whom the mutineers were inflicting the most odious treatment, and it was then that we had been disembarked, politely enough, in the vicinity, so the ringleaders said, of a certain island X, the steep shores of which could be distinguished four or five miles away, close to the equator at ninety degrees of longitude—which is to say, on the shipping route traveled by the Australian mailboats.

We were left with the alternatives of marking time there, uncomfortably, while awaiting the first passing steamer, or making for little island X, where French colonists had been established for some years, who could not fail to give a good welcome to two of their compatriots...

All that evidently did not represent a desperate situation, but you'll grant me that it was also not one that warranted a vote of thanks to the Demiurge that holds the threads of our destiny. During the hour and more that I plied the oars, we made rapid progress over a flat sea, and island X was no more than the range of a rifle-shot away. The spectacle of its shores, which one might have thought painted by a master landscape artist, even drew a cry of admiration from my wife. It was then that, already habituated to mistrust her enthusiasms, I let go of the oars in order to turn round and contemplate the scene in my turn.

Truly, the view was delightful. One might have thought that a mysterious curtain had just risen over a magical setting; a low strand appeared, rosy and green, making a kind of bright girdle for a delicate screen of little wooded mountains, whose jagged outline seemed more cheerful than severe, and which might have been taken, at a distance, for a fan of green feathers. In brief, that lost island, designated in the special tablets of our mutineers by the most algebraic and enigmatic letter in the alphabet was a pastel, a miniature.

My wife's eyes, very wide and very blue—a violet-tinted blue—have an astonishing faculty of refraction. Some feminine eyes reflect the sky, the sea, and everything they contemplate; hers break up the luminous rays as surely as a prism, only retaining a kind of luminous dust in the utmost depths of the pupils. That, at least, was what I had found every time I had plunged into her gaze, and it is, I believe, that power of refraction in her eyes that ensures that no one ever knows what she is thinking.

On that score you might tell me that the eyes of other women are generally true mirrors, but that one still doesn't know what they're thinking, because mirrors don't think, and again we'd be in agreement.

When I've added that my wife resembles a little girl in terms of her stature, but that the hardness of her eyes, her quivering nostrils, the willful curve of her slightly plump nose and the imperious arc of her pepper-red lips reveal a temperament of fire and iron, in spite of her blonde hair and a skin as delicate as rose petals, I can't see any possibility of painting a more revealing portrait for you. I know that novelists affect to describe the features of their characters scrupulously, but I don't believe any of them has ever given his readers a sensation of the man or woman he is trying to paint, because the physiognomy of anything whatsoever—even a banal hill, let alone a human face—always escapes those who pretend to fix it with the aid of simple words in the guise of a brush or pencil.

"Do you think?" said my wife, suddenly, "that we'll get out of this sorry adventure safe and sound?"

"I don't believe that our chances would weigh very heavy in the estimation of an insurance company, but after all, if this island X really is inhabited, and if it is by Europeans, especially Frenchmen..."

"By whom do you expect it to be inhabited?"

I hesitated momentarily, very tempted to enlighten her as to certain probabilities supported by the most elementary geographical and ethnographical knowledge—to wit, that quite a few of the islands lost in the Sunda Strait still shelter ferocious cannibals. And in truth, if I didn't yield to that malicious impulse, it was purely out of admiration for the composure she had shown thus far.

"By no one," I replied, simply.

"A desert island!" she said, smiling. "Bah! They no longer exist except in adventure stories; rents are too high everywhere for any abandoned island to exist anywhere without becoming the prey of some entrepreneur of colonial settlement. In any case, we have everything we need to subsist by ourselves while we wait for the next steamer to pick us up and repatriate us."

I nodded my head, but without conviction, occupied precisely with taking an inventory of the limited food supplies, weapons and ammunition that we had been able to bring along with our trunks, hammocks and a few rusty tools that I did not know how to use. From a distance, we must have had the appearance of carrying toward the equator the contents of one of those handcarts containing the precarious possessions of the victim of an eviction from his lodgings. And I clenched my fists in rage at the thought of the wretches who had done us that bad turn, and the dirty Portuguese coaster whose sail had now completely disappeared over the horizon.

Oh, the swine! If only there had been gendarmes in that watery desert! Only the proximity of my two revolvers and my six-shot carbine—a superb weapon bought from the best gun-smith in Paris—defended the coquettish silhouette of the island where we were about to land from the invasive flood of excessively desperate suspicions.

My wife, with her eyes glued to the binoculars, was studying the shore that was getting closer and closer: a beach of fine sand, which the surf was fringing with a line of foam.

"It's delightful," she murmured, "but there's no trace of human beings." Suddenly, however, she uttered an exclamation. "There, in that clump of trees that seem to be falling into the water..."

"Mangroves." I specified.

"...I seemed to catch a glimpse of bare skin...of human skin, perhaps..."

I seized the binoculars in my turn, and made out the form of a creature that plunged precipitately into the branches of the mangrove—rapidly enough, at any rate, for it to be impossible for me to make any judgment as to its species. Was it an animal or a human? Its haste to disappear from the field of the binoculars, if it was not fortuitous, surely indicated a human—and, what is more, a civilized human.

"You see," said my wife. "Those scoundrels were telling the truth."

We landed. We were about to find out.

In the meantime, in order to have the upper hand in any kind of confrontation, I seized my carbine and passed my two revolvers through the flannel belt knotted, for the occasion, over my shirt—for I was in my shirt sleeves, in view of the heat, and with the abstraction of my weapons, believe me, I did not have a martial appearance at all. In Paris, on the boulevards, I would have been taken for a madman, and had it not been for the gravity of the moment, my wife would certainly have made fun of me; she had not allowed far less propitious opportunities to escape.

I think, in reality, that she had not taken an exact account of our situation until the moment when we touched that unknown land, where death might perhaps be lying in wait for us, for I saw her suddenly go pale, and she drew closer to me, talking to me with soft inflexions that I could previously have believed to be absent from her vocal register.

"Are you really sure of yourself, Maurice?" It was the first time that she had called me by my forename.

"As sure of myself as of you," I said, in the same tone, not without smiling internally at the ambiguity of the response.

And we disembarked, our eyes and ears on the alert. It might have been seven o'clock in the evening. It was September, and the sun was declining rapidly over the horizon, ready to plunge between the sky and the sea.

Our first steps on the sand put a group of giant tortoises to flight, and flocks of aquatic birds nesting among the reeds of a marsh that extended into the interior of the island in an inlet. Immediately behind the marsh, whose muddy banks we prudently went around, woody promontories overlooked the strand, overhanging a gorge with gentle slopes carpeted with a dense jungle, in which, it being twice or three times our height, we would have disappeared. There was no trace of a path anywhere, and although I affected the most perfect calm in the laconic responses I opposed to my wife's optimistic hypotheses, I was much less reassured than her, because it appeared increasingly evident to me that if the island was inhabited, it was not by civilized people.

The worst of it was that those accursed promontories were multiplied all along the strand, veritable cliffs some thirty meters high, cutting off the view and allowing nothing to be divined of what might be behind them. At all costs, it was necessary to scale one.

I confided one of the revolvers to my wife, who waited for me by the boat while I risked the climb.

"Above all, my dear Yvonne, no untimely alarms. A gunshot would cause a mighty echo here, and it's not a good idea to attract curiosity-seekers before finding out what race they belong to, and what their intentions might be. Furthermore, it's necessary to be economical with our ammunition."

"All right, but don't be long, Maurice."

Delighted with the new progress implicit in that remark, nuanced by a semblance of tender inflection, I was just setting forth, carrying a kind of boarding ax, which played the role of the machete employed by trappers and pioneers, when a violent sneeze nailed me to the ground, in the pose of comical fury mitigated by distress that I struck every time I was formally menaced by a cold in the head.

"Damn—that's all I needed!"

And I smiled myself at hearing the traditional phrase falling from my lips, naively astonished that a cold in the head could extract exactly the same stupid expression from me on the equator as in Paris.

"Bless you!" mocked Yvonne—but she was almost immediately punished for her sarcastic intention by a sneeze even more violent than mine. At the same time, an acrid taste grabbed us by the throat, and I suddenly understood. After taking a few strides, I had reached a point on the shore from which I could see the mountains of the interior again. My wife followed me.

"Volcanoes!" I said, smiling and indicating the blue-tinted summits, now plumed with pale gleams, very visible in the crepuscular sky.

My joviality annoyed her. "An aggravation of our situation," she groaned.

"Pooh! Inactive volcanoes retired from employment...which is to say, somnolent and three-quarters extinct. Besides which, isn't the worst of possibilities preferable to the certainty of a cold in the head?"

"I don't know—I've never had one."

I drew away rapidly, disdaining to comment on that mendacious assertion, surely a corollary of inveterate feminine coquetry.

The ascension of the cliff was relatively easy, but I bloodied my hands and face as copiously as possible, avoiding the inoffensive thickets of rhododendron and mint, and throwing myself in preference into the ferns and thorny creepers strewn over the plateau. Was it not necessary to acquire a halo of heroism in Yvonne's eyes, in order to smooth out the path of repentance into which she had entered?

In any case, the result of the little expedition was negative. As always happens when one scales unknown cliffs or plateaus, I did not discovery any new horizon, but merely a host of further plateaus and promontories, each more enigmatic than the one before. The part of the island embraced by my gaze seemed to be divided up into a series of thin slices extending more-or-less symmetrically toward the sea. Along their declivities and in their interstices, the virgin forest extended its mystery all the way to the foot of the line of volcanoes—which is to say, over an extent of some fifty or sixty square kilometers, for, although the nearest of those crests was scarcely a league to our left, detaching a buttress that seemed to plunged into the sea, the entire chain curved away, plunging into the interior and only approaching the shore again at the opposite extremity of the island.

Fortunately, my compass enabled me to determine our orientation—or, rather, that of the shore: a splendid beach following the arc of a circle with a southerly exposure, where Frenchmen would certainly have built a casino a long time ago.

"From which you conclude," said my wife, when I had communicated my impressions to her, "that those wretched sailors were mistaken."

"Who can tell? It might perfectly well be the case that the colonists, if they exist, having only cleared the north of the island, have founded some important center on the shore opposite to this one, behind the natural screen formed by the mountain chain."

"The best thing would be to go and see."

"Tomorrow," I replied, without flinching—and we looked at each other with the satisfied expression of people who have just decided an excursion to Saint-Germain or Fontainebleau.

My wife added: "What a pity it is that you've got your trousers in that state."

I made no reply. As soon as I had reappeared, a tender emotion had shone in her eyes, and she had almost taken it upon herself to staunch the blood paling along my scratches, but now she had got a grip on herself again, and doubtless for fear of sliding down the slope of pity, had caught hold of the rips in my trousers. It was, however, her nuptial voyage, and she was my wife! And I was still sufficiently crazy about her to be astonished that our situation, so thorny, and the real perils hanging over us and getting worse—in our conjectures, at least—as night fell, had not yet persuaded her to throw her arms around me and beg my forgiveness.

I don't know whether her imagination was exploring, at the same time, a field adjacent to those reflections; at any rate, she broke our silence to ask me in the most natural tone in the world what arrangements we were going to make to spend the night.

"It's quite simple. I'll disembark our essential luggage and haul the boat up on to the shore as far as that cleft, where we'll have nothing to fear from the tide. We'll install ourselves therein as best we can, and as I'm not sleepy I'll keep watch until dawn while you sleep. Furthermore, there are plenty of dead branches, bamboo and brushwood in the jungle back there. We'll make use of it to light a big fire, which, if it doesn't attract the attention of some steamer or sailing ship, will at least preserve us from indiscreet visits by wild beasts and carnivores, including snakes and mosquitoes."

"That's true—I've read about that in books of illustrious voyages."

"Me too—that's one more thing we have in common, isn't it?"

A mocking smile illuminated her lips, proving that she appreciated the quip.

My work of haulage and the preparations for the fire only took me an hour. However, night had fallen abruptly when I was finally able to sit down next to Yvonne, who had taken her place in the dried-out boat.

"To table!" she said to me, in a tone that was almost good-humored.

And I praised her, not only for having conserved her appetite in such circumstance, but also for having extended condescension to the point of preparing personally, and disposing on a white napkin placed on the central bench of the boat, the tinned food making up our menu.

"I'm a wife like any other," she agreed, a trifle naively.

My God! What was she saying?

Eternal magic of the tropical skies! As the darkness thickened around the ring of flame that protected us, we slid into a torpor, in the profound security poured over us by the tranquil starlight, and the sudden, seemingly religious silence of the nocturnal immensity.

We had abandoned the remains of our dinner to a large red monkey that had been bold enough to approach the line of fires. Its capers amused my wife a great deal; as for me, I appreciated its audacity and its familiarity too, but not without wondering whether they implied the absence of any human beings from the island. I refrained carefully from making my wife party to those reflections. Lying in the bottom of the boat on a bed improvised from clothes and a travel blanket, she was already falling into the semi-consciousness that precedes sleep.

It was only when I was alone with my own thoughts that I finally took account of the fact that there was not, in this accursed adventure, the hundredth part of the gaiety that we had forced ourselves to put into it, and a discouraged, peevish, exasperated lassitude overwhelmed me, to which sleep would have been a hundred times preferable. Why was I not lying down at that moment in the coolness and absolute calm of my little entresol in the Avenue Marceau? When and how would I be able to return to the surroundings that were dear to me, the familiar harness so well-adapted to my quadragenarian eccentricities?

And for the first time, I felt a sentiment of hatred against the woman who was the indirect cause of that odious bifurcation of my destiny.

I had always slept so abominably lightly that in Paris, the squeaking of a mouse reaching me through three floors caused me to sit up in bed. I was, therefore sure of a sleepless night, even though fatigue and ennui were inciting me to drowsiness. Insects—flies and moths—were roasting their wings in the flames and then whirling around us with an enervating sizzle and buzz. On the sand close by, the furtive slithering was audible of more or less heavy and slow-moving beasts, for which I experienced the profoundest disgust. Furthermore, the forest itself was no longer entirely silent, for I had already heard the distant snigger of some wild beast or nocturnal bird on several occasions.

I don't know whether you're like me, but my brain is terribly similar to my stomach; neither of them ever takes the slightest rest. Even at night, while I fall unconscious, they continue to function, emptily, crushing ideas and aliments, populating their leisure and my sleep with frightful nightmares. In case of insomnia it's even worse; indescribable horripilations keep me breathless on the pillow, and I have no other distraction than reading, which I hate.

This time, again—toward midnight, I think—I had recourse to that extreme remedy, hazard having placed it within range of my hand in the form of a copy of *Graziella*, the only volume that my wife had felt obliged to bring on the voyage. Thirty years previously I had read that book without being impressed by the classical beauties that lovers of Lamartine find therein.[7] This time, I opened it with the firm desire to rectify the doubtless-erroneous judgment of the boy of old, and I smiled in thinking about the singular and complicated combination of circumstances that it had required to impose

---

[7] Alphonse de Lamartine's fictionalized memoir of his youth ostensibly tells the story of his first love, for a fisherman's daughter, during his first visit to Italy.

on the man of today the reading of a work once judged tedious by the child he had been.

I reopened it, as I said, ready to reread it with a fervor and an impartiality for which I was praising myself in advance...and less than five minutes later, I was profoundly asleep.

II

When I opened my eyes again, a livid dawn was painting the contours of our shelter with gouache, and I was immediately conscious of the fact that my awakening had not been produced naturally. My first gesture was to reach for the weapons that ought to have been within arm's reach. They were still there.

At the same time as I made that reassuring observation, there was a sound of light, furtive, fleeing footsteps behind me. I turned round and clearly distinguished a human silhouette slipping between the now-extinct fires of the camp. Judging by his accoutrement—an Indian waistcoat and a short skirt retained at the waist by a belt—it had to be a Malay.

While a perfectly legitimate hesitation froze my arms and legs, the individual turned round, and my perplexity changed to amazement. The suspicious and anxious eyes that looked at me for the space of a lightning-flash were gleaming in a white face, completely hairless, the general type of which, rather than its symmetrical outline, at first glance, went back beyond the present time, beyond known races, abstracted from any definition as from any ethnographical classification. I mean that it would not have been possible for me to say whether the strange creature was young or old, male or female, Aryan or Semitic—any of the particularities that are discernible at the first glance in an ordinary visage. At any rate, our gazes had no sooner met than it launched itself beyond the charred branches with a single bound and vanished into the jungle.

As you can imagine, I did not dwell on the more particularly anthropological enigma implicit in the apparition. First of all, it was important to know whether the nocturnal visitor was simply an isolated thief or curious person, or the delegate of a hostile group with which we would soon have a bone to pick.

A rapid inventory of our luggage convinced me that nothing had disappeared—nothing except the book, which I thought at first I had mislaid, but which proved definitively undiscoverable.

I ended up by recalling, moreover, that the mysterious individual had been holding an object in its hand exactly similar to a volume—and a mild hilarity invaded me at the thought that a more-or-less savage individual had thought to skim the cream off the unusual fatalities that had cast us up on this tropical island by filching a terribly soporific book for which a Parisian book-dealer would not have given five centimes.

What followed will prove to you once again how often we are mistaken in the judgment we make of actions whose meaning escapes us, as if life did not offer hazards and diversities such that a book, so denuded of value for the rest of humankind, can become an inestimable treasure in the hands of a predestined individual.

"Why are you laughing?" asked my wife, whom my comings and goings had finally woken up.

"Because I'm cheerful. And I'm cheerful because I have the firm hope that we're soon going to get out of trouble. While you were asleep I've had a look round, and I've discovered a trail of fresh footprints…European footprints…"

"I didn't know you had that talent…"

Me neither. You'll appreciate that it was a white lie, a story improvised to mislead her and permit me to leave on my own in search of the mysterious individual—for a person who was content to steal a book when he could have put his hand on infinitely more precious booty, notably my weapons, could not be a dangerous adversary.

Thus, it was important that I make a friend of him, or at least an auxiliary, as soon as possible, and I had firmly decided to launch myself in his pursuit without wasting a minute. It was necessary, however, to have no thought of taking my wife with me. Even assuming that she would be able to follow me through the jungle, I dared not associate her with such a hazardous expedition. Better to entrust her with guarding the camp; it was, therefore, appropriate not to alarm her, by means of the little lie that represented me as an expert tracker.

"If you're not afraid to guard the house," I said to her, smiling, "I'll go right away—and I'm convinced that within an hour, we'll be informed as to the quality and dispositions of the islanders."

"I won't be afraid...if you promise me not to go too far away."

"Understood. Anyway, I'll leave you the two revolvers, and as I won't go beyond earshot of a detonation, you only have to fire one in case of alarm. But I'm absolutely certain now that the inhabitants of the island are civilized and, in consequence, inoffensive."

She accepted that slightly risky assertion without argument, and we kissed one another...on the forehead. Then, ax in hand and my carbine slung over my shoulder, I left with a light tread.

To my great surprise, it only took me a few minutes to pass through the curtain of jungle that had appeared to me, the previous evening, to fill the whole of the profound cleft of the promontory. The long grass and reeds ceased abruptly, giving way to arborescent ferns in which I naturally lost the trail— visible until then—of my book-thief: a trail that a child could have followed as easily as me, the man not having taken any trouble to hide it, whether because he was disdainful of my pursuit or because he judged it impracticable.

The ferns themselves only grew in a very limited area of the gorge that they transformed into a somber tunnel, the floor of which rose up gradually, and which I took longer than a quarter of an hour to pass through because of piles of sandy or granitic rocks, over which I sometimes stumbled painfully. My eyes gradually got used to the gloom, and I began to see clearly in spite of a new vault, this time of creepers, intercepting the bright light that gilded the upper reaches of the fissure.

Here the route ceased to be tiring; a delightful coolness reigned in the shade of flowery arbors populated by birds. So, even though I had completely lost the trail of the unknown individual, and the walls of the gorge were drawing together in a disquieting fashion, I resolved to continue my route, convinced that it must lead somewhere.

For a little while, in fact, I had been haunted by the near-certainty that humans passed along this natural corridor as often as animals. What am I saying? At times, I had a sensation on the surface of my skin of the proximity of numerous individuals, whose senses were apparently more subtle than mine, since it was impossible for me to grasp the sound of their footfalls, while they perceived my approach and withdrew as I advanced. Doubtless they were companions of the unknown individual, who preferred to beat a retreat rather than confront my presence. But why were they afraid of me? Why, on the other hand, did they seem to be hiding, like owls, in the darkest excavations of this promontory?

Perhaps it was because the low-lying land, broken up by ancient earthquakes, only presented a succession of ravines invaded by the sea. That hypothesis explained why, in the course of my bird's-eye inspection the previous evening, I had not been able to perceive any trace of human activity. But then, how did they know about my approach? How could the theft of the book be explained, and the hectic flight of the strange man who had committed that petty larceny?

Those questions pressed up one another in my vigilant brain, even imposing themselves on my nerves, overexcited by an increasing, almost palpable sense of mystery. Slightly out of breath, I sat down on a block of quartz, and took advantage of it to mop my face copiously, for a steam-bath temperature reigned once again in that part of the corridor, and the flannel if my shirt was soaked. At the same time, I pricked up my ears, and heard quite distinctly, some distance away, the splash of a waterfall, and, closer at hand, a discontinuous rustle, like that of an intermittent rain of sand. Did that rustle come from a retreating troop of humans or a band of monkeys moving along the walls of the ravine, which was sandy in places? I got up and moved forward, almost running this time, in haste to clarify the matter.

A disappointment awaited me; the route was blocked, for after a hundred paces or so the ravine abruptly broadened out and abruptly opened, at a right angle, over a veritable defile of sinister basaltic rock, between the walls of which roared an impetuous river, strewn with rapids, whose course was almost perpendicular to the road I had been following thus far.

However, on examining the river a little more closely, I found that it was more noisy than dangerous. I even observed, with pleasure, that my route continued on the opposite bank; at any rate, directly opposite the place where I stood, there was a crevice very similar to the one from which I had emerged. And as the bed of the river was encumbered at that place by black or micaceous blocks, some of which emerged from the rapids, I concluded that there was a series of stepping stones serving as a passage for all those following the route. Thus, I really was on a genuine path, which led somewhere, and on which I would inevitably end up encountering someone. It was simply a matter of going on.

Crossing the river was relatively easy, for I am still a good jumper, and the stepping stones were no further apart than an ordinary jumping distance. Having arrived on the other bank, which was rather steep. I climbed up to the top in two bounds. And I was already heading for the gaping fissure by means of which—in my imagination, at least—the national route of this strange country continued, when an apparition surged forth from one of the angles of the fissure, the mere sight of which paralyzed me with horror.

Imagine an octopus with a human face, standing upright on one of its tentacles while the others while the other dangle inertly around it. The comparison is perhaps not completely exact, because the upper tentacles were more reminiscent of a mane or branches than prehensile appendages. The entire body, soft and segmented in places, gelatinous and as if diffluent in others, devoid of precise contours, was transparent to the daylight. Denser than the rest, even the head was translucent, at least in certain positions; it constituted a kind of oval bud at the top of the body, but the face, glaucous in appearance, with opaline nacreous gleams here and there, presented regular features, astonishingly human, with an abject, bestial expression, a linear mouth, a fish-like nose, two enormous, fluorescent eyes, split vertically, which were fluttering with a kind of tenderness, all of it veiled by a mysterious halo, one of those blurred patches that one observes on spoiled photographic prints, giving the impression of an image perceived through liquid layers. The tegumentary substance of the monster, tentacles included, was clad in long, rigid tongues, which trembled with a continual spasmodic movement.

It goes without saying that the majority of these details only struck me later, when I had had the opportunity to examine other specimens of the species at closer range. For the moment, my horror was so profound that it abolished any spirit of examination, and I would certainly have fled at top speed if the most elementary prudence had not advised me to put on a brave face. The monster, in any case, had not perceived me yet. When its gaze fell upon me, the impression produced was such that my fear vanished instantly. Its first movement was to leap backwards, and then to throw itself flat on the ground and stick there, as if it would have liked to enter into the surface.

At the same time, I noticed a change in the hue of its body, which suddenly took on the tints of the rocky terrace on which it as encrusted, and I then recalled a host of inferior animals enjoying a mimetic facility that allowed them to take on the color of their ambient environment in order better to evade their enemies. Thus, the monster was afraid of me, and the offensive was entirely indicated. At the first forward step I took, however, it leapt up in a single bound, literally rolled itself into a ball, and, spinning around, drew away, its tentacles and tongues accelerating the movement of rotation that projected it along the river-bank, at the first turning of which it disappeared at a prodigious speed.

I sat down momentarily, half-suffocated by emotion, compressing my heart, which was beating as if to burst, with both hands. I have never had the slightest inclination to superstition, nor to supernatural speculation, and so far as I know, I am utterly refractory to hallucinations. I could not, therefore, believe for a single moment in a fantastic apparition, much less a vision engendered by my nerves or my brain.

I was, in consequence, obliged to admit the reality of a being representing, in the biological order, a bridge between humans and the most primitive mollusks: a being that, in spite of the laws of evolution, had acquired a few human traits while conserving the overall form of a cephalopod. In the final analysis I was forced to conclude that the isles of Sunda, to which we already owe *Pithecanthropus erectus*,[8] that fossil link between man and apes, also contains unknown monsters, very much alive there, teratological exceptions to the animal scale, having escaped the investigations of naturalists just as *Pithecanthropus erectus* itself had, until recently, escaped paleontological excavations.

That would have been all well and good if I had been a scientist on an expedition, for whom the most extraordinary discoveries are as many windfalls susceptible of giving him the key to one more biological enigma. Personally, I was merely a man accomplishing, very reluctantly, the most singular of nuptial voyages. And I was in a hurry—oh, how much!—to see the end of it, rather than desirous of extirpating any of the secrets of that inhospitable island, producing nothing but monsters or dubious specimens of humanity, which were prowling around in search of books to devour, as in the *Apocalypse*.

---

[8] The author inserts a footnote at this point, saying that a note on *Pithecanthropus erectus* has "gone astray." Presumably it would have noted that the discovery of humanoid fossils in Java in 1891 and 1892 by Eugène Dubois had been widely touted as the "missing link" between humans and apes whose existence had been deduced and popularized by the evolutionist Ernst Haeckel. It would not have been able to note that the fossils in question have since been reclassified as *Homo erectus* by the taxonomist Ernst Mayr in 1950.

Those non-very-cheerful reflections having stimulated my energy, I decided to continue my exploration, and without further delay, I penetrated into the fissure at the entrance of which the monster had appeared to me. I was, however, obliged to stop after a further fifty paces. Enormous blocks of black granite, mossy or glazed in streaks, like those in the rapids, were piled up to a height of at least twenty feet—the same height as the walls of the fissure—and there was no doubt at all that they had been extracted from the bed of the torrent and piled up expressly to block the passage. In fact, they rendered it totally impracticable, and I was reflecting on what to do next when the sound of light footfalls coming from the entrance to the fissure caused me to turn around abruptly.

Another monster almost exactly similar to the one I had put to flight was advancing with a prancing gait on two of its tentacles, which it was placing one before the other like human feet.

It had not perceived me because of the gloom prevalent in that part of the corridor, but as I was fearful of its viscous contact I took a few steps in order to emerge from the dark zone. Instantly, the gelatinous being assumed a defensive posture; its tentacles retracted, it rolled itself up as the other hand and began rotating like a wheel, while its tongues, because of the speed it obtained, formed a nimbus around it like a pale cellar, and produced a strident hum.

I made a movement, and the humming ball, which had not progressed until then, shot up the facing wall, which was almost vertical, and disappeared over the summit.

Thus, these hallucinatory beings, found in gyration, combined with the tactile force of their tentacles, pendants or vibratory cilia, a strength and velocity of projection that no other animal possessed, and which freed them almost completely from the law of gravity! And I thought, as an aside, that it was fortunate that their natural inoffensiveness and timorousness—apparently, at least—surpassed their agility, or I would have cut a sorry figure before such adversaries, especially if the idea occurred to them to attack me in numbers.

All those reflections could only increase my profound confusion and mental distress. I have, as you know, traveled a great deal and seen a great deal, and my imagination, extreme in its flexibility, adapts quite easily to the most unexpected and the most extraordinary circumstances. I could not, however, contend this time with the sentiment—more crushing with every passing minute—of my weakness in the presence of the fantastic unknown, in which I had been wallowing since the outset of an expedition whose goal was to find a means of extracting my wife and myself from a situation that was already critical enough in itself.

My wife! It was nearly an hour since I had left her, and it would not have taken much for me to have forgotten her completely, so true is it that violent emotions exercise ravages upon the intellect capable of obliterating the most solid presence of mind. Her image now reinvaded my memory with the force and tenderness inherent in the returns of consciousness that follow certain nightmarish inhibitions. I relived the charm of her first tender kiss—the one she had given me on the forehead at the moment when I left her, and I felt that my duty, before the unknown perils that lay in wait for us, was to return to her immediately and not to leave her again.

Without losing a minute this time, I retraced my steps. I was getting ready to cross the rapids again when, to my great consternation, I saw that the stepping stones no longer existed. The half-immersed rocks with the aid of which I had crossed the river in a few leaps seemed to have been torn up and tumbled along the bed, into muddy depths that had engulfed them. But that was the work of a Titan, and debilitated creatures like those I had seen could not, in spite of their prehensile organs, have accomplished it in such a short time.

The increasingly discouraging inductions that I took from this new mystery were soon increased by the anguish caused by a summary sounding of the water. Its depth was such, at the place where I found myself, that there was no possibility of crossing over other than by swimming, at the risk of being dragged away by the current. Upstream as well as downstream, moreover, that was the only place where there seemed to be a bank; everywhere else the river ran between two vertical walls of rock designing a corridor similar to the one from which I had emerged.

Completely demoralized this time, I nevertheless felt the imperious necessity, even at the peril of my life, of getting to the other side, and I was just about to take off my flannel shirt when, fixing my eyes on the bend formed by the rapids fifty meters downstream, I saw the slender prow of a vessel emerge, the hull of which was still masked by the bend. It was coming upstream with great difficulty, to judge by the slowness with which the visible part of the prow was progressing.

I had time to take a few steps backwards and flatten myself against the angle of the blind corridor in order to be able to observe the newcomers before they saw me.

Two mortal minutes went by, and then the entire boat finally appeared in my visual field. It was manned by six individuals, the sight of whom initially caused me a prodigious surprise. Their dominant feature, in fact, consisted of uniformity, and the almost perfect resemblance of their six equally hairless faces, which reminded me, so far as I could remember it, of the visage of my nocturnal thief. They were, moreover, all dressed in the same costume as him and coiffed in white helmets similar in all respects to the one I was wearing myself.

Their slightly tanned faces had the disconcerting aspect that I had earlier attributed to the absence of any ethnic characteristics; seen at close range, their features expressed nothing but naivety or indifference, although their gaze appeared to me to be melancholy, with the hint of astonished bitterness that is fixed in the eyes of individuals in exile. Again, they did not have any determinable age, nor could I make any conjecture as to their sex, in view of the fact that their chignons and short skirts are common to both sexes in Malaysia. And I could easily have taken them for Malays—of either sex—had my knowledge of the principal Asiatic types not been profound.

Malays are short of stature, muscular but coarsely framed; their bone-structure is that of the primitive peoples of Polynesia, their faces broad, as if flattened, with snub noses. Furthermore, Malays have prominent cheekbones and oblique, dark eyes like those of big cats, shrewd and sly beasts. The soul of a pirate, incompletely freed from cannibal ancestry, floats in their menacing gaze, and the projection of the cheek-bones emphasizes jaws made for breaking bones. The people I had before my eyes were tall and slim, and their general aspect, setting aside the dark chignon and skirt, related them confusedly to a host of present-day civilized types.

Here, permit me to open a parenthesis. I contend, in fact, that homogenous races no longer exist among civilized peoples The European races themselves reproduce all the ethnographic types of the entire world, from the most obvious occidental type to that of the most bestial Oceanian savage. The faces of white negroes, for instance, abound in Europe, and every day we rub shoulders with Parisiennes who, in the feline lines of their faces or their eyes like those of umbrageous beasts, might as well have been born in Malaysia or Polynesia. What conclusion can be drawn from that fact if not that humans really do descend from a single unique stock whose branches are infinitely variable, and persist in reproducing more or less accidentally, in accordance with some law of embryology or atavism, the original type—which is to say, that of the anthropomorphic ape?

That is said in order to make you comprehend that, in spite of the tanned faces of the unknown people, their hair and their slightly misleading costumes, and even in spite of their primitive armaments—an ax and a machete—I was not tempted for a single instant to mistake them for Malays. With the result that by the time the one who appeared to be their leader commanded: "Stop!"—an interjection more English than French, but which nevertheless tickled my natal fibers delightfully—I had firmly resolved to enter into negotiations with them.

They were coming to a standstill alongside the bank when I quit my hiding place. For the sake of prudence, I only advanced a few paces, my right hand riveted to the butt of my carbine.

The effect of my appearance was as bewildering as it was unexpected. With a single movement, the six individuals, standing up and about to disembark, folded themselves in two, applying their chignons to the edge of the boat; then they raised their upper bodies slowly, while keeping their heads bowed in an attitude of devout respect.

Although somewhat stunned and abashed, like any man who suddenly finds himself invested with a prestige for which he cannot perceive the reason, I strove to make my voice form in order to break the ice without compromising anything.

"Do you speak French, my friends?"

"We know no other language," replied the chief, in the purest French.

From then on I was completely reassured. While I was searching for a formula adequate to the situation—which is to say, terms susceptible of initiating them into my critical situation without prejudice to the pedestal on which their fearful respect had placed me, the chief added: "If Monsieur has need of us, let him command."

And with one voice, the group added: "We are the humble servants of the divine."

After everything I had seen in the last hour, my provision of astonishment was very nearly exhausted, so I did not manifest any at all. My deification, however, amused me ferociously, and I had some difficulty aborting into a grimace the ambiguous smile that tugged at my lips. When the crisis had passed, I approached the chief and told him, in a few words, what he needed to know.

While our conversation lasted, I did not lose sight of the others, and for the first time in my life I savored the enjoyment of being literally contemplated by several pairs of ecstatic eyes. My face was dishonored by an indecently uneven and bushy beard, inevitably unkempt—the veritable beard of an

Assyrian god, which would have disgusted me if a mirror had showed me my own image. That beard was, however, the focal point of all those pairs of eyes, the ritual object of their deferential and humiliated admiration. And I had no doubt that the last adjective held the key to the respect I inspired in those implausibly, abominably glabrous individuals—glabrous to the point that one could have counted with the naked eye the rather coarse freckles on their tanned and sun-baked skin. You will see in due course that I was only partly mistaken.

Without further ado, the chief offered me the hospitality of the Pure land—his own land—situated about two kilometers upriver. Understandably, I did not have to be begged to accept it.

In a few words it was agreed that he would wait for me with his people on the little bank, while I went to fetch my wife from the camp. I ought to note in passing the eminent curious detail that the word "wife" seemed to flay his lips; he only made use of it himself after having heard me pronounce it several times and with the hesitation of a schoolboy articulating a word whose meaning and scope his does not know. Out of self-respect I refused the escort that he wanted to attach to me.

Our luggage would, in any case, be conveyed by the personnel of another, larger boat which had just completed, conjointly with theirs, a police patrol on the lower river and which ought to catch up with them at any moment. Their mission consisted of unblocking the course of the rapids over a certain extent and giving chase to the refractory Unclean Ones who persisted in building crossings there and trespassing in the Pure lands.

The word "unclean" struck me and I asked for an explanation, but only obtained one that was very vague and obscure. All that I could gather was that the Unclean Ones, of which I had just encountered two specimens, were "primitive" and "impure" beings whose origin they, the Pure Ones, did not know, or pretended not to know. They had reduced them to slavery, restricting them to a clearly delimited residence, and only communicated with them by certain routes specially adapted for traffic, deliveries of tools, machines and manufactured goods. Access to Pure territory was, moreover formally prohibited to them, as was navigation of the river, for which they manifested, even more than for the sea, a "disorganized" penchant.

In spite of all the precautions taken, however: rigorous repression, river patrols by day and night, the blockage of essential issues from the Unclean Valley by means of artificial landslides, unsubmissive individuals still broke the prohibition, overcoming all the obstacles by means of their extraordinary agility, defying all orders, infesting and degrading the most remote Pure districts, especially those on the coast, until iron reckoned with them.

"For, remember this well," the chief said to me, in conclusion, "firearms can do nothing against the Unclean; bullets go through the without doing them any harm; it is necessary to cut off their heads—*when they have one*. That is the sole means of killing them. If ever you have a quarrel with one of them—although there is no known instance of their attacking a divine—a simple blow with an ax or a machete will rid you of it."

The chief said that coldly, in the uniformly unctuous and puerile tone that seemed to be the natural timbre of his voice—a timbre that was admirably appropriate to his facial expression. A child among us would not have spoken more innocently about crushing a slug, vivisecting a fly or breaking the shell of a snail.

I was somewhat dazed but, I repeat once again, I adapt very rapidly when necessary because, having strong nerves, and a cerebral stomach more adept at savoring the spicy sauces of the extraordinary, even when peppered with the unreal, than digesting the most substantial everyday dishes.

Ballasted with that good advice, I set out toward the camp. I walked briskly this time, feeling, in spite of everything, a hundred times lighter than at the beginning of my expedition. I was bringing good news to my wife. What am I saying? I was bringing her salvation. Thanks to the encounter with those worthy folk, we were going to find ourselves sheltered from all need and all danger, able to await in complete quietude an opportunity for repatriation.

On the way, I applied myself to trying to grasp the significance of the words "unclean," "pure" and "divine" in order to get my bearings within a situation that was somewhat confused, in spite of everything, and whose substratum still escaped me entirely.

Sliding a little further than was appropriate down the slope of humorous hypotheses, I even came to wonder whether the Pure Ones were not simply a colony of escaped lunatics. But no, that was impossible. Their type, unique in the world, their identical faces and silhouettes, which made them, in a sense, interchangeable and devoid of individuality, excluded any banal explanation, surrounding them with a mystery as opaque as the one in which the Unclean Ones existed.

It was that irritating double mystery that I was laboring with all my mental faculties while stumbling through the basaltic blocks of the tunnel of ferns when I heard a humming behind me almost comparable to that of an electric motor. I knew, this time, what—or rather who—was making it, and as it was rather dark I judged it prudent to step side in order not to be knocked down or bowled over by the monster.

It was as well that I did, because it went past me like a tornado, almost brushing me, and leaving behind it a malodorous wake, like a trail of musk, seaweed and brine. Evidently, it had not seen me, but it had scented me in passing, for it suddenly immobilized in the light, at the place where the wood of ferns opened up before the jungle, and I felt faint with horror.

For as long as I live I shall have before my eyes the hideous apparition that pranced amid the long grass, oscillating on its tentacles as if it were marking time, ready to bound forward. The monster had no head, but in the bosom of the swollen cushion that took the place of an abdomen two fleshy peduncles protruded, terminated by faceted eyes, which it darted in all directions, and a snail does with its horns.

Sensing that audacity would pay, I continued to advance. Soon, we were only separated by an interval of a dozen meters, and I was then able to distinguish, through its transparent dermis, immediately above the two peduncles, the sketchy form of two nostrils and a human mouth. The horrible creature grimaced, open-mouthed, and its trembling lips, convulsively, transmitted to brief sonorous vibrations to the bladder, like hiccups.

Suddenly, I lost my head and, seizing my carbine, I fired it almost point-blank into the breast of the human cephalopod. Several holes appeared at the places where the pellets had penetrated, and closed up again almost immediately. The mocking mouth had not ceased to grimace and cluck like a hen laying an egg. Only then did I remember the recommendations of the Pure chief and, grabbing my ax, I launched myself at full tilt toward the monster—which, struck in the body, was literally cut in two.

Curiosity taking precedence over disgust, I leapt forward, and was able to witness a spectacle that seemed magical. The two truncated halves that lay on the ground elongated and stretched toward one another. They ended up fusing together again. But the tentacles had retracted and been subject to a rapid resorption. In less than a minute the sketch of the nostrils and the mouth melted, vanished like an overexposed photographic plate becoming veiled.

I no longer had anything before my eyes now but a trembling, creased, green-tinted mass, secreting a viscous humor with a strong odor. Life, however, was far from having abandoned the monster, for while I leaned over it with a mixture of fear, disgust and I don't know what indescribable pity, I was able to discern, in the diaphanous thickness of the subjacent cells, an intense circulatory flow. Furthermore, under the effect of those internal waves, I saw it decompose, and metamorphose, as if its substance were running backwards through several phases of its evolutionary progress.

It took on, successively, the form of a reptile and then that of a fish, and finally that of a medusa, whose invaginated leaves ended up dissolving into the protoplasmic mass. And nothing any longer remained but a uniform pool of colorless jelly, which began to move gradually through the jungle, doubtless heading for the sea.

At that moment, a piercing scream rang out from the direction of the beach. I recognized my wife's voice, calling for help, and I sprinted in the direction of the camp.

I arrived just in time.

Revolver in hand, my brave Yvonne was holding two Pure Ones at bay—who, as she told me later, had approached her with apparent gestures of cordiality and suddenly, prodigiously intrigued, had begun to palpate her and lift up her garments in the most indecent fashion, like savages who had never seen a European woman. It was then that she had begun to call for help, while aiming the revolver at them—of which, she judged, it would be prudent only to make use as a last resort.

At the same time, the shot I had fired had rung out, and the two Pure Ones, who had leapt backwards at the sight of the revolver, had frozen, as if petrified by terror.

I expected to see them collapse before me in the humiliated ritual posture of the others, but, either because they did not expect any mercy from an angry divine, or because they judged that the best way to escape a punishment was simply to flee, since it would be impossible for me to recognize them later among their peers, they greeted me with an oblique genuflection—the gesture of choirboys in a hurry—and then made off as fast as their legs could carry them.

You can imagine that I did not attempt to delve deeper into an incident of which only the continuation of our story could provide us with an explanation. In any case, my wife did not give me the time. Convinced that my martial appearance alone had sufficed to put her aggressors to flight, she fell upon my breast, conquered forever, glad to hug in her arms the athletic torso that radiated strength and protection.

Entirely given over to those effusions, so new to me, I was in no hurry to reveal my good news. I only resolved to do so after having—somewhat as a marauder, alas—expressed, to the last drop, the ambrosia of that young and overflowing tenderness.

The announcement of the success of my expedition won me further marks of recognition, the duration of which, to my great regret, I was obliged to limit this time, for fear that the Pure Ones who were waiting for us might get impatient and leave without us.

They were true to their word, however, and we found them at their post when we arrived. Their number had doubled, or even tripled, increased by the personnel of the second boat, which had rejoined them in the interim. I noticed in passing that all those individuals, with the exception of the chief, stared at my wife with an intense curiosity, from which the respect that they showed to me seemed excluded: another enigma that we would have to decipher later.

Already, the boats were drawing away from the bank, fraying a passage through the foaming waves. The difficult ascent of the rapids commenced, with its complicated, sometimes dangerous, maneuvers; and as all the Pure Ones, including the chief, were employing the best of their physical and mental energy in that task, there was nothing for us to do, in order not to get in anyone's way, but to chat in low voices about the new phase into which our bizarre nuptial voyage was entering.

III

Today, still, on thinking about it, the impression that dominated the beginning of our sojourn in the land of the Pure is that of an exquisite and excessively short honeymoon. None of the deplorable climatological, geographical, orographical or even ethnographical preoccupations that are normally inseparable from a voyage of any long range came to assail us. The weather was splendid, the heat moderate, the natural surroundings entirely cheerful and perfumed. The brief and frequent periods of rainfall had the effect on us of showers of rosewater, even though the roses were absent, replaced by orchids of all colors with violent perfumes.

What is admirable about the tropics is that the most brutal atmospheric crises are as ephemeral as they are sudden. Once the rain and the thunder have stopped, no trace remains of them, and the sun reappears, triumphant and invincible, as if it has not rained for years and will never rain again. In Europe, by contrast, it is the rain that invariably communicates the discouraging impression of never going to cease, while the disappearing sun incites belief in an irremediable and definitive catastrophe.

Even the mores of our friends, so profoundly different from ours, did not inconvenience us in any fashion, because those differences related to details too intimate for our purely superficial relationship to be affected by them.

It is necessary to say right away that the entire Pure nation was limited to some thirty individuals, and that the districts over which they seemed to reign scarcely measured a dozen kilometers along the two banks of the river. That did not prevent them from talking about their country as people deprived of any notion of comparative geography and inclined to take themselves, and their island, as the center of the universe.

Their *campong*, to make use of the Malay expression, was on the slope of a plateau overlooking the ravines, gorges, defiles and other depressions hollowed out by the plutonian fires on the southern coast of that strange island. Each individual had his hut: a little wooden house ornamented by a flowery belvedere and flanked by a garden. Those huts and their annexes were scattered without any order along the gentle slope of the plateau like the contents of a toy-box overturned by accident. Between these huts, quite distant from one another, there were no comings and goings, no animation at all; the Pure Ones were not neighborly, and only communicated with one another for matters of collective interest: commercial traffic, road maintenance, general policing, etc.

Their exactly similar garments completed the disconcerting uniformity of their silhouettes. My wife had even founded on their interchangeability the anodyne joke of asking me how each of them was able to recognize his own hut, or to recognize himself. They all wore a while jacket and a Malay sarong. A sarong is a very ample piece of calico or cotton draped around the hips, the ends of which are attached at the back after having passed between the legs at knee height, so as to form a kind of culotte-skirt. That costume was completed by an ample Malay belt and a white helmet, the only European note in their uniform.

In that regard, is it not interesting to remark that it is with the head that civilizing modifications begin among exotic populations—modifications that then propagate gradually toward the feet, so that the coiffure is always several years ahead of the rest of the accoutrement, especially of the footwear. That is the case, for example, for the transplanted Chinese who decide to adopt the fashions of the environment in which they live. They wear European hats for a long time while they still persist in wearing the triple-soled Oriental slippers that singularize the feet of the majority of Celestials so strongly. One can say the same of the Japanese.

That psycho-physical law found one sanction more among the Pure Ones in that those enigmatic beings, very

modern in the helmet, French by language, and, in sum, sufficiently civilized in their public actions, only wore precarious
cotton sandals. A few of them even eluded the decisive Rubi-
con of footwear and remained barefoot as much as they could.
But let's pass on.

Now, you might say to me, how is it that you were no
longer anxious to know who these beings were and where they
came from? Remember, my dear friend, the words of Ecclesi-
astes: *there is a time for every purpose*; and don't lose sight of
the exigencies of a honeymoon delayed by several months
from the anticipations of the Code and custom. I was so happy
finally to have conquered my wife, and Yvonne had such a
considerable backlog of felicities to recuperate herself. For
want of other reasons, those would have been sufficient to
justify out mutual insouciance—but we had others.

The most determinate resided in the very character of the
Pure Ones: unsociable, excessively taciturn, deprived of any,
as it were, *impersonal* bonds between them. I believe that they
were ignorant of solidarity and all the sentiments deprived
therefrom. Between themselves they met and quit one another
without a gesture or an amiable word. In any case, they spoke
and gesticulated as little as possible, and never smiled, with
the result that one could not tell whether they were happy—
and perhaps, in reality, they were not, in spite of the proverb
concerning people with no history.

The one who brought us our nourishment, and who was
perhaps not always the same one, disappeared as he had come
without unclenching his teeth. His—let us say *their*—attitude
toward us was nevertheless imprinted with the most obsequi-
ous deference, with a hint of slyness only with regard to my
wife, on whom they never ceased to spy covertly.

I'm abbreviating. What the Pure Ones had of
verdachtlich,[9] in sum, only awoke our analytical curiosity af-

---

[9] Author's note: "German adjective almost equivalent to the
word 'suspect,' but with a less pejorative implication." The
word appears to be rather esoteric in its original language.

ter returning from an excursion to the north, upstream of the first rapids. In that place the river snaked through an idyllic valley illustrated by the triumphant flora of the tropics, which magnified, at that matinal hour, an intensely green light, the delightful light of European underwoods. To begin with, there was an avenue of cinnamon trees, areca palms, tamarinds and cabbage-palms with frail dentellate foliage along the bank, as if crushed beneath a sumptuous curtain of flowering lianas, with glimpses of the freshness of noisy tributary streams. Then the watery road disappeared at a bifurcation, and the avenue rejoined the edge of a wood of cedars and maples.

In the silence and the obscurity—an impressive obscurity and an almost religious silence—reigning in that wood, a thousand little flowers paths were interlaced, felted by delicate mosses that scarcely conserve the imprint of forest. Suddenly, there was a gap in the leafy arches; oblique sunlight glided over a glimpsed grayness. We arrived at the foot of a kind of immense set of crudely-sculpted stone shelves excavated with a range of niches like those designed to contain Buddhas, but absolutely empty.

"A temple," suggested my wife, "from which the gods have moved house."

"Unless they never adopted it as a domicile," I suggested—because there was no evidence that the empty niches had ever contained the images of any divinity. Their pedestals and friezes were, however, illustrated with crude scenes in which the silhouettes of Pure Ones were killing wild beasts and apocalyptic monsters for which the Unclean Ones had undoubtedly furnished the model.

"Perhaps," I said, "they're waiting for their god to die to raise statues to him and worship his image."

"What if they have no god?"

"They certainly take us for divinities."

"Speak for yourself."

That precise reply on Yvonne's part finally spurred us to confront the troubling questions that neither she nor I had yet dared to ask aloud:

Why did my wife seem to be excluded from the veneration of which I was the object?

Why was the worship of the Pure Ones for their god, whoever he might be, not given any external symbol?

How could their absence of individuality be explained, and why could no precise age or definite ethnic filiation be assigned to them?

Why was their social group so restricted?

Why were they totally illiterate?

Who had taught them French?

How were they buried, since there was no cemetery in their territory?

Whence came the Unclean Ones, the teratological, abortive creatures redolent of nightmare and the frying of Hell?

Why were the Pure Ones all hairless, and why were there no women or children among them?

"Perhaps," my wife put in, "it's with that question that we ought to have begun, for it alone can give us the key to the puzzle. I have an idea that the Pure Ones aren't men—which is to say that they can't lay claim to the male sex."

"They're women?"

"Not that either."

"So?"

"They have no sex."

Disturbed, I looked at Yvonne. Her simple logic had just clarified, in a flash, the mystery in which we had been floating with a truly unconsidered quietude. Once again, triumphant feminine perspicacity swept confusion away. At least her explanation illuminated the majority of the dark faces of the Enigma.

Yes, the Pure Ones were asexual beings. That hypothesis alone explained some of the strange things that had struck us.

Everything, moreover, corroborated it: the glabrous faces of the Pure Ones, and their veneration for the beard, which they considered as the absolute and exclusive attribute of virility, and also as an indication of a superior essence that they qualified as divine. Their colorless voices, and their general type, disconcerting at first sight, came precisely from the fact that they were scarcely imprinted by anything except what was common to the two sexes divided by nature, and seemed not so much a compromise between the two but a third sex, perhaps appearing on earth for the first time—for, thinking about their strength, the vigor of their muscles, the light rhythm of their movements, their noble and proud gait, we were not tempted for a single instant to assimilate them to the category of eunuchs.

But what, then? Were they a special product of the island, a biological accident, a temporary error of nature? No, nature is neither an enchantress nor a witch, and she does not proceed by abrupt leaps. Furthermore, she is never deceptive. The Unclean Ones were, in that sense, more "natural" than them, for they at least had ancestors in the lower branches of the genealogical tree of the animals. At any rate, normal human beings deprived of any sexual sign or attribute are never seen.

We were, therefore, obliged, in the final analysis, to consider the Pure Ones as *artificial* beings, in spite of the frisson of terror and repulsion attached to that conjecture. Yes, artificial beings, which a mysterious and perhaps maleficent will, in any case, as omnipotent as that of the God of Bibles, and perhaps more so, as the power of creating all of a piece was only deployed by our Biblical demiurge during the short period of genesis—a human will, in consequence—had extracted these beings from nothingness to project them into normal life, where they would become what they could.

And doubtless it was that same will to which it was necessary to impute the responsibility for the deplorably spoiled trial of the Unclean Ones.

Without pausing on that supreme hypothesis, which gave us vertigo, we then resumed the series of posed equations, successively translating them as functions of the putative x.

A mysterious will, some human Demiurge, had succeeded in fabricating, all of a piece, two categories of viable phenomena.

To those of the first category he had given the name of Pure Ones, because they were asexual and, in consequence, liberated from the base servitudes of the flesh.

The name adopted for the Unclean Ones was justified by contrary analogies.

The Pure Ones had made the beard divine, because their Demiurge was bearded.

Opposite reasons, taken from their own image, explained their absence of respect for female effigies.

The Pure Ones only spoke French because their Demiurge, French himself, had only taught them that language.

"It's very amusing," my wife interjected, "to apply algebra to psychological inductions. Soon we're going to discover that the Demiurge in question is an old scientist with spectacles and white hair, who takes snuff and nourishes himself on frogs' legs."

And we burst out laughing, in spite of an increasing irrational apprehension showing us our pretended mental and material security in the process of dancing a jig on the nearby volcanoes.

In sum, the Pure Ones now appeared to us from the only viewpoint from which they were intelligible. Their creation must date back to a relatively recent epoch, and that explained why they had no cemetery—apparently, at least. As for the absence of women and children, that followed logically from the premises. Only the fact that they were illiterate remained definitely inexplicable, but that point was only of secondary interest.

For the moment, it was becoming urgent to suspend the pursuit of our syllogisms, subtle as they were, to submit the results to the sanction of the Pure Ones themselves. Although we had decided by common accord to prolong our sojourn on that island of dreams, which made a marvelous frame of color, silence and recollection for our nascent honeymoon, an elementary prudence intimated to us that we ought to elucidate its troublesome mysteries as rapidly as possible.

When our excursion was concluded, I went on my own to the chief's hut. I found him sitting on veranda, reading—and good God, with what application! The effort of understanding was making his temples stand out, evoking the image of an Orientalist at grips with a Tamil manuscript.

At the first glance I recognized the volume over which he was poring in that fashion: it was our copy of *Graziella*.

"You found that book in our luggage, didn't you?" I said to him, smiling benevolently in order not to intimidate him.

A bluish halo circled his eyes—doubtless his fashion of blushing. "I was going to return it to you immediately, believe me—but it is so very interesting..."

I didn't give him time to finish.

"Keep it, my friend; I'm only too happy to give it to you, and believe that my gratitude will not be limited to that modest souvenir."

He bowed, and offered me a seat. Without losing sight of the essential objective of my visit, I expressed my astonishment that he was able to read, his comrades seeming considerably less advanced than him.

"Indeed...we have not been taught either to read or to write. So I had unusual difficulties in learning...on my own. I believed that it took me years...or months at least."

Evidently, he was a trifle uncertain of the respective duration of months and years.

"This book," he added, while his eyes were ringed again, "which doubtless seems to you to be simple and easy to read, I can only succeed in understanding by deciphering it sentence by sentence."

There was an embarrassed silence. My gaze wandered over the interior walls of the hut. They were ornamented by colored engravings, apparently cut out of illustrated periodicals.

"Where did you get those pictures?" I asked.

He bowed his head. Then, slowly, with a visible effort, he said: "I found them in the vicinity of the Residence."

"What Residence?"

A further hesitation. The orbits of his eyes had become livid. His index finger pointed northwards. "Out there," he announced, "beyond the mountains."

"So the north of the island is inhabited?"

"Yes."

"Why didn't you say so right away?"

"Because the Father has forbidden us to do so, under the most severe penalties. In any case, no one else has ever disembarked in this island, which belongs to him."

"Who is the Father?"

"He is the Omnipotent. He lives in the Residence with the divines, men made in his image, who command the winds, the lightning, the animals, and all creation."

Although I had expected that response, which confirmed all our hypotheses, I could not help shivering. The chief had stood up, prey to a profound anxiety. He took a few paces on the terrace, and then stopped in front of me.

He went on: "He is the one who created us...to our misfortune. We believe that he also created the Unclean Ones."

"Why do you say *to our misfortune*?"

A further silence; then, the chief articulated, slowly: "I cannot reply to you...at present. First, it is necessary for me to finish reading this book...and then...I will tell you; I will explain everything...and perhaps you will condescend to intercede on our behalf with the Father. Perhaps, I mean, you will deign to be the echo of our legitimate aspirations."

I stopped him with a gesture, estimating that his reticence was casting too much obscurity into our dialogue.

"That's agreed, my friend. I accept with closed eyes the mission that you want to confide to me—all the more willingly because I'm burning with curiosity to meet the extraordinary individual to whom you think you owe the light of day. If he is our compatriot, as I suppose, he will gladly consent to allow us to plead your cause, whatever it is, and furthermore will doubtless furnish us with the means to return to the continent. But once again, why didn't you say something immediately?"

A grimace of pain contorted the chief's features.

"How do I know? We are poor beings plunged in the darkness of the most terrible ignorance...we do not know how to confide to others what is happening within us...the majority of us do not even take account of the fact that they think. And then, listen: I am not entirely sure that dolor exists for us, but I am certain that we do not know pleasure, any pleasure."

As he repeated the assertion that they did not know *any* pleasure, his voice took on a heart-rending tone.

"We are not like other beings. We have so little in common with these men and these women of whom there is question in your books. My companions do not feel...do not feel anything...they are neither joyful nor sad, neither gentle nor violent; they are not passionate about anything whatsoever; they scarcely exist in themselves. Life flows in them, and they perform actions without awareness.

"I swear to you they have no suspicion of the world, the true world. For them, humanity is limited to the little they see of it, and the habitable universe does not extend beyond the limits of this island. I, because I can read, since I have known how to read, I have seen the world is a new light. Your volume has finished opening my eyes, clarifying my doubts, my presentiments...

"I know now than an existence like ours is not worth the trouble of being lived..."

While soliloquizing thus, the unfortunate individual had fallen into his seat, with his forehead in his hand, in front of the volume from which he had extracted these ferments of revolt. His eyes remained dry; his organism doubtless did not include the lachrymal secret—but a bitter rictus creased his beardless cheeks, furrowed his brow and clenched his jaws, giving rise to an image of distress more gripping than that of a man in tears. His natural taciturnity seemed, moreover, to have been exhausted by that oratory effort, for he did not pronounce another syllable.

Impotent to offer him any consolation, and only suspecting, in any case, the real cause of his emotion, I contented myself with shaking his hand; then I left him, almost glad at the idea that the wings of nightmare still deployed in the sky above our imaginary bed—for we slept in the open on the terrace of our hut—were finally about to stop beating.

IV

I have often asked myself since why I left that poor devil, whose rudimentary internal consciousness was perhaps un-
dergoing a unique expansion, so abruptly. Would it not have
been more interesting to observe the first whimperings of his
consciousness in awkward evolution, which was about to loi-
ter along the river with the mischievous gamine who took the
place of womanhood?

Perhaps, but I must say by way of explanation that the
immediate proximity of the chief, especially now that I had
almost determined the truth with regard to his origin, caused
me an insurmountable malaise, somewhat analogous—if one
can compare a physical sensation to a mental one—to the one
I had once felt in the presence of a dog-man presented to me at
the Society of Anthropology.[10]

Then again, I was in a hurry to submit the fresh news to
Yvonne, and pour out the eulogistic tribute due to her triumphant sagacity. Alas, I think today that it was our very ardor to
unwind the reel of mysteries with which Yvonne was toying,
like a kitten, that haste to know everything, to get to the bottom of things, which precipitated the progress of the terrible
catastrophes suspended over the island. I tell myself that, and I
would like to attenuate our responsibility, as far as possible—
but I owe you the truth, my dear friend; otherwise, my story,
especially now that it will shortly arrive at the most frightful
twists and turns, would no longer be worthy of your attention.

The Demiurge of the Pure Ones, the man to whom we referred, in jest, from then on as "the man of the Residence,"
was beginning to take shape in our minds, in the fever of divi-

---

[10] I have translated *homme-chien* literally as "dog-man"; I
cannot find any clue as to what, exactly, the protagonist might
have encountered at the Société d'Anthropologie under that
label.

nation. Only two hypotheses remained in presence, and they were of a secondary order: either he was a great scientist, or he was a trickster on a vast scale. In either case, the scope of the individual and his role advertised a man of genius. In the second hypothesis, moreover, the Unclean Ones remain too enigmatic, so we were obliged to incline toward the first.

A great scientist had found the secret of artificial genesis, of spontaneous creation. He had fabricated a certain number of human specimens, had brought them up as best he could, and then become disinterested in them, as every creator of genius becomes disinterested in the created work once it is finished. As for the Unclean Ones, doubtless they were a trial that had gone awry, a first experiment, an accident independent of his will.

"Yes, that's right," said Yvonne, sarcastically, at that point in our exchange of views. "An accident: someone knocked over the genetic cooking-pot..."

And she did not suspect, all proportions retained, how right she was.

While chatting in the fashion, we had climbed a kind of rocky spur that had been indicated to us the day before, offering a view of the entire Valley of the Unclean.

"In any case," she suddenly added, "if the Unclean Ones didn't exist, it would almost be necessary to invent them, because of the services they render. Look..."

The valley that we had before our eyes was almost parallel to ours, irrigated by a foaming torrent, doubtless a tributary of our river. The narrow and bare plateau whose edges we were following separated the two territories. On the "Unclean side" that edge fell almost vertically, and faced another ridge no less steep. Between those two slopes the Valley of the Unclean was contained, about a kilometer wide, forming a veritable ravine into the depths of which our gaze could not plunge. At either end of that strangulation there was a village. But what a village! The huts of tropical rag-pickers, scattered along the two banks of the torrent, all askew and shaky on their reed supports. Some even gave the impression of having fallen into the water, where they were floating as best they could, wedged on rickety black pillars whose remains were being disputed by the erosion of the waters and the depredations of rodents.

To the west, the sequence of huts suddenly ceased, a spacious avenue heading straight for the foot of one of the hills of the Pure Land, and traversing it by means of a tunnel sealed by a portcullis. It was the busy traffic of that avenue that had provoked my wife's exclamation. Under the surveillance of two indolent Pure sentries who distilled the bleak ennui of our police posts, two uninterrupted files of sketchy, deformed cephalopod beings, some acephalous or horned, were coming and going. Those in the descending file were carrying bales or baskets, in which they lost interest as soon as they had deposited them on the ground, in order to join the ascending file, unconstrained and prancing, all giving the illusion not of a chore accomplished but of a ritual celebrated in a popular ceremony dedicated to the god of free exchange and mutuality.

"Slaves who take things in good part," my wife sneered.

And I thought, privately, that it was doubtless independent of their will, by the sole effect of an instinct as old as the world, that those semi-human monsters illustrated by example the biological maxim by virtue of which labor is the exercise of a natural function. They were monsters even so; worse than that, beings isolated in creation, unable to prevail upon any ancestry, having nothing to expect, nothing to hope for, either from evolution or natural selection—but you will see that I was mistaken about the later point and that their biological future was on the contrary, assured.

Undoubtedly, they only had an embryonic brain and consciousness, and did not even know whether life, existence, is a state preferable to non-existence. Organisms scarcely evolved, at least in their ensemble, they were only connected by vague traits to humanity, whereas, on the other hand, they retained a thousand defects and gross imperfections, of which some were capital, such as their asymmetrical and bestial anatomy. Furthermore, they were mute, following the example of all animals, only emitting gurgles, wails, hums and other inarticulate sounds.

My wife became anxious about my meditative silence and, ever ironic, suggested that the comforting spectacle that we had before our eyes would gain from being seen at close range.

Remembering my unfortunate encounters on the lower river—encounters that I had thought it best to pass over in silence—I brought up the danger that there might be in entering into contact with the rabble of the Unclean, but she was obstinate. A Pure One had told her that they were completely inoffensive. And she added, sarcastically, that if the Unclean were intimidated by the Pure, there was all the more reason why they ought to fear the divine. Then again, finally, were we not both armed, she with a revolver and I with the machete that I had obtained from one of our hosts, and from which I was never separated?

I was obliged to give in, and I cannot deplore that sufficiently today, for the catastrophic outcome of our expedition must certainly have played an influential part in the progress of the redoubtable events that were in preparation.

We reached the tunnel that gave access to the commercial highway that I have just mentioned. The portcullis was lowered, because it was normally only raised in order that merchandise could be carried from the doorway to the wagons sliding on a double iron railway track. The Pure One on guard, however, made no difficulty about opening a postern masking a small lateral passage. He recommended nevertheless that we not stray too far from the zone under surveillance.

That, however, did not suit my wife, whose insatiable curiosity was passionate to see precisely what could not or ought not to be seen—the domestic mores of the Unclean Ones— even more than their life in the open. She dragged me in her wake in the direction of the ravine of which we had seen the somber outline from the height of our observatory. She hoped to surprise the inhabitants of the Valley in their petty intimate and familiar occupations.

We went past a few isolated huts, temporarily unoccupied, whose low-set and warped openings yawned before a fuliginous interior. Those primitive redoubts, made of thatch and reeds, grew like excrescences on the edge of a bleak, silent arm of the stream, among the roots of mangroves, whose rapid growth would certainly end up shoving them into the water. Some of them already seemed to have suffered that fate, for they were positively floating on the bundles of bamboo that served as their supports. In certain places the water had dried up and the hut was simply resting on mud, or encrusted on a foundation of rhizophores.

The majority of these aquatic refuges served as a habitat for a species of small and hideous cephalopods, the embryonic heads and clinging pseudopods of which we saw several times between the reeds of the roofs and the floats. Were they the true owners of merely temporary guests?

On the threshold of one of those floating hovels, infinitely decayed, rotten and dilapidated, we chanced to witness a spectacle that settled the question without leaving room for the slightest doubt. A scaly, horned Unclean One with the face of a crab suddenly surged forth, grabbed one of those parasites, skinned it alive in a trice, and then, sitting on its fundament—which is to say, the folded and considerably reduced caudal appendage, like that of a crab—progressively gobbled it up, until the very last tentacle had disappeared between its sticky palps, which quivered with pleasure: a titillation whose astonishing clockwork motion my wife admired for a long time.

We left that almost deserted region where the vegetation grew, not between the paving stones but on the water itself, which ended up disappearing beneath nenuphars and lotuses. We saw other empty huts and other arms of marshy water, where a rotten odor floated that seemed to be the odor of the stagnant water itself.

A large silent area solicited us because plump black pigs were wandering there, amid the discouraged prowling of two errant dogs in quest of improbable nourishment.

We were already thinking that we had gone astray, for we had been wandering for nearly an hour in that nauseating territory, when we finally perceived the entrance to the ravine that we had decided to explore. One might have thought it a hole of triangular verdure opening over a narrow thalweg of pink earth. The path followed the sinuosities of a torrent scarcely detectable under the tangle of branches, in which true miniature humans, jolly blond and bearded monkeys, were gamboling.

We plunged into it. Nothing moved. The silence became even more profound; at the most we heard behind us the particular crepitation, the infinitely light and tentative rustling that distinguished the tread of an isolated Unclean One. Strollers were no less rare here than elsewhere.

The path suddenly inclined in a shallow slope. The sky was almost effaced. Sordid huts emerged from the warm, dense shadows of the ravine; unreal warts growing between the multiple trunks of fig-trees, some seemingly suspended from the low braches of the self-reproducing trees, others one might have thought carved out of the rock, or perched more highly still, showing a fragment of a precarious and frowning roof, half buried under dangling lianas.

In one of those low huts a frightful spectacle was offered. An acephalous Unclean One was sitting between a bark receptacle in which an unspeakable green jelly was quivering, and a heap of no less sickening segments of snakes or sliced-up and peeled cephalopods. It was picking up the pieces one by one, dipping them in the jelly, and then plunging them into a circular depression that was visible in the center of its abdomen—a navel, mouth or eliminatory passage; it was impossible to tell, so abject was its form. The depression hollowed out into a funnel, and the aliment was drawn into the flesh, which closed over it: a system of digestion and nutrition that as doubtless raid and convenient, but which was too reminiscent of the mouth-cloaca of primitive Monera.[11]

"And yet," my wife observed, ever prompt in whimsy, "who can tell whether such a simple digestive apparatus, acquired by humans, might not liberate their intellectual faculties from the eternal tyranny of the stomach?"

I was about to protest on behalf of my stomachal mind, which I deemed to be as interesting, if not as noble, as the other, when Yvonne nudged me with her elbow.

On the threshold of another lair, two insignificant creatures were prancing face to face. They approached one another and there was a moment of hesitation, of solemn emotion, translated by the grotesque trepidation of their tentacles. Then they came together and, through the tangle of the diaphanous limbs we discerned their two conjugated bodies, blended together, and which, materially, now formed a single whole.

A prodigious spectacle, resuscitating the earliest ages of animal genesis! Was that not the simple mode of conjugation of the protozoa? And what was about to become of that instantaneous, miraculous metamorphosis of two beings into one?

I had advanced to the very threshold of the hut. The amorphous mass was no more now than a unique organism through which intense circulatory currents ran. After a few minutes, a tremor agitated the internal cells of the being, intensified, and was localized at a precise point, which appeared to me to swell up gradually. Was I taking for a reality the ar-

---

[11] The term *Monera* is nowadays used to refer to a realm of prokaryotic organisms (i.e., organisms whose cells have no nuclear membrane), but at the time the present novel was written it was a hypothetical term invented by Ernst Haeckel to describe the most primitive organisms in his "evolutionary tree." The protagonist's reference is to the single aperture employed for ingestion and excretion possessed by such primitive organisms as the hydra, then frequently cited as a kind of archetypal primitive organism analogous to the ancestors of all animals.

dent desire that I had to see the principles of reproduction by budding made concrete and verified before my eyes? At any rate, my scientific curiosity wanted satisfaction, and I then had the idea of repeating the barbaric experiment that had marked my first expedition into the island's interior.

Without the slightest suspicion of the frightful danger that I was about to bring down on our heads, I drew my machete and cleaved the gelatinous mass from top to bottom.

I ought to declare in my justification that the latter, increasingly amorphous, had completely ceased to give me the impression of a living being. Already, remembering what had happened in the jungle and savoring the absurd vanity that magnified didactic actions – the vanity of the pedantic schoolmaster and amphitheater show-off—I was announcing in advance to Yvonne the strange phenomena that were about to be produced before her eyes when a kind of strident and savage racket burst out behind us.

Turning round, I saw a large form moving between the trees—doubtless the being that I had heard walking behind us. But it turned its back on us and, in the gloom, seemed to be drawing away rather than moving toward us, while bellowing in an ear-splitting fashion.

Very sensitive, with her habitual intuition of the imminent, every time that imminent deviated from the norm, Yvonne was the first to sense the threat in the air. She asked me whether I didn't think that we ought to quit the theater of my sad exploit immediately—but I reassured her, sniggering, and offered the opinion that the fleeing monster was afraid for itself, with its osprey-like screech. She insisted, however, that we should go, and as she took me by the arm, I yielded, regretfully dismissing the pedantic teacher astride my intellect and tongue, ready to interpret the magnificent lesson in transformist theory consequent on the thrust of my blade.

We had scarcely taken a few paces when Yvonne stopped me with a pressure on my elbow and said: "We have to go back."

My gaze traveled up the slope of the ravine. The monster was now outlined, motionless, in the bright orb of the entrance, and was howling with all its might. Distant clamors were responding to it in the same fashion, even more frightening because we could not see the beings uttering them. We stopped advancing in order to take stock.

In a matter of seconds the voices appeared to have come considerably closer, and a frisson seized us at the thought that we were under threat.

"It would be imprudent, I think," my wife said, "to continue in this direction. Better to go back and go deeper into the ravine, until we can find an exit to the Pure hills."

That was, in fact, what we did, straining our ears—not without a commencement of apprehension that we dared not admit, regarding the frightful tumult that was filling the ravine behind us. It rose up in fits into a furious crescendo, and then, abruptly, there was a deathly silence—a silence of several seconds, more terrifying than the rest.

In the interval of one of those silences a hum passed through the trees, against the overhanging wall, and two gray horns poked through the lianas, at the end of which were two eyes that peered us with a ferocious expression. I say "peered" because the triviality of the term almost conjures up the basely grotesque nuance with which the entire tragedy was impregnated, but the slang term "gawk," inherently more ignoble, perhaps conveys it better.

We now found ourselves in an increasingly restricted and dark section of the defile, and our situation might have become critical had a lateral bend not offered to facilitate our retreat. Not that we were really afraid of the monsters, by we dreaded—my wife especially—their viscous and stinking contact. The atrocious din was, however, getting closer by the minute. Although we were out of breath and soaked in sweat, we started to run, scrutinizing as we passed by the slightest projections in the rock.

Fortunately, my wife was wearing a culotte-skirt, which did not hamper the movement of her legs, and we were thus able to run for quite a long distance. How long would it go on? I had no idea, but when we finally thought that we were safe because the sky had reappeared in a gap in the trees and creepers, which ceased to form a vault, it transpired that we were trapped.

A hundred paces further on, in fact, an enormous rock-fall of quartz terminated the ravine in a dead end. We must have reached one of the points of the frontier that the Pure Ones blocked, in the fashion I have described, and I knew from experience that it was futile to attempt to climb the steep slopes, where neither the hands nor the feel could find any purpose.

The flood of monsters was now arriving on our heels with a frenetic clamor compounded out of shrill ululations, like the sobs of a nocturnal bird, which chilled us with fear. Doubtless they were celebrating in advance the certain climax of the hunt, knowing that we no longer had any means of escaping them.

A few trunks of fig-trees served to hide us momentarily from their sight, but when they were almost upon us, I said to my wife: "I'm going to show myself in the full light. Perhaps my bearded face will hold them in respect. Load your revolver, and if they continue to advance, fire into the mass."

With one bound I placed myself in the middle of the path, facing the braying horde, but my body froze in my veins at the sight of the one leading the host. It was a half-fossilized larva of a man, with arms and legs like ours, an imbricated skin covered with ichthyosis, a stitched, varicose, mangled face in which two nyctalopic eyes were blinking, and whose lips and nose, as if ossified, were combined in a raptorial beak. The head, scarcely attached to the torso by a kind of fibrous bundle, was wrapped in a sheet of hair the color of rotten seaweed. Surely that one had nothing in common with the Unclean Ones. Where had it come from, and why was it at their head?

Everything, in the meantime, suggested that it was the most dangerous of our assailants. It marched straight toward me, uttering raucous grunts, and a hideous fluttering of its triple eyelids, inconvenienced by the diffuse light reflected from the rocks. It only stopped when it sensed in front of its face the air current produced by the circling of my blade.

At the same time, a detonation rang out in the nearby branches, reverberating in the depths of the gorge in formidable echoes, and I saw one of the monster's scales shatter—but the bullet had doubtless only ricocheted from its filthy armor, for it did not flinch.

My wife discharged the other five shots from her weapon in quick succession, at the creature or its entourage, without obtaining any other result than a deafening din.

Our aggressors responded by yelping, croaking, bellowing and jostling one another in such a way as incessantly to narrow the space that separated us from them. Some of them, drowned in the melee, climbed on the backs or shoulders of their neighbors, brandishing their impotent tentacles at us. There were some who chose that aerial route to reach the first rank, where their improvised mounts caused them to fall by shaking them off, and trampled them underfoot.

The entire ravine was now billowing and swarming, invaded by legions of those sickening creatures, which came running without knowing why, without understanding, perhaps obedient to the instinctive pressure of panic, which already, in the times of animal battles for the possession of territory, had to group individuals of the same species together for salvation or destruction. The air had become suffocating, unbreathable, and the host of monsters continued to grow as newcomers incessantly arrived at the entrance to the gully. Every path up above must have been disgorging them in hundreds.

At one moment, a few virtuosos scattered in the crowd started forming wheels and gyrating, flying like dull bolides through the branches of fig trees and along the asperities of the rocky wall. Then a band of large monkeys, frightened by that infernal vision, launched themselves out of the somber foliage, grabbing the acrobats and tearing them to pieces. The bulk of the assailants appeared to weaken and disband.

I judged that the moment had come to act. A little audacity and a few good knife-thrusts might convert the panic that had just burst out into a stampede. But my simian auxiliaries had already disappeared. To complete my misfortune, my blade snapped in two against the shoulder of the being with the head of a scarecrow. Its beak sketched an atrocious snigger, and with its palmate paw, with long hooked and clawed fingers, it drew the horde's attention derisively to the stump of the blade that remained in my hand. A clamor of victory underlined the gesture, and a new surge by the monsters covered the small area that the hideous tide had left vacant until then.

I understood that we were irredeemably doomed.

I threw myself in front of my wife, who was half-dead with terror, and made a rampart of my body, while striking at our assailants at random, with all the energy of despair. I felled a few; others were pierced through by my broken blade—but I knew full well that sooner or later, I would succumb to the weight of numbers.

I remember that in that terrible moment, when my life flashed before my eyes, an infinite regret gripped me: that of seeing my honeymoon abruptly interrupted by those brutes, who had no idea how difficult it had been for me to edify it.

And why did they want my death? Because, moved by a curiosity that was perfectly legitimate, since it was scientific, I had sought to discover the secret of their genesis.

The critical phases of our life have a kind of light of their own, more dazzling than lightning, which preferentially outlines the tenuous ridges of our consciousness, with its essential folds. Thus, the puerile doubt I had had regarding the legitimacy of the machete-slash that had killed a couple of Unclean Ones in the process of budding, was gradually grafted on to my amorous regrets, and remained the unique pivot of my supreme meditations.

Everything that happened thereafter has the effect today of a dream—or the end of a nightmare, if you wish. The old scarecrow reappears at times with a fragment of quartz in his hand, and takes aim at me so adroitly that he hits me on the right elbow—an extremely sensitive spot, as you know. The stump of the blade escapes me; I'm disarmed. The entire infamous pack rushes upon us with savage cries, a pullulation of human rats, and I can already feel their sticky and fetid contact on my skin. Sly tentacles palpate my garments, applying suckers to my skin, winding around my limbs; others, lashing the air, seek to seize us by the neck and by the hair.

However, I still have one arm free, and that arm thumps, staves in, squashes; crania burst with a soft sound, spreading the milky ichor of their brains over my garments; carapaces shatter, eyes are popped out; a sticky jelly trickles and drips viscously where my boots are slipping and turning...

But my strength is exhausted, I'm out of breath, deafened by the piston-thrusts of my own arteries—and the fecal breath of the monsters is blurring my consciousness...

I close my eyes in order not to see anything any longer...

And all of a sudden, I open them again.

A salvo of gunfire has just made the air vibrate up above, at the stop of the slope down which the howling flood poured; then a succession of profound, lugubrious appeals, like those of a powerful gong, make the walls of the gorge resonate. The tumult of the Unclean Ones dies down, as if by magic. As far as my eyes can see, their turbulent waves seem to have fallen flat.

At the first stroke of the gong, I felt the odious grips that were polluting my body and paralyzing my limbs relax The gigantic serpent of beings in delirium that was writhing from one end of the gorge to the other has been abruptly immobilized; its coils, which were writhing a minute ago, are frozen; one might think that it has been stunned by the formidable sounds that are making the air tremble and groan.

A further volley of strokes of the gong restores them to movement, but in the inverse direction...

I breathe. There is a general rout. The old lemur[12] has vanished like a specter. With a single uniform surge the monsters flood back toward the top of the slope, and their backs, bladders that roll and heave, huddled, flat and wan, crowd into the narrow passages, simulating from a distance the undulations of an immense reptile in flight.

That is because, in the distance, human silhouettes— truly human, these—have just appeared, threatening, brandishing blades that glitter in the sunlight. It is the Pure Ones. They cannot join us at first, hampered as they are by the fleeing host. For minutes that seem to be centuries to us, they remain immobile, as if entangled by the hideous swarm that divides around the obstacle and joins up again behind it.

I observe that they are not striking, but are content to whirl their weapons terribly over the heads of the filthy livestock, whose heads are seen to dip momentarily under the mortal wind that brushes them, to rise up again immediately and then bow down again, as if hypnotized, and disappear into the confusion of the rout.

A few moment later our liberators are in front of us, but our emotion is such, on either side, that no explanation is possible. It could not be heard, in any case because the tocsin of the gong continues to resound from the head of the valley, and it is mutely that we set out follow the handful of brave men who have just saved our lives.

My head is reeling slightly now, and I gaze dazedly at my clothes, ripped to shreds and polluted. Yvonne's reaction is more intense; she has fainted, and when she comes round,

---

[12] It is not obvious how the creature described warrants description as a *lémurien* [lemur], although the term is clearly not being used in the strict biological sense, but merely employed to give an implication of the exceedingly primitive, with regard to human ancestry. Nor is it obvious why the narrator applies the terms *fossile* [fossil] and *larve* [larva] to it, except that they share similar implications.

she feels so weak that I decide to carry her, in order not to slow us down.

The entire locale had fallen back into a flat calm. The last vibrations of the tocsin die away. It really is a gong, the chief explains; the Pure Ones readily make use of that instrument against the Unclean Ones, in whom it provokes a kind of hypnotic stupidity, especially if the sonorous waves are associated with luminous waves: vivid flames, flashing blades, metallic reflections, etc.

The Valley is still slightly disturbed, but our approach caused a gap to open everywhere, and the avenue that leads to the Pure land appears to be completely deserted at the moment we steep on to it.

Soon, my wife and I find ourselves safe and sound back in our hut, where Yvonne finally dissolves in tears, her dear weeping face glued to my cheek, her arms enlacing me in a desperate embrace.

She begs me not to stay one day longer in this infernal valley, all the more so as we are now certain of finding out there, beyond the mountains, civilized beings, veritable humans, Frenchmen capable of offering us a hospitality that is less precarious and, all things being equal, more worthy of us.

And she is so reasonable that I declare myself ready to lift camp immediately, if I can persuade the Pure Ones to supply us with guides and ensure the transport of our luggage.

V

It is a case of recalling here the old proverb: What a woman wants, God wants.

The day after the dramatic incidents I have just recounted, my wife's wish was granted. We set out for the mysterious Residence.

You have not forgotten the vague promise that I had given the chief to intercede with the Demiurge—let us use that title for the moment—with regard to the difference, still obscure for me, that divided them. Thanks to that promise, renewed under oath, I was able to obtain what I wanted from him. Formed by his care, our convoy was composed as follows: four scouts changed with clearing a path through the parts of the forest that were still virgin; a kind of narrow two-wheeled cart carrying out most indispensable luggage, drawn by an old asthmatic buffalo; and finally, the bulk of the troop, consisting of my wife and me, the Pure chief and four of his fellows, all mounted on little ponies native to the island.

The ponies were charming beasts, scarcely taller than mountain dogs, slender and intelligent, with mischievous eyes—"but whose species is nearing extinction by the day," the Pure Ones confided to me with the indifferent tone of beings absolutely closed, and for good reason, to the mysteries of the amelioration and reproduction of species.

The possibility of making the voyage by sea had been raised briefly, but the numerous reefs of the northern shore would have rendered the landing too perilous. In any case, my wife had no desire to see the boat again that had carried our destiny before the honeymoon, and I was eager to yield that witness of our defunct discord graciously to our friends and saviors.

Our definitive itinerary, mapped out in advance, comprised three stages, of three days; its route passed through the very heart of the forest and ought to reach, by the end of the third day, the limit of divine territory—which is to say, the foot of the highest massif on the island. There were would separate from our guides, for access to the Residence situated on the northern slope of that massif was, it appears, forbidden to the Pure Ones within a radius of several kilometers. The chief affirmed that two of theirs, having ventured beyond that limit, had paid for that act of temerity and insubordination with their liberty. That was a shadow on the picture, but there was no reason to think that the so-called divines would reserve the same welcome for shipwrecked compatriots.

The nightmarish scenes of the previous day still haunted our imagination so forcefully that they served as the unique theme of our conversation during the first hours of the march. When I say "conservation," reduce that to verbose questions asked by me of the chief, and the rare and parsimonious responses that I had all the difficulty in the world extracting from his invincible laconism. It seemed that his brain, at grips with some insoluble problem, had no effort to spare for contingencies unworthy of its attention. Think of Archimedes searching for the law of the specific weight of substances.

Was it the enigma of *Graziella* that had upset him to that degree? Perhaps, for there was, as you will see later, a close link between the reflections suggested to him by reading that book and the desires and demands that I was engaged to lay at the feet of the Demiurge, of which I was as yet ignorant. It had been agreed, in fact, that the text of those desires would only be communicated to me when the moment of our separation arrived, either because the chief had insufficient faith in my memory, or because their substance was not yet sufficiently ripe in the mind of their author.

In sum, therefore, and in spite of the affectionate testimonies of gratitude that I lavished on him during the times when we chance to be riding side by side—testimonies by which he was visibly touched—the character of our exchanges with regard to the incidents of the previous day was summary. The chief clamed, in any case, not to be able to explain the cause of the sudden and unprecedented uprising, and I dared not submit to him my own explanation, which was that by sectioning the two conjugated beings, perhaps before the eyes of a member of their family, I had struck a criminal blow against the future of the race, and that it was that crime for which the Unclean Ones wanted to punish me. You will agree that our friend was too insufficiently initiated into the mysteries of genesis to follow me on that terrain.

As for the old lemur, it remained, for the chief as for us, a repulsive enigma. Its existence was totally unknown to all the Pure Ones, and it was necessary to admit, as a last resort, that the superlatively fantastic creature in question had a domicile in some subterranean excavation from which it only emerged by night. I note in passing that the chief seemed very sorry not to have been able to capture it. Had he wanted to submit it to an interrogation of a nature to enlighten his religion with regard to some of the more particularly impenetrable sorceries of the island? That was a question that I asked myself idly, but on which the future—an imminent future—was to cast a very sinister light.

In a general manner, the Pure Ones explained solely by their physical and mental superiority the ascendancy that they exercised over the Unclean Ones and the blind submission of the latter. They would not have governed them by constraint, but they approved, by their attitude at least, of violent means with regard to the refractory and unsubmissive. The Pure Ones, in any case, never treated the mass harshly. The intervention to which we owed our salvation had been of a purely mental order, for they would not, for anything in the world, have risked their prestige, and hence their future security, in a brawl in which their numerical inferiority might be turned against them. Bladed weapons were, in their hands, primarily instruments of hypnotism; as for firearms, they made use of them for appeals, summons, and rallying signals. As has been explained to us summarily already, the Unclean Ones adored detonations, the resonance of the gong and, in general all loud and deep sonorities. And in that regard, the chief, becoming momentarily loquacious, declared himself convinced that with a rudimentary orchestra composed of powerful instruments, one could lead them to the end of the world.

I was later to remember the somber and meditative expression he took on when he confided that idea to us, which initially struck a chord with us simply because of the grotesque images that it called up, and also because the Pure chief seemed to be confusing—like so many others, alas—music with noise. Even the rumbling of thunder, he added, threw the Unclean Ones into ecstasy, while it inspired a mad terror in the Pure Ones, from which only he had ended up freeing himself, since he had started reading, and striving to scrutinize nature.

By a singular coincidence, that particular psychopathology of the Pure Ones was about to be put in evidence before our very eyes. The weather had been threatening since our departure, and toward midday a storm burst.

Everything is exaggerated in the tropics, the best as well as the worst, but the worst especially. It was an atmospheric tragedy of a quarter of an hour, but how terrible! Uninterrupted flashes of lightning striped the sky, as black as ink; soon, cataracts of water drowned the visible world, as in diluvian times.

At the first thunderclap, our scouts uttered cries of anguish and disappeared into the undergrowth. As for the riders of the escort, they departed in all directions, with bridles lowered. They all came back, however, as meekly as anything, as soon as the storm had dissipated. The chief was content to shrug his shoulders and deplore the pusillanimity of his fellows, but that trivial incident undoubtedly affected him more than he wanted to show, for his brow remained furrowed, and we arrived at the end of the stage without him having said a single word more.

Another detail of that first day comes back to me, which I am reporting to you in passing, as a curiosity. Perhaps, in harvesting all these crumbs of observation, you will succeed in forming a vague idea of the mentality of our strange friend.

The route of our first stage passed through the wood of cedars where we had discovered the sketch of the temple that I have already mentioned. Questioned about the origins of that work of art, the chief told us that some of his brethren had amused themselves by sculpting and chiseling those stones, without really knowing whether they were obeying a purely artistic sentiment, or an innate instinct of iconolatry—the word is not his; I'm simply making use of it to summarize his somewhat confused explanations. And on that score, the religious question that I had deliberately touched upon suggested some reflections that were even more astonishing.

"We have no religion. Why would we have one? Religion can only be an individual conception more or less transformed, and we, unfortunately, are not individuals; we are similar specimens of a species, to such an extent that the Father has not even given us distinctive names, as is done among you. He designated us, and we still designate ourselves, by numbers. The epithet 'divine,' which we apply to the other humans of humanity, those who are bearded like our Father and you, does not have the significance for us that you give to it. It corresponds more closely to the word 'extraordinary,' or 'superior,' or 'supernatural,' qualifications by which we distinguish you from us, the ordinary, the inferior, the natural, and which, until recently, entailed a hint of respect and veneration on our part."

His face had darkened. He added, slowly, with a sensible bitterness: "To the Father, above all, I had, in the early days, when I was not thinking and could not comprehend, avowed a pious, bewildered admiration, which all my brethren shared and which caused us to kiss the tracks of his feet... Today we no longer know what attitude we ought to take to him. We do not know...we know longer know...whether the...singular...life that he has given us ought not to excite our scorn and our hatred rather than our gratitude... It is up to him to decide."

That evening, when Yvonne and I found ourselves alone under the leafy shelter that served us as a tent, she reminded me about those words, barely intelligible to her, and then said: "Who could have divined what might occur in the primitive consciousness of these poor phenomena? Among us, one has a soul under the skin—under the skin of the face, at least, for it is relatively easy to read in the features. Their faces give the impression of a closed book—a book whose binding, however, is fraying and deteriorating with a disconcerting rapidity. Have you noticed how much they've aged in the last fortnight?"

I had not noticed that at all, but it was true, and I had once again to admire my wife's subtle vigilance, incessantly occupied in discovering the physical imprints of the mystery that was drawing us in its wake, while I limited myself to scrutinizing the ideal substratum, weakly. If I evoked the Pure Ones as they had been at our first encounter, I was forced to admit that they seemed to have aged nearly two years. Their step had become heavier, their features more austere; rings had appeared around their eyes, the skin of which was chapped—and the wrinkles on their foreheads and at the corners of the mouth, especially those due to the facial contractions produced by solar light, were hollowed out, as if by the effect of an acid. Finally—a sign of accelerated maturation more remarkable than all the rest—their temples, which had still had a juvenile aspect a fortnight ago, garnished with hair as perfectly black as that of the rest of the head, were beginning to go gray.

I have no need to tell you, my dear friend, that we did not waste our time that night, nor the following day, in searching for the probable cause of that new anomaly, which might depend on a thousand biological influences. The editor responsible for all those strange things would soon inform us himself; our curiosity could give him credit for forty-eight hours.

In addition, our journey was becoming superlatively captivating, and dawn found us ready to accord our exclusive attention to the virgin forest that we were entering. The sun had not yet risen when we were moving in Indian file—the baggage cart closing the march—through the crackling lacework of ferns, among the smooth sleekness of coconut-palms and bananas, in an atmosphere heavy with unusual odors, and a phantasmagorical silent penumbra.

But I can see your brow darkening, my dear friend; you fear one of those descriptions in which the fabricants of extraordinary voyages excel. Well, no; I shall sheath my lyre. The truth is that those two days of marching through the woods were, in sum, tedious and enervating. I lost all my illusions regarding the charm of virgin forests. As a general rule, even the most picturesque landscapes do not gain from being seen at close range.

"Nothing gains from being seen closely," the Persian poet says, "because our breath tarnishes even the mirror in which we gaze at ourselves." The admirable Schopenhauer, for his part, expressed the special disappointment of a forest location very well in making the remark that once one has penetrated it, it is no longer a forest; one is simply among trees. Virgin forests lead to that same pessimistic conclusion, raised to the nth power.

First of all, it is dark in broad daylight, because of the opacity of the leafy vaults and domes that the overabundant lianas transform into veritable vegetative catacombs. On the other hand, one stifles there, for the calorific rays traverse everything, like X-rays. Then again, in that heat and obscurity, millions of diabolically aggressive insects live, not to mentions wild beasts and snakes, imperfectible and backward animals that have never been able to accustom themselves to the proximity of humans unless they are protected from them by the solid bars of a menagerie cage. Finally, a virgin forest is designed to discourage travelers, on horseback or on foot, for the thorny thickets, the fallen tree-trunks and the more-or-less trenchant grasses transform an ordinary march into an odious exercise in acrobatics. The humus itself seems to join in, by distilling an unknown poison which gives life and glamour to prestigious flowers, which decorate the trees but with whose effects on one's person it is not a good idea to experiment.

Fortunately for us, our scouts continually found trails that were already partly cleared, rendering the wielding of the machete almost unnecessary, with the result that we advanced rapidly enough and our second stage took us a little beyond the envisaged point—we had gained several kilometers. Thus, before noon on the following day, we reached the region of the solfataras: that of artificial colds in the head, as Yvonne put it, informed by my sudden sneezes—I have an olfactory sensitivity—as to the geological ambiance long before the Pure chief had declared that we had arrived at the limit of our journey.

After half an hour's march, in fact, during which we skirted the still-invisible mountain, the forest thinned out, and the sea breeze refreshed us and caused our ponies to whinny. We crossed a bank of blue-tinted clay and finally set foot on the foot of a vast rocky terrace at the top of which, a few minutes later, we saw, in the depths of a bay shaped like an amphitheater, the Promised Land—which is to say, the cluster of buildings comprising the Residence.

There was, at first glance, a minuscule citadel of verdure encrusted in a steep cliff. The surrounding wall—in granite, that one—was supported at an acute angle on the inferior steps of the mountain, and then its two sides opened up and descended toward the strand. Behind that wall, a few buildings made white patches against the dark clumps of trees in which they were inserted. Immediately below the citadel, the surf threw up a haze over the reefs that framed the bay, and the profoundly blue see rose into an even bluer sky. At our feet, rice plantations extended their green carpet, alternating with other plantations, arranged in steps, which seemed to be linked by a road departing from the foot of the citadel.

All that was in a unique fissure in the cliff, resembling, seen from a distance, an immense green satin stripe cut into the surrounding granite masses. The rest of the mountain seemed to be infertile, charred and eroded, reminiscent of the most desolate landscapes of Judea.

Fifteen hundred meters above the citadel, the principal volcano raised its peak of mystery and anguish, flanked by two or three smaller craters, extinct, as black as smokers condemned to repose. Half way up one of those craters, a round, dilapidated stone construction simulated a ruined gasometer; the chief declared to us, not without some embarrassment, that he had never known its purpose.

And when I asked Yvonne what she thought of that impressive panorama, she simply responded, in her typical elliptical fashion: "I'm now convinced that the man of the Residence is no trickster."

VI

If I were writing my story instead of narrating it to you summarily, I would think myself obliged to devote a chapter to the emotional adieux of the Pure Ones, and to the chimerical mission with which the chief charged me—chimerical in the sense that that its very objective removed it to the realm of the radically unrealizable. Then I would undertake to detail in order our own states of mind in confrontation with the colossal mystery at the door of which we were about to ring. But I know the provision that needs to be made for your vagabond attention, and that an implacable train will be waiting for you at exactly midnight at the Gare Montparnasse, so I shall cut the story short.

I shall allow the brave individuals to whom we owed our lives twice over to draw away, without permitting myself the slightest sign of emotion, and remain as mute as a carp regarding the mission, on which the continuation of my story will oblige me to cast sufficient light.

Duly fortified, as we have seen, the Residence had only two entrances, one at the summit of the triangle that it sank into the mountain, the other at its base—which is to say, on the shore itself. The one at the summit, the chief had told us, was "forbidden" to the profane, because it gave access directly to the Demiurge's private gardens. The one at the base, on the other hand, was the public entrance, and it was toward that one that we headed in following the pathway through the terraced plantations, which brought us to the foot of the citadel in less than half an hour.

It had been agreed that as soon as we were admitted to the enclosure we would sent someone to fetch our luggage from the Silver Table—that was, it appeared, the name given to the micaceous rocky shelf on which we had made out last halt. Until then the Pure Ones would keep watch on the cart from a distance. They would raise camp as soon as they saw the men from the Residence approach, resolved as they were, in view of previous experiences, not to make contact with the divines under any pretext. They would, however, return exactly a week later in order to enquire as to the results of my mission, and their reappearance would then be signaled to me by a large fire, which they would light on the evening of their arrival at the Silver Table. Now that the path had been cleared, it would be very easy for them, the chief declared, to travel the forty or fifty kilometers for which we had required three stages.

Night was falling when we reached the entrance to the Residence: a round and low portal, over which were inscribed the words: *Maritime Zoology Station.* Our use of the knocker unleashed a concert behind the door such as we had never heard. Combine in thought all imaginable animals, and a few others besides, and imagine that from that Noah's ark a formidable vocal explosion departs in unison, each one attempting to make its personal diapason dominate. An interior bell that doubtless responded to our knocking reestablished a relating silence, and then a spyhole opened behind its grating.

"Fisitors?" queried a cheerful thick voice, seasoned by a strong German accent.

"Shipwreck victims," I replied, "requesting hospitality."

"Ah! ferry cud, ferry cud...berfect."

The invisible individual had said that in the jovial tone with which one excuses oneself to old acquaintances that one cannot immediately recall.

A further ring of the bell, and the door opened slightly in order to let us through. A sequence of white arcades opened into a distant courtyard, where a streak of residual daylight remained.

"Gome in, chentlemen, laties, the gompany!"

A tall fellow in short-sleeves, with a marmoset on his shoulder, his head buried in shock of flaxen hair, wisps of which hung down over his eyes, bowed to us with the most comical ostentation. At the same time he launched behind him a resounding; "Chut ub, Maria!" evidently addressed to one of the voices in the savage concert, which recommenced more loudly—but which one? I shall tell you immediately that we never did find out, as much because of the large number of animals populating that strange farmyard as because of the clownish character of the porter. The latter was an amiable half-mad Alsatian who, having spent the best years of his life in a sort of menagerie, seemed himself to be a kind of menagerie in miniature, from whom some unexpected clucking, unjustified laughter, fluttering of wings or croaking in the void—all the onomatopoeias of animal language—continually escaped.

He was rubbing his hands now, in the cheerful and urgent manner of a hotelier who sees important clients arriving, and he repeated, ineffable and blinking: "Ferry cud... ferry cud... von knows vot...ah, ja! The paggage...von vill haff them vetched right avay, the chentleman's und laties' paggage...vrom the Silfer Taple...ja..." (An interval for me to summarize our story.) "Ja! Ja! Zat's discusting! Zo zat is how the chentleman, the laty, vound zemselves apantoned on our islant...not efen the vay to dreat a tog...! (Rapid allusion made by me to our generous welcome by the Pure Ones.) "Ah! Ja, ja! Berfect, berfect...ferry droll...the Bure Ones, the Baubers...as I call zem..." (Formidable explosion of laughter, with which the Noah's ark makes a chorus.) "Ja...the Baubers...von knows vot zey are...ve haff two of zem here...the zame ones I zend for the paggage"—a bell rings—"at the Silfer Taple, no?"

He disappeared, flying away with the maladroit flutter of a chicken, and came back capering like a goat. "It's done, I've giffen the orters...ah! It's chust that I haff to take off the cloves to talk to zem, those Astecs...zey eat the vool off your pack...not that zey are pad beople, but zere's alvays somezink grumpling und grunching petween zair deeth...pefore zere were chenuflexions und zirs und votever you font. Ah, zey are ferry chanched zince peing vith us...if one knew vere dey came from...tvins, the poss's aide zays...zat's all I know...but the ozzers, out zere in the zoth, vere you haff peen, it's all kif-

kif like vaces, it abbears...vunny, no? And vorse, zey's valse saffages, zince zey're vite, like us...and zey speak Vrench, like us, only zey're vite men who haff never done military serfice anyvere...me, vit do you expect...I don't atmit peings who haffent carried a gun..."

We had sat down in order to allow the Alsatian's verbosity to run dry, and it was only then that I noticed how livid and leaden his complexion was. One might have thought that he was being eaten alive by anemia, with his drawn, ageless features, only a few bristly hairs above his linear mouth and dull hollows replacing the soft flesh of his cheeks. The outline of his face was further elongated by a commencement of acromegaly, which gave him a chin like Polichinelle. And what was more disconcerting still was the contrast between his stupid gaze and his simian volubility with the contained and meditative silence of the marmoset that was studying us from the height of his shoulder.

I took advantage of the first hiatus in his loquacity to clarify the situation, giving him to understand that, although his society delighted us, we would also be glad to see the "poss." That unleashed a further babble, from which we extracted the following scarcely encouraging tidbits:

As for the boss, quite simply, one did not see him, one never saw him, he says that he is not to be seen, and besides which, he doesn't have the time. Monsieur Moustier, his laboratory chief—for the Alsatian insisted that the boss was "a great chemist, a very great chemist"—has been charged once and for all with standing in for him with regard to any stranger who presented themselves. They are extremely rare, as one might imagine. The boss, moreover, has designated a bungalow—the very one to which he was about to escort us—to be put at the disposal of visitors required to stay at the station for a few days, but it is rare that he has any direct dealings with them.

"I whom am speaking to you," said the Alsatian—I shall give up mimicking his accent[13]—"have only see him two or three times, two years ago, when I went into his house, and not since." A shudder passed through his body, as if under a cold shower. "Oh, no—not since." The shadow of a retrospective fear passed over his gnomonic nose, and then he burst out laughing under the effervescent effect seemingly produced by the said cold shower. "And I haven't come to any more harm, as you see."

"He's a complete idiot," Yvonne whispered to me. "Ask him to take us to the strangers' house; once installed, we'll have to get rid of him."

My requests were finally understood by the strange individual.

"Very good, very good," he said. "One knows what's what. I'll take you to your bungalow. It's chic, comfortable…let me know. Don't pay any attention to the menagerie…they're not malevolent, all the birds…just a bit noisy. Shut up, Maria! What do you expect—it's my passion, birds…"

We traversed the interior paved courtyard, where the most bizarre specimens of the avian realm were frolicking, principally predators: pelicans, cranes, ibis, cassowaries, storks, etc. On its four faces, barred cages contained a host of other animals: carnivores, climbers, rodents, a great many monkeys, and also a seal.

"They once served for laboratory experiments," the Alsatian explained to us, while administering an amicable slap to a chained-up gibbon that had grabbed hold of the hem of his white trousers.

The courtyard opened up on an immense park, where the slope of the cliff immediately became steeper. Avenues of trees of every species departed from a central lawn and rose up

---

[13] In the original, the author continues to employ an atrocious eye-dialect to represent the Alsatian's speech, but as the character's speech is ostensibly being filtered through an oral narrator, I have taken the view that it might as well be translated.

in flowery streets to lose themselves in a prodigious mass of verdure dominated by the majestic summits of cedars and banyans. Each avenue led, it seemed, to one or two bungalows lost in the vegetable tide to the point of being quite invisible. Ours had the advantage of being half way up the slope, very close to the surrounding wall, directly above the beach, from which it was only separated by a wooded slope of a hundred meters. The house—a small cubic structure of white stone, was ornamented by a portico and a slim colonnade flanked at each corner by the crown of a banana tree or a parasol pine.

There were climbing roses all over, and, by virtue of an already-inveterate habit, my wife picked two bouquets, which would, she said, ornament our mantelpiece—which provoked a merriment in our gangling guide that was as silent as it was enigmatic, justified a few moments later by the revelation that there was no mantelpiece anywhere.

The interior of the house was entirely furnished in the oriental style, with caskets and divans, with green plants arranged along the walls—and that was all. But the rooms, opening on to the patio, were exquisitely cool, and as the daylight was disappearing rapidly, we hastened to explain to the Alsatian that we were eager to obtain a well-earned repose. He did not raise any objection, all the more so as, he told us, he "slept like the chickens." Before going out he showed us, in the vestibule, a panel of electric buttons, whose bells corresponded to the various internal services—meals, baths, wardrobe, etc.—each of which was assumed, he explained, by a "platoon of coolies" who would respond as soon as they were called.

At the same time, he turned a commutator, and the enchantress Electricity became softly resplendent amid the whiteness of the arcades.

"Electric light!" exclaimed Yvonne, as soon as he had gone. "Valets, waiters, cooks—and a fortnight ago, we thought we were landing on an island of cannibals!"

For two pins, she would have danced with joy. I joined in with her enthusiasm myself, but not without a few reservations regarding the "fly in the ointment" represented at the very outset of the adventure by the precarious mental equilibrium of the Alsatian. That one would surely give us a headache. But my wife saw him as one more proof that the master of the Residence really was the man of our hypotheses.

"Only great scientists," she adjudged," surround themselves with such a personnel."

That first night, however, reserved a few slight disappointments for us. Firstly, an aubade provided by thousands of crickets extracted us from the reparative slumber on which we were counting. Then howling moneys started abusing one another in a nearby wood, and only shut up after having succeeded in making some old night-bird sob. Then, from the direction of the farmyard, two other guttural voices rose up, doubtless those of parrots or macaws, one of them shouting loudly for an imaginary "boy," the other insulting the enigmatic Maria, whom the Alsatian had so often commanded to shut up.

There was also an extraordinary saurian, which, from the depths of its lair, pronounced emphatically, seven or eight times in succession, the name "Hugo," after which it commented on the disdainful silence into which its appeal fell with a dolorous sigh that resembled a stifled hiccup.

Shortly before daybreak, a resounding reveille was sounded in fanfare by all the porter's poultry, and his own jovial voice was eventually heard enjoying the most animated conversation with them.

Then, finally, the sun rose, and we were able to go to sleep.

VII

As soon as we got up, we continued to assimilate the surroundings. The Residence was decidedly a little Eden—you'll
permit me, won't you, to continue to make use of the word
Residence, simpler and shorter than the scientific title of the
station—for décor as well as climate, the heat not surpassing
thirty degrees, and with regard to moral standing. The rare
white men we encountered from time to time in the pathways
of the park seemed a trifle surprised to see us, but their salutes
nevertheless preceded ours, and they passed by without asking
us any questions. In any case, they were, for the most part,
simple artisans, and I thought I recognized in them electricians, mechanics, factory foremen, sailors and waiters.

Women must have been exceedingly rare, because we
only encountered two, one a chambermaid and the other and
old spinster who, we were informed, was a stenographer. The
domestic staff consisted entirely of male Hindus with majestic
flowing beards, an ethnic prerogative that earned them the
most reverent salutations on the part of the two Pure Ones,
who had indeed been retained as a disciplinary measure.

The latter had been convicted of espionage—a detail of
which the porter seemed to be unaware, let it be said in passing—and now, condemned to remain there for months, they
felt lost in a society that they did not understand, without any
real contact with people who probably suspected their dubious
origin. They had remarked themselves the previous evening
that the affectionate tone in which we thanked them for bringing our luggage gave them a sensible pleasure, for no one in
the Residence spoke to them except for the porter, a true churl,
and they did not speak to anyone.

From the little bastion occupying the western corner of
the enclosing wall, we could see, successively, the high thickets of the park rising up to the first buttress of the volcanic
massif, which simulated from a distance a triangular green

carpet thrown over the sinister rocks of the solfataras; the inferior arbors, the lawn at the intersection and the central courtyard; and, lower down, the two rocks at the corners of the surrounding wall, which broadened out progressively as it descended to the shore, its two extremities joining up with the two rocky jetties of a small natural harbor.

To the east, beyond the wall, a few trees indicated the zigzag path that led to the Silver Table, whose very visible bare platform seemed, at that distance, a livid wound eating away the edge of the forest. To the west, a veritable rocky chaos caused to float above the sea the harsh and desolate impression of the edge of the landmass.

From one side of the bay to the other, the reefs to the north of the island projected a chaplet of black rocks, like the spines of a semi-submerged monster, the fantastic tail of which seemed to writhe in the rush of the waves—for the sea here was seething and foaming, ejaculating geysers in plumes and fans, in which the sun painted delicate and ephemeral rainbows.

Suddenly, as we were leaning a little further over the redan, the same exclamation escaped from our breasts, inflated by delight: "Saved!"

In a little internal port that we had not perceived at first because it was shielded by the overhanging bastion, a pretty white yacht lay dormant on the rusty steel of dead water, seeming slightly dead itself, with its deserted decks and its extinct funnel, giving the impression of having been abandoned there for years. Doubtless no one in the Residence bothered to render it life and movement.

But we were there now! And as emotions always have their action and their reaction, the certainty of salvation temporarily removed the desire to realize it, in order to orientate us urgently toward the means of penetrating the mystery that weighed upon the island.

The next day, I had myself introduced to Monsieur Moustier, the Demiurge's laboratory supervisor. His bungalow was situated at the top of one of the vaulted avenues that radiated toward the central lawn from the summit of the station—avenues that were almost rectilinear, of friable soil whose red clay stood out amid the green of the grass, reminiscent of the bloody entrails of some gigantic watermelon.

I had scarcely handed my card to the Hindu domestic who appeared on the veranda than the latter introduced me into a modest study, where I found myself in the presence of a man about forty years old, correct and cold to begin with, but who gradually became animated to the extent of raising his tone to the most exquisite amiability.

I can still see his distinguished features today: his clear and healthy complexion, and his thinker's forehead labored by precocious wrinkles. He had gray eyes—the eyes of the races of northern Europe, which seem to be looking inwards but never avoid the gaze of an interlocutor. He assured me from the outset of our conversation that he knew my name, having read it at the end of many a magazine article, and that he would make every effort to obtain for me, as soon as possible—which is to say, within two or three days—an interview with "the boss," Monsieur Brillat-Dessaigne.[14]

I jumped at that name, which no one in the Residence had yet pronounced in my presence. So the fantastic Demiurge on the subject of whom my wife and I had so often exercised our verve, was none other than Brillat-Dessaigne, the illustrious chemist, the pioneer of the synthesis of simple substances, one of the most highly-reputed scientists in France and Europe. And I suddenly recalled that, having reached the apogee of his glory, Brillat-Dessaigne had disappeared fifteen years before, when the rumor had spread that his health, severely compromised by overwork, had condemned him henceforth to live in the most absolute retirement and seclusion.

---

[14] The first part of the double-barreled name would immediately remind a French reader of that of the great gastronomic essayist Brillat-Savarin, while the verb *saigner* means "to bleed," thus giving the whole an impression of fancy cookery of a bloody nature.

Doubtless out of discretion, Monsieur Moustier did not ask me any questions about the purpose of the interview I had requested. I thought I ought to take the initiative, and without any oratory precaution, I narrated our adventures very sincerely, with the exception of the perilous skirmish in the Unclean Valley, which appeared to me, because of the initial role played by our curiosity, liable to do us harm in the estimation of our hosts. I expressed nevertheless my ardent desire to hear the great scientist explain to me from his own mouth the double mystery that made the south of the island a kind of annex of a teratological museum.

My interlocutor's expression darkened. He thought the matter thorny. There was every chance that "the master" would refuse to explain. He had never opened up to anyone. Alone among all the staff of the station, his laboratory supervisor was initiated into the secret of the experiments, and knew the role that they had played in the genesis of the Pure Ones and the Unclean Ones. As for the two prisoners interned in the Residence, into which they had slipped one day disguised as Hindu coolies, he had forbidden then *on pain of death* to speak to anyone whatsoever about what they knew or believed about their origin.

"In any case," Monsieur Moustier added, "if they have been kept here, it is only to set an example, to put a brake on the espionage of the Pure Ones in general, which might become very troublesome if it laid bare the scant consistency of our prestige and our inaccessibility."

We discussed for some time the fact that, having discovered and penetrated by myself at least the superficial layer of the secret, I could not be reckoned a simple curiosity-seeker. Furthermore, it went without saying that if I were to divulge what I knew after my return to Europe, it would only be with the assent of Monsieur Brillat-Dessaigne. Monsieur Moustier ended up admitting that the weight of those arguments, combined with my personal worth, might persuade the Master to make an exception. Everything would depend on my diplomacy and the present state of mind of the illustrious chemist. The cycle of great biological experiments had, in any case, been completed several months ago and their divulgence in Europe—supposing that I were to divulge them—could not have any troublesome consequence.

In the final analysis, Monsieur Moustier renewed his promise to plead my case.

"If I ask you for two or three days," he said to me, as he showed me out, "it's because Monsieur Brillat-Dessaigne is busy at this very moment evaluating the definitive results of an experiment in vegetal chemistry whose phases he has been tracking for months, with the result that his door is rigorously forbidden. I shall not be admitted to see him myself for at least forty-eight hours. That leaves me some forced leisure time, which I shall be delighted to devote to you if I can be useful to you in any way."

I seized the ball in flight. My wife and I would be glad to visit the immediate surroundings of the Residence, including the volcanoes, if he would deign to serve as our cicerone. There must be many curious things to see.

The scientist finally smiled. If we wanted to anticipate the Master's eventual revelations, we were in for a disappointment; there were no "monsters" to be seen anywhere, and the territory of the Residence scarcely differed in appearance from any other Javanese region. He would nevertheless place himself at our disposal—and on the same day, as soon as the heat declined, we began our excursions under his direction.

Our first visit, naturally, was to the port. We were eager to contemplate at close range the yacht that remained the pivot of our dreams of an imminent return to the continent—a return in which it could not fail to be involved in one way or another.

A surprise awaited us on the deck of the vessel. Three artillery pieces, including a machine-gun, were arranged on the poop deck.

"A whim of the boss," Monsieur Moustier explained. "He bought them in Batavia at the same time as the yacht, about two years ago, to garnish our bastions. Since then, they've stayed on board, Monsieur Brillat-Dessaigne having neglected to issue any instructions in their regard. The yacht itself, unused, is a veritable floating arsenal in miniature. You'll find powder and shells in the liquor-store, and the saloon, as you can see, is cluttered with sabers and rifles, the majority deplorably rusted by now, good at the most for being transformed into theater accessories. I think that the boss had the intention, for a while, of transplanting the inhabitants of a neighboring island here, whom he intended to subject to various experiments in accelerated civilization. These weapons were destined to hold them in respect if the experiment turned out badly, but I only tell you that with all reservations."

The "floating arsenal" into which the object of our hopes had suddenly mutated saddened us slightly. We could not easily see ourselves sailing in a vessel overflowing with powder and piratical weapons, with cannons on the deck instead of rocking-chairs. For my part, I was calculating the time that it would take to unload that cumbersome cargo on the day we were authorized to confide our two lives to the yacht. The calculation was complicated by a thousand dark points, ending in an insidious question that I put to Monsieur Moustier with the most innocent expression in the world.

"How many Europeans are there in the Residence?"

"Exactly a dozen," he said. "Thirteen if you count the porter." As my wife started at the number thirteen he added: "But he doesn't count, for the poor fellow is half-addled."

"Only a dozen," I said, in a sinister tone. "And the service staff comprises nearly two hundred Hindus. Frankly, I won't hide it from you that in your place, I'd rather see all these weapons and all the ammunition inside the place rather than outside."

But the scientist burst out laughing. "Our Sinhalese are the most inoffensive people in the world. Their meek and servile character is a characteristic of the race. There could be a thousand here and you could sleep easy."

I said no more, but I remember very clearly that I dreamed that night that, having chartered the yacht to take us to Ceylon, we hastened to disarm the floating arsenal by throwing the cannons overboard. As for the powder, we used that to put on a splendid firework display as we were crossing the equator.

The next morning, very early, we set off for the volcanoes, still in the company of our amiable cicerone. A spiral path, interrupted by potholes, marshy jungles and more-or-less sulfurous streams, passed behind the northern point of the citadel, winding around three craters, which, up to a certain height, formed a single body. It then divided into two threads that plunged into creepers and ferns to reappear a hundred feet higher up in the form of oblique steps linking the last ragged vegetation of the forest to the denuded and devastated passes of the two superior craters.

As we arrived at the fork in the path, on the edge of a kind of pool of muddy clay framed by a few meager mint bushes, my wife suddenly stepped back and said to me, in a low voice: "I've just seen something slithering in that grass."

"A snake?" I asked.

"No," she said. "It as a very small creature with lots of legs and skin…extraordinary…a skin…"

She did not finish, by I understood by her pallor that the beast she had glimpsed had evoked by its form or its hue the horrible vision of the creatures of the Unclean Valley. I caught up with Monsieur Moustier, who was marching a few meters ahead of us, as a scout.

"Are you sure," I said, "that the monsters of the south of the island have never given rise to descendants in your region?"

"Not so far as I know. In the first months following their accidental birth—the Master will explain to you what I mean by that—the creatures, more repulsive than dangerous, infested our region, where they had come into the world, but there were only fifty, I believe, and the Master and I soon drive them back into the southern ravines, from which they never emerged again."

I communicated this response to my wife, who shook her head, saying: "All the same…what I saw wasn't natural."

I smiled, and was searching, in order to reassure her, for some witty remark to make about the uniformly supernatural incidents of our nuptial voyage, when a distant hum that our hearing could now discern only too well nailed us both to the spot.

Monsieur Moustier turned round. Seeing us distressed, he smiled compassionately.

"Didn't you hear it, then?" I exclaimed.

"Yes, I heard a vague buzz, perhaps a rumble, and if you have no objection, I'll willingly attribute it to the flatulent entrails of this essentially volcanic ground."

The phlegm and placidity of the man were beginning to irritate me.

"You're completely mistaken," I said, in a bantering tone, "and if you hadn't just affirmed that the region has been rid of its…teratological fauna for years, I'd attribute that same sound, which you suppose to be plutonian or seismic, to the gyration of an Unclean One in the process of stretching its tentacles.

Monsieur Moustier started to laugh loudly, so comical did the idea appear to him.

It was becoming evident to me that, not knowing about our tragic entanglement with the monsters, he did not have the slightest idea of what had become in the course of the years of the strange chemical products with which their laboratory had endowed the land. It appeared to me, too, that by dint of living in the midst of the extraordinary, of manipulating the unreal and the prodigious, the scientist had lost the notion of normal nature—so it is true that habituation to the strange broadens ordinary human vision, at the risk of deforming it, just as the contemplation of banalities limits and impoverishes it.

We arrived on a flat area where the path became easy.

"Look," said our guide. "There, properly speaking, is the cradle—the womb, if you prefer—of all those beings that intrigue you so much, the Pure Ones as well as the others."

His index finger pointed toward a cylindrical stone edifice, open to the sky, at the foot of which our route passed: the same bizarre structure partly encased in the wall of the mountain, the sight of which had struck me at a distance on the day of our arrival, and which I had compared previously to a ruined gasometer.

With the aid of a few superimposed stones I was able to reach one of the breaches in the circular wall and cast a glance inside—but I was greatly disappointed, for the grass had grown back thickly in the depths of the enormous vat, and the walls themselves presented nothing particular, except that they were still coated in places with a thin layer of the gelatinous emulsion that they appeared to have contained.

It was giving off an unspeakably sickening odor, which Monsieur Moustier compared, laughing, to that of a factory of animal charcoal.

Festoons of moss, ivy and climbing plants were insinuated in all the crevices of the cylinder, serving as attachments for the green weave that prodigious equatorial nature had hastened to hurl to its conquest. My eyes, probing the vegetal thicket at the bottom ended up discerning, at one point, a circular swelling almost deprived of grass, which resembled a large rusty disk fastened to the ground.

"It is indeed a disk," Moustier explained. "An iron disk, which constitutes the secret seal of a cellar excavated beneath the vat, in which we store our provision of dynamite."

"Dynamite!" I said, with a start. "But..."

The scientist interrupted me, having divined the connection I was about to make.

"No, it's not a supplementary arsenal—a simple powder store at the most, a powder-store that was offered to us by nature, for it was lightning that did the work of excavating the hole in which we installed our dynamite, by means of a strike nine or ten years ago, the course of a formidable electric storm.

"In the wake of that storm, which put an end to our experiments, the fissures of the vat having allowed the escape of all the precious substance on which we were operating, Monsieur Brillat-Dessaigne had the idea of taking advantage of the excavation produced by the lightning, enlarging it by means of an incision contrived by dynamite, susceptible of opening the flank of the mountain—for it's necessary to tell you that this crater, the smallest of the three, as you can see, conceals in its bowels a lake of boiling water, exceedingly sulfurous, and the bottom of that lake corresponds, according to our calculations, to the rocky stratifications of which the floor of the vat forms the external crust.

"By means of a few charges of dynamite, Monsieur Brillat-Dessaigne, thought that those stratifications could be cracked, so that the lake could flow through, and that it's bed, still hot—which is to say, the immense funnel that it would leave behind—would become a new laboratory of biological chemistry for us. The idea was as grandiose, was it not, as it was bold? It was too bold, for—just a minute…stand here, Madame"—Moustier had led my wife to the edge of a precipice formed by the very slope of the mountain, almost vertical at that point—"and look straight down at your feet…do you see that little white cube buried in a triangle of verdure? That's Monsieur Brillat-Dessaigne's bungalow, at the extreme tip of the station. You understand now why the boss's project was impracticable."

"Of course!" said Yvonne, always extra-lucid. "There was a risk that the dynamited mountain would fall on your heads, with everything it contains."

"Exactly. And as that's a genre of risk for which no insurance has been invented…"

"In truth," I said, "I won't hide it from you that I'd be very curious to visit that little crater, given that it's still intact, and bathe my feet in the lake in question."

"I advise you against it…and for good reason. There are other excursions to make here, especially in the company of a lady. The shore, for example, offers charming viewpoints…

"As for the volcano, it's very curious at a distance, even the relatively short distance at which we are at present, but only on condition of not diminishing that distance any further. Believe me, it's necessary not to trust too much in the innocent appearance of these 'sacks of lava,' as our facetious porter calls them; in addition to their alleged complicity with the earthquake that coincided with the electrical storm I mentioned to you a moment ago, they conceal within their flanks an entire sizzling inferno with which it's not good to come into intimate contact.

"In places, there are holes filled with hot water that give off suffocating acidic fumes; in others, there are filigrees of crystalline sulfur that the slightest breath of wind causes to break like glass, little mounds of burning embers, gigantic Turkish pastilles made of sulfur and vegetable debris, which doubtless offer Pluto the homage of their deadly vapor. Elsewhere there are the charred or boiled specters of trees whose inconsistent cadavers crumble and fall into dust at the slightest touch.

"And all of that would doubtless be interesting to see at close range...yes, it would perhaps be interesting to perch above one of those gaping holes in order to hear the dyspeptic entrails of the earth moaning and growling...but the most curious of the curious would feel his ardor congealing in thinking that the formidable cauldron is only waiting for a favorable moment, or a mysterious word of instruction from nature to spread ruin and mourning through the human world, as in Martinique.[15]

"From here, where we're standing, you can make out with the naked eye the external edges of the small crater, which rises up about five hundred feet over our heads; on the great massif the spectacle would be exactly the same, but you'd have at least six kilometers of steep slope to climb simply to reach an observatory as convenient as this one..."

My wife declared that she would not insist; she now had a clear idea of the charm of excursions on volcanoes, and we could go back.

---

[15] Mount Pele in Martinique had erupted in 1902, destroying the city of Saint Pierre.

The descent was effected briskly, and we soon saw the fork again where the incident had occurred that provoked the scientist's skeptical remarks. We had scarcely taken a few steps along the edge of the marsh when he signaled to us not to continue advancing. He had stopped, freezing in the attitude of a hunter on the lookout for prey. Suddenly, we saw him bound forward and throw his helmet on the ground, and then lift it up again cautiously, in both hands.

He had just captured the animal whose appearance had so frightened my wife. It was a creature with a soft carapace, scarcely incrusted with a few grains of agglutinated sand: a sort of giant crab, which offered a reduced image, completely animalized, of the most hideous of the monsters of the Unclean Valley.

The scientist turned the animal this way and that, while an immense perplexity contracted the muscles of his face.

"Curious, curious!" he murmured. Then, seeing that we were in quest of an explanation, he pronounced, in a hesitant voice: "It really is one of our laboratory reactions of eleven years ago...the period of trials and probes... But in those days, we only obtained evanescent forms—which is to say, very ephemeral, whose existence did not surpass the season in which they were born. I can, therefore, only attribute the survival of this creature to a phenomenon of encystment, which would also explain the present state of its carapace, to which a few siliceous grains are still adhering. Another phenomenon, that of revival, common enough among the Protozoa, its phylogenetic ancestors, must have extracted it from that period of encystment, which must have lasted more than ten years. It will then have resumed living, and resumed something very like the form in which we see it now."

We were triumphant this time, my wife and I, the apprehensions on the subject of which the scientist had mocked us having been justified beyond measure. Who, then, could affirm that other escapes had not been produced, and that the as-yet-unexplored ravines of the island were not populated by similar "laboratory reactions," more or less evolved, which must have brought to the population of the Unclean Valley a supplementary contingent of monsters still unknown to the scientists themselves? When the rules of nature are violated, is it not necessary to expect anything, and was it not already a symptom of an evident transposition of the laws of evolution that these essentially protistan faculties of encystment and revival had deferred to animals as developed as the one we had before our eyes?

"You can see, at least," I observed, in a sarcastic tone, "that I had some right to draw your attention to the possible...aberrations...of the fauna with which you have embellished the island: a fauna that we perhaps know better than you at present, having made contact with it on several occasions."

Moustier smiled, without conviction. "I lay down my arms," he declared. "You can confide your observations to Monsieur Brillat-Dessaigne himself, who, I'm sure, will record them with the keenest gratitude. Perhaps, in fact, our attitude has been a trifle...light...with regard to the creatures and larvae of creatures to which we have given life, but the continuation of our experiments absorbed us to such an extent... Then again, it's necessary not to exaggerate...even if the entire island were populated by these little monsters, there would be no reason for anxiety...they are, I repeat, simple laboratory reactions, phantoms of beings, almost inconsistent skeletons...and the proof, look..."

He dropped the creature that as still imprisoned in his helmet on to the ground, and, placing his foot on it, showed it to us reduced to a formless pulp.

"You see," he concluded, "one can get rid of them with a simple gesture."

At that moment, all three of us heard, quite distinctly, the hum that had already caught our attention when we were passing the mud-hole; it seemed to be emerging from the brushwood on the mountainside, which was garnished in that area with thickets impenetrable to the gaze.

Moustier blinked, as if in amusement, and shrugged his shoulders saying: "There's the nonsense starting again."

My wife and I abstained from any comment this time, for fear of taking on the role of those people bewildered by magic, who utter loud cries at every pass of the enchanter's wand.

We went back to the Residence, chatting perfectly placidly. I noticed, however, that the scientist willingly let the conversation lapse, and that his visage, when at rest, was hollowed out by a worry-line that was not habitual to him.

VIII

More than ever, my dear friend, I regret not having the gift of evoking the color of things, the material atmosphere of any environment whatsoever. I would have liked to give you an exact and tangible idea not only of Monsieur Brillat-Dessaigne, but of the frame, uncomplicated as it was, in which he appeared to me on the memorable day of our first conversation.

I can doubtless depict for you, very nearly, a visage whose photograph is found in all the display-cases in which our Parisian celebrities are featured; I can also describe the impressive physiognomy of the study in which he received me: a low-ceilinged room with squat pillars, almost devoid of windows, and where there was, however, sufficient illumination to be able to read, write or mediate, with sumptuous carpets on the floor. In one corner, there was a divan on which the Master sat to "think," and where he lay down to sleep at night. Three walls out of four disappeared behind rows of bookshelves; the fourth presented a reinforcement fitted out for rapid and summary chemical manipulations, encumbered by retorts, test-tubes, barbaric machines, lenses, prisms, instruments of micrography or micrometry, and a few other instruments whose very silhouette was completely unfamiliar to me.

My narrative talent could give you an idea, approximate, at least, of all of that—but what I cannot describe is the special atmosphere resident there, the magical circle in which in which the Master appeared to me, and which was, perhaps, a mere mirage of my fearful imagination—and perhaps also the direct suggestion of the magnetic scrutiny of that visage, whose mat pallor manifestly hid the inexpressible, the indecipherable, almost the intemporal.

Permit me to add, in case I am forced to touch on it here, that in spite of that, the man had nothing cadaverous about him. I mean that he did not in any way give the slightly unfortunate impression that, in current parlance, associates the stereotypical image of the scientist with the reek of death.

The visage gave the appearance of fifty years at the most. Younger still was the malicious smile that accompanied his sallies, the ludicrous images, the faceted words, with which he willingly spiced the terrible vocabulary of a biologist. You're familiar, in any case, with the celebrated profile, the slightly bulbous forehead, the forceful, sinewy nose, the ascetic cheekbones that extent into an alchemist's beard; you also know the extraordinary steely gaze that once burned in the depths of the bushy orbit of the eyebrows. You can easily picture that same gaze today, magnified, sublimated by the dogged combat that thought had sustained there, for fifteen years, against the associated mysteries of life and nature.

You can imagine mine even more easily, respectful and attentive, entirely adapted now to the fantastic enormity in which I had been wallowing for days, so well adapted that it would not have taken much for me to think of myself as a simple laboratory reaction, more or less evanescent, who had nothing of which to be proud in the superiority that a more highly-developed cerebrospinal system gave him over other animals.

You are, therefore, sufficiently "polarized" to substitute for the impressive note that I lack, and I can allow the Master to talk in accordance with my stenographic notes, passing over in silence my own interruptions—those, at least, that did not have the purpose of marking some essential detail of our anterior adventures.

We were sitting facing one another, him with his head upright, his chin in his hand, his speech loud and clear, slowing from the source, occasionally with a slight Alsatian accent that was reminiscent, at times, of the unspeakable porter, thus annihilating another common link, the idea of race, since the same human stock—the scientist and the porter both having been born in Colmar—can produce types so very different from one another.

"Yes, I understand that it must appear strange to you that I have succeeded in fabricating living human substance—men, in sum, almost similar to us. I myself, had the discovery been made by someone else, would only have believed it after seeing it and touching it, as you have. Let is not exaggerate however. My part was, in fact, fairly modest, since not only did I take advantage of the work of my predecessors, firstly of all those who created chemistry and secondly the masters of current chemical synthesis, of biology and its associated sciences—all those, as I say, who took steps on the same path or parallel paths before me—but my discovery, like the majority of great discoveries, also benefited from the collaboration of hazard.

"For a long time, like many others, I dabbled in the deceptive rut of *ad hoc* syntheses. I isolated the primitive elements of a substance, and, after having determined its formula, I tried to reproduce the substance by combining its elements slavishly in accordance with the discovered formula. I have no need to tell you that the magic spark was always lacking, the very principle of life: movement. For it is in movement that the entire secret resides of the transformation of inert matter into living cells—which is to say, the secret of spontaneous generation, and expression that signifies, in my thinking, the production of living beings without preliminary procreation.

"I don't say without fecundation of any sort, for any genesis, no matter how simple it might be, supposes and implies the intervention of a fecundating principle, or, if we want to set aside that old word, a principle of multiple affinities, which, in the presence of identical or contrary affinities, combines with them and gives rise to germination, to proliferation, to dehiscence—to all the phenomena constitutive of embryonic life, properly speaking: phenomena of which the subsequent growth of the being is merely the overt repetition of the occult phases.

"I am leaving aside, of course, the puerile so-called artificial fecundation, for if you fabricate a flower-seed, for instance, by fecundating the pistil of that flower with natural pollen, you are not creating anything at all, but merely complicating things by substituting your maladroit hand for the magical hand of nature. If, on the contrary, you succeeded in fecundating the eggs of a starfish by means of carbonic acid, as Professor Yves Delage has done in his laboratory at Roscoff,[16] then you have created, because you have given life to an inanimate substance—the carbonic acid in question. That is, therefore, already a kind of spontaneous generation.

"Personally, I wanted to go much further. And as it is necessary to commence everything with the small extreme— nature has given us the example of that herself—it was toward the infinitely small that I turned my attention first. Yes, I devoted the better part of my years in Paris to the search for the synthetic formula of a primitive cell, of an infusorium, and, in fact, I found it, or very nearly. I had succeeded, in fact, in obtaining an entity that reproduced the morphological type of the plastids in general, but on a scale thousands of times larger, of course, since it had the dimensions of a small egg and ordinary plastids are microscopic creatures. Except that it lacked one thing: life. I had neglected to light my lantern—and you shall see that that image is more accurate than it might seem.

"My lack of success at least had the fortunate result of redirecting me on to the right path: the preliminary and exclusive study of protoplasm. You know—or perhaps you don't— that in the general opinion of my predecessors, protoplasm differs entirely from all other known chemical substances. Well, that's true and it isn't. That simple and unique differ-

---

[16] The zoologist Yves Delage (1854-1920) wrote numerous books, including works on embryology and evolution, as well as his six-volume *Traité de zoologie concrète* [Textbook of Physical Zoology] (1896-1903), but at the time the present story was published he had not yet published his then-definitive work on *La Parthénogénèse naturelle et expérimentale* [Natural and Experimental Parthenogenesis] (1913, with Marie Goldsmith), for which the experiment mentioned here was one of the significant demonstrations.

ence separates them: life—which is to say, once again, movement. Protoplasm is a living substance.

So, therefore, the entity that I had fabricated, the one that constituted my giant infusorium, was not endowed either with Brownian motion,[17] or amoeboid motion, or any motion whatsoever. Why was it not alive? Because it had no nucleus. I had omitted the nucleus, which scientists call the egg of a creature on a higher rung of the animal scale. It was with the egg that it was necessary to begin, since it alone is the origin and hearth of all life, the vital principle confused, in sum, with the reproductive principle. Yes, but that egg was itself composed of living protoplasmic substance, and I was incapable of creating that.

"How was I to get out of that vicious circle?

"Perhaps I never would have escaped from it without Haeckel's work on the Bathybius. Do you know the Bathybius? Yes? No? Vaguely? I wouldn't want to pontificate to someone who has signed up to scientific fantasies susceptible of being understood by a four year-old child. Allow me the number of barbaric words strictly necessary, and I promise you to be clear with regard to all the rest, except for a few formulae that I am still obliged to hide under a bushel. Among other secrets that I can't explain further is that highly fermented human serum would figure in the composition of my first nuclein—don't utter loud cries without knowing what's involved. Proud to pay, in his turn, his tribute to science, our porter, a compatriot of mine, put at my disposal all the blood in his veins.

"In any case, he bled himself frequently as a measure of health, as one purges oneself, and it is to the abuse of those

---

[17] The random movement of particles suspended in a liquid first observed by Robert Brown in 1827 was explained by Albert Einstein in 1905, but Hoche would not have read the paper in question, so he is mistakenly assuming, as many people did at the time, that some kind of "vital energy" is involved in the phenomenon.

bleedings that I attribute his present anemia, as cerebral as it is muscular. Eventually, in any case, I renounced the employment of the serum, which had become unnecessary. So let us not mention it again.

"I shall now summarize, briefly, the history of Bathybius, or the "creature of the abyss"—so-called, as you will have divined, because it is only found on the sea-bed, and extreme depths. The first known specimen was, at any rate, brought up from a depth of 8,000 meters, by the drag-nets of an English ship on a scientific expedition in the Atlantic. It was a kind of animate jelly, capable of imperceptible movements. It could grow, and elongate indefinitely—and that property subsisted, when it divided, in each of the parts, with the addition of the extraordinary particularity that if the two parts encountered one another again, they fused again as if they had never been separated.

"My regretted and celebrated colleague Huxley studied this phenomenal being and gave it the name *Bathybius haeckelii* in order to give pleasure to Haeckel, who was already the godfather of the Monera and who gratefully assumed the grave responsibility of that new tutelage. I say 'grave' because Haeckel had naturally quarreled with all those who were not partisans of the single and simple origin of life. It was nevertheless demonstrated that we were finally in the presence of the famous primordial slime, the *urschleim* of the Germans, that immortal and individual entity that remained the living witness of the flora and fauna with which it had populated the world.[18]

---

[18] The English biologist Thomas Henry Huxley gave the name *Bathybius haeckelii* to a substance he found in a mud-sample that had been dredged up from the Atlantic sea-bed in 1857 and stored away until 1868, in which he thought that he had identified the primordial *urschleim* hypothesized by Haeckel. Huxley sent a sample of the substance to Haeckel, who was naturally overjoyed, and integrated its discovery into the later editions of his best-selling book on evolutionary theory, which

"It is from Bathybius, I told myself, that it is necessary to demand the solution to the great problem of the synthesis of living beings. I therefore searched for Bathybius, and I ended up discovering on the shores of this very island, to which we had been led after long and fruitless trawls along the marine routes from Europe to the Far East. An extensive layer extended here over calcareous ground only a hundred meters deep.

"As soon as the size of the deposit had been confirmed by a summary sounding, I had a great stone reservoir constructed, the ruins of which you have seen half way up the small crater, above our heads. At the same time, I entered into negotiations with the Dutch government to lease this almost-deserted island. Then I gathered in my reservoir all the Bathybius that we were able to dredge up, and I commenced my experiments, with the aid of my devoted collaborator Moustier.

"In the interim, I had actively pursued the chemical synthesis of animal eggs, naturally commencing with the eggs of inferior animals, notably hydras and mollusks, and I had obtained very satisfactory results. It therefore only remained to replace the artificial nuclein and insert in my egg the veritable germinative plasma furnished by the very substance of Bathybius.

---

was very popular in France. Skeptics, however, suggested that the supposed *urschleim* might be the result of chemical decay in the stored sample, and Huxley recanted his "discovery" in 1875, when a chemist attached to the 1872 *Challenger* expedition, which had failed to find any trace of *Bathybius* during its intensive study of the sea-bed, found similar manifestations in other stored samples and worked out how they had been produced. Haeckel initially refused to recant, and continued to promote *Bathybius* as proof of his thesis until 1883, but he too eventually threw in the towel. Hoche was probably aware of the fact that he was quoting an obsolete thesis in crediting Brillat-Dessaigne with this process of invention, but was prepared to overlook the fact in view of its utility to his story.

"My first living animal egg inevitably led me to the human egg. I could doubtless have been mistaken, but my reasoning was supported by the known verity that the egg stage is common to all living beings. The human egg is, in that sense, merely a nucleus of the perfected plastid. To these 'horrible details' I will add the statement of two laws of selection that are entirely my own and which permitted me to vary and complicate the primitive egg in a gradual manner, all the way to the terminal type, the human egg:

"Firstly, the law of embryonic equivalents, by virtue of which each of the parts of an inferior animal embryo can, in certain conditions, such as those of a retardation or acceleration of evolution, acquire the distinctive faculties of the corresponding parts of a much higher animal, the later being itself merely an aggregate of colonized plastids.

"Secondly, the law of retrograde adaptation, which attributes to the embryos of superior animals, even very specialized, when placed in the aforementioned conditions, the faculty of adapting and developing in the fashion of inferior animal embryos that are scarcely differentiated.

"But I do not want to give myself more gloves than I could put on; you will notice that the second law, in sum, is, in reality, merely the reciprocal of the first, the terms of which it almost inverts. I will even add, to give Caesar his due, that the two theses both follow more or less directly from the great biological law that every embryo, in the course of its development, reproduces in a more-or-less abridged fashion the evolutionary phases of its ancestors—a law confirmed, notably, by the human embryo, which passes through the stages of the gastrula, fish, reptile, chicken, etc.[19]

"I ought, therefore, to have been able to achieve ascendant series in my geneses be retarding or accelerating the de-

---

[19] "Haeckel's law," usually stated briefly as "ontogeny recapitulates phylogeny." It is not true in any rigorous sense, although patterns of vertebrate embryonic development do lend it a superficial plausibility.

velopment of my eggs, as necessary. But that was the snag. One cannot catch a devil that has no hair. I could not influence the development of my eggs because they were not developing. They were alive, giving evidence of circulation and appreciable heat by means of my micrographs, but that was all. Once again, I had run into a dead end.

"This time it was radium that got me out of difficulty. A communication from the Cavendish Laboratory in Cambridge had just been circulated in the press, announcing that a young scientist, Butler Barke, had just succeeded in a new experiment in spontaneous generation. That experiment simply consisted of placing a particle of radium in a rigorously sterilized solution of gelatin. After an hour or two, microscopic examination revealed the existence of cultures formed of black dots that slowly increased in volume and subdivided into several new elements when their growth attained approximately one sixty-thousandth of an inch.

"That was a flash of enlightenment for me. Yes, perhaps it was radium, that new and mysterious dynamic agent, that contained the force susceptible of loosening the bonds in which nature was obstinate in keeping the creatures I had created captive. I therefore deposited some radium in the reservoir in which my eggs were simmering, protected against climatic variations by a layer of unemployed Bathybius.

"Alas, I had probably overdone the dose, for the eggs perished, and I had to begin all over again. My collaborator and I went back to work, and within a year, the damage was repaired. Although we renewed the radium experiment with various doses, however, our new eggs persisted in living without developing. I was beginning to tear my hair out in despair when the fortunate hazard to which I made allusion at the beginning of my little lecture. Hazard, the *deus ex machina* of inventors and scientists, finally intervened.

"In the course of one of those formidable storms accompanied by seismic shocks in which our latitudes are prodigal, lightning struck the reservoir and caused our eggs to...hatch, or germinate. What the radium had been unable to do, atmospheric and telluric electricity had accomplished at a stroke. I cannot describe the poignant emotion that gripped my entrails when, leaning over the first egg observed after the lightning strike, I recognized in the invaginated leaflets of the blastoderm the sketch of a vertebrate embryo presenting all the characteristic signs of a human fetus.

"Nor can I describe my horrified stupor in the presence of the amorphous monster which grimaced behind the translucent wall of another egg. The products of base cuckoos had slipped in among our eagle eggs! And we had no one to blame but ourselves, for only our inadvertence could have allowed our human eggs to be mingled with that laboratory debris.

"Perhaps, my collaborator Moutier suggested, it was necessary to file that stroke of witchcraft under the heading of 'singular effects of lightning'—the lightning that had overturned our cooking-pot, or had at least stirred it so thoroughly the no trace of Bathybius any longer remained.

"A simple joke, but rooted in a fact that was only too certain: our provision of Bathybius had disappeared, as if volatilized, and at a stroke, our experiments came to an end, because I no longer had the capital necessary to finance further dredging expeditions in the Indian Ocean. The bottom of the reservoir was dry and only its breached walls, at the most, still presented a few vestiges of grilled protoplasm reeking of burned horn.

"I thought at first of destroying the abortive seeds, whose suspect anatomy was perhaps only attributable to the incompetence of our manipulations, but after mature reflection I did nothing, thinking that their subsequent development and activity might enrich teratogenetic science, still so young and tentative.

"You know now how the Pure Ones and the Unclean Ones were born. You certainly know the latter better than I do now. Moustier has told you how we drove them into the south of the island, where their simple and rapid multiplication, in the fashion of protozoa, could only be a phenomenon relevant to the law of retrograde evolution that I cited just now. It remains for me to talk to you about the Pure Ones, whose story is much more complicated, and also more worthy of interest, since it is a matter, after all, of human beings that are almost normal.

"I can only say 'almost,' because it did not take me long to perceive that they were, unfortunately, afflicted by two congenital defects that placed them in an intermediary echelon: they had no sex, and their duration was excessively limited. In the early days, they grew and matured visibly; after two years they had attained their present stature and development, and I was then able to calculate that senility would arrive for them in about the tenth year—which is to say, imminently, since it has now been approximately nine and a half years—and that, in any case, they would not surpass the maximum longevity of a Newfoundland dog. The observations and information that you have brought me prove, moreover, that I was not mistaken in my anticipations. There are thirty of them in all, and as none of them has died as yet, it's probable that they will all die at the same time, and in the near future.

"I have, of course, as a matter of principle, renounced interfering in the social life of beings so highly organized. The members of my entourage, with the exception of Moustier, were unaware of their origin and of their physiological defects, and the moment had not yet come to divulge the secret of our experiments. We therefore kept them shielded from all profane curiosity, and as soon as they were fully grown I sent them to found a closed colony in the south of the island, were the Unclean Ones had not yet settled.

"It was only then that I realized that that group of asexual, non-individual beings, without roots in the past or any veritable human attachment, liberated from all the passions derived from the sexual instinct, represented a new formula of humanity, a totally unprecedented moral and social type, the observation of which might furnish an interesting contribution to the history of artificial selection.

"My work as well as my personal inclinations dissuaded me from undertaking such an absorbing study, but at that time

I had offered hospitality to a university professor on an intertropical botanical expedition, who wanted to explore the southern part of the island. He accepted enthusiastically the mission I confided to him, feeling that he had all the more aptitude for it because he had, he said, missionary blood in his veins.

"I ought to have mistrusted that blood, since, after all, it was not an apostolate that I was confiding to him. At the most, he was charged with giving my wards a semblance of an education in conformity with their organism and brief passage on the earth. But you can't stop a university man from playing the schoolmaster. He fabricated for the usage of those poor devils a grim theodicy, which gravitated around me, their Father and their Providence, which also included 'divines'—which is to say, all the bearded men on the island. In sum, he had no difficulty inducing in them absolutely false ideas about the world and its origins, concealing all the secrets of life from them, including the mystery of the sexes, and fashioning a kind of anthropocentric consciousness for them, limited to the region they inhabited and from which it was, in fact, forbidden to them to leave.

"It is also to the unfortunate bequest of that maniac—he has died since, let's be indulgent—that my wards owe their bizarre label of Pure Ones, as opposed to the others, who became Impure, or Unclean. Fortunately for them, the symbolism of those labels cannot torment them, since they do not know…they do not know anything about anything. It is to conserve for them, at least, the benefits of their total lack of culture that I subsequently decided to leave things in the *status quo*.

"I'll explain what I mean. The more I thought about their singular situation, unique in the world, the more I told myself that they represented a theoretically and perfectly happy humankind—a humankind that does not exist, and never has existed, but certainly will exist at the end of the human era. That humankind will, indeed, be ignorant of womankind, because there will be no more women, and it will be the ultimate neuter product of ancient sexual differentiations.

"I can see you smiling, but I shall soon prove to you that the supreme stage of human evolution will be marked by the suppression of the sexes—which is to say, the suppression of antagonistic male and female types, which will be confused, as is only just, with the extinction of the species. First, let me explain what I mean by the theoretically happy humankind, to which I assimilate the Pure type.

"Happiness, as you know, is a negative condition of being. No other definition is possible. Thus, the happy humankind is one that has no histories[20]—in the plural, no?—one that does not torture itself with the spur of sex; one that is not ravaged by the need of reproduction, of procreation; one, above all, on which the damnation of genesis does not weigh; one, in sum, that is ignorant of amour and all the catastrophes that it implies. And it really is that humankind that our artificial eggs have produced—but it is also, or will be, the humankind of the terminal stage of human evolution, and this is why:

"The history of general evolution shows us that the faculty of reproduction is perfected and diminished as the animal becomes more complicated. Among the unicellular creatures, it is both primitive and unlimited. The cell divides, and can continue to divide indefinitely. As we ascend the animal scale,

---

[20] It is relevant to note here that French has an ambiguity that English does not; the word *histoire*, as well as meaning "history," also means "story." Although the speaker is here ringing changes on the oft-quoted dictum that "happy peoples have no history," usually considered to have been derived by Thomas Carlyle from Montesquieu before being cited more succinctly by Tolstoy, the statement could be interpreted as applying to literature as well—an alternative reading encouraged by the role attributed in the plot to *Graziella*, and also by the emphasis here on the plural: on "stories" rather than a single "(hi)story."

we see fecundity diminishing at the same time as the reproductive organs are perfected and diminished.

"Among the segmented Metazoa, there are still several
pairs of reproductive organs, and already the faculties of budding or binary fission have disappeared. The propagation of
the species is limited from then on, as is the life of the individual. In the same way that in the vegetable realm, as the
types are perfected, we see them renounce the genetic profli-
gacy that permitted agamic or cryptogamic reproduction, her-
maphroditism, parthenogenesis and other aberrations of nature
in delirium. As a general rule, as soon as the sexes are differentiated sufficiently to become concrete in individuals, reproduction decreases.

"Among humans, finally, there is no longer anything but
a single consensual sexual union and an extremely limited
faculty of multiplication, which is diminishing from day to
day and will soon be reduced to zero. And then the reproductive organs will disappear, having become useless, as everything that is useless disappears in nature. The sources of human virility will dry up; women will cease to give birth. At the
very most, we shall see temporary parthenogenetic faculties
appear in a few stubborn females, as a transitional phenomenon preceding the total extinction of human fecundity. But the
generations thus conceived will no longer know amour, for the
'shameful' and puerile mystery of the sexes will have disappeared with the distinctive attributes of the sexes themselves,
and the life of the last humans will be a striking commentary
on the theory of absolute happiness—that which resides in the
absence of any passionate emotion..."

For the first time in the half an hour and more that he had
been speaking, the scientist stopped dead, as if afflicted by a
vocal weakness. He passed his hand over his eyes, and then I
saw his gaze flutter and mist over. Was it the passage of a
poorly disciplined emotion? At any rate, that gaze did not
seem to be plunging into the chimerical distances he had
evoked, but into a dolorous sentimental past: the ineffaceable

past that we all bear in our wilted hearts, and in the name of which we anathematize amour and its generous illusions.

What was embarrassing for me at that moment was that hazard had designated me to be the bearer of a complete refutation of his subtle theory of a perfect happiness founded on the disappearance of the sexual spur and the misunderstandings of amour. For that refutation was the very substrate of the mission with which the Pure Ones had charged me. A cruel hesitation held me momentarily in the impossibility of articulating a single syllable.

You know that I have never been very bold. In the present circumstance, not only was boldness scarcely within my scope, but I did not even enjoy any liberty of judgment, having all the difficulty in the world conserving the integrity of my conscious self in the midst of the formidable and chaotic impressions, alternately obscure and luminous, that the scientist's conversation had evoked.

"Have I left you somewhat nonplussed?" he said, suddenly, with the contrived smile of the master of a house apologizing to a guest who does not seem to be sufficiently amused. "I beg your pardon, but I could not edify you, even summarily, as to the mysteries of the island without showing something of the chemist."

I protested. His story had, on the contrary, interested me greatly. More than that, his conclusion, in particular, had overturned all my ideas, all the more so as—my, God, how artful I was!—the Pure Ones themselves had charged me with bringing him a request, doubtless vain and sterile in advance, but which nevertheless allowed a glimpse of a state of consciousness on their part that was not at all in conformity with the formula he had just stated.

"Damn!" The scientist guffawed. "If you're going to be amphigoric in your turn...would you care to explain?"

Well, no, I would have preferred to put off that vain explanation until another day. By explaining myself immediately, I would seem to be trying to cast a stone into the prodigious anthropological garden of which his genius had just given me a tour. My explanation, moreover, would be redolent with the profound trouble in which my intellect was still struggling, and it would then take on such a ludicrous expression that I would risk passing for an imbecile.

While I did my best to excuse myself, asking the Master for time to collect myself, a whistle-blast resounded behind a curtain next to the desk at which we were sitting. A short exchange took place via the intermediary of an acoustic conduit. A moment later, a coolie appeared, and presented the scientist with a small cephalopod exactly similar to the one from the peat-bog.

He examined it at length, and then turned to me, frowning, more nervous than he wanted to appear.

"It was an animal of this sort, wasn't it, that you encountered in the course of your excursion with Moustier?" On my affirmative nod he added: "Well, I'm told that our plantations are being sacked at this moment by thousands of similar creatures. If we want to avoid famine within a matter of months, it will be necessary to take immediate and energetic defensive measures. I shall therefore leave you, my dear Monsieur, asking you to come back tomorrow at the same time. In the meantime, I'm counting on having found a means of halting the progress of the scourge that has been brought to my attention, and we'll be able to resume our chat in complete security. We shall meet again on the very theater of their exploits...adieu! If, once again, I can understand...oh, the filthy beasts!"

He was on his feet, gesticulating nervously, no longer talking to anyone but himself. I had my wish; it only remained for me to consent and leave, and that is what I did, in haste to ascertain the extent of the disaster, which was far from leaving me indifferent. Already, however, the scientist had changed his mind, and he caught up with me in the vestibule.

"In fact," he said, "why don't you come with me, if your time isn't otherwise committed? In a few strides we'll be on the site of the disaster, and you'll see a spectacle such as you have certainly never seen before...nor I, either."

A labyrinthine path took us to a small iron door in the surrounding wall, at the summit of the triangle formed by the Residence. After the manipulation of a heavy lock, we were outside.

IX

The first thing that struck me was that the admirable silence that ordinarily reigned over the country, especially at that hour, no longer existed. One might have thought that thousands of little pairs of scissors, albeit invisible, were carving and slicing the air, uniting their clicking voices in a continuous, tremulous modulation that embraced the entire space.

From the place where we stood, we could look out over the sloping carpet of plantations of tea and coffee whose terraces rose up along the road leading to the Silver Table. At the foot of the carpet the line of rice-plantations undulated; it was from that direction that the noise was coming. We went toward it along a lateral path.

"How many Unclean Ones do you think there are, out there in the south?" the scientist suddenly asked me.

I hesitated, an absurd false shame seizing me by the throat—the same one that had prevented me from telling the whole truth to Moustier: the panic of the child who, having disturbed a wasps' nest, dare not complain about them to the owners of the tree. However, an obscure presentiment had been haunting me since the previous day, of I don't know what disastrous possibility, which I ought to ward off by speaking—with the result that this time, I made up my mind.

"There are at least five thousand...perhaps ten thousand...perhaps even more."

Monsieur Brillat-Dessaigne seemed astounded. His surprise, however, was scarcely perceptible, so much self-control did the man have. After a few seconds of silence, he went on, in the most ordinary tone.

"It's evident, then, that they've reproduced in the fashion of the inferior animals."

"How can that fact be explained, among beings as elevated in their organization, almost human in some respects?"

"It can't be explained by the biological theories that I was recounting to you a little while ago. In the embryonic state, these monsters must have benefited from a considerably accelerated evolution, initially by virtue of our chemical reactions, and then by virtue of the combined dynamic influences of the radium and the lightning. Other biomechanical influences might have been involved.

"I've just told you that atmospheric shocks and variations have a manifest repercussion on embryogenesis. We therefore find ourselves in the presence of beings that, while usurping the morphological advantages of a species much more highly evolved than their own, have remained adapted to the organic conditions of the humble type from which they originated. And take note that that explanation is entirely consistent with the phylogenetic theory—let's say biological theory, in order not to multiply barbaric terms unnecessarily—that shows us the greatest evolutionary progress realized by the retardation of sexuality.

"The Pure Ones have only obtained the intensity of evolution that has made them perfect humans at the price of the total suppression of sex. In the same way, the rapid evolution of the Unclean Ones has coincided with the stagnation of their gross, barely-sketched sexual modality. They are, in sum, and in accordance with the most concise formula, highly evolved beings adapted to very backward functional actions. In which case..."

The scientist hesitated, looking at me in an embarrassed fashion, as if, in spite of everything, he did not feel completely secure behind his rampart of hypotheses, and he fell silent.

"And the little cephalopods that are playing the role of locusts at present?" I said, trying to make a joke of it. "What do you think of them?"

"Pooh! They really are mollusks—cephalopods...laboratory cephalopods, of course. At the beginning of our experiments, it was with the simplest reactions that we obtained animals of this moderately complex type. Why? I never found out, any more than I know how they've adapted themselves to terrestrial life—nor, above all, how they've managed to remain hidden until now. As they emerged from the matricial urn we replaced them in the layer of Bathybius in the reservoir. After the electrical storm, we didn't see them again.

"Moustier, who is a convinced partisan of my theory of retrograde adaptation, has suggested that the survivors, hidden in the depths of the vat, were able to manifest, at a given moment, the phenomenon of encystment that is observed in certain infusoria. That's possible—but it's also possible that they simply emigrated to the south of the island in the wake of the Unclean Ones, toward whom they were attracted by a mysterious instinct of homology.

"They've reproduced thereafter by budding or binary fission—which is to say, in accordance with the modality of the phase through which they passed in our retorts: a modality that they've rediscovered by retrograde adaptation, the necessities of life demanding that they multiply rapidly, exactly like the Unclean Ones. Perhaps the latter domesticated them subsequently and kept them in captivity, either because of their edible quality or for some other reason...

"Anyway, it doesn't matter, since none of that explains why these degenerate and...disaffected...squid, if I might be permitted that improper but amusing terminology, have come to ravage our plantations today."

"Perhaps," I said, taking a risk, not without some intention, "we might question the two Pure Ones interned at the station. There's a chance, at least, that they know something about the habits of these creatures."

"Our two prisoners! Blockheads, my dear Monsieur; I've never been able to get a word out of them, never been able to obtain the slightest information, either about themselves or the Unclean Ones. I was on the point of mounting an expedition to the south when you arrived. I think, in reality, that those fellows fear me like the plague...as Israel feared Jehovah!" he added, laughing.

At the same time he plunged his arm into the long stems of the rice-plantation.

"Aha!" he said. Here's one that will pay for the others, while awaiting reprisals on a grand scale."

His right hand emerged, clutching a cephalopod, which disgorged a flood of ink.

"That was the only faculty it still lacked!" the scientist exclaimed. Then, showing me the parrot-like beak fixed in the hideous mouth, he said: "Look—that's what's making the noise of scissors that you can hear—it would cut, I'll wager, the strongest sugar-cane—and it really is the mandibular apparatus of the classic octopus. Their trunk, however is more reminiscent of *Phrynosoma*, a kind of lizard with the false appearance of a toad, of which I once dissected a rare specimen originating in America.[21] You'll notice, moreover, that most of its tentacles have been transformed into rudimentary organs of locomotion. It doesn't matter—I'm not proud of my work, and the proof..."

With a disgusted gesture of the left hand, he tore the head of the cephalopod, and threw away the two pieces, still palpitating.

Almost instantaneously, we were surrounded by a dozen of the monsters, which disgorged over our boots the fuliginous contents of their ink-sacs. A few energetic kicks got rid of them.

"A plague on these animals!" the scientist grumbled, while we accelerated our pace. "They're as intelligent as wasps—perhaps more so. Fortunately, their ink is inoffensive." He turned toward me. "One can't always say as much for yours, Messieurs the writers!"

I did not rise to that benign gibe. We were no longer in sympathy with one another, it seemed.

---

[21] *Phrynosoma* is the genus of horned lizards, sometimes popularly known as "horned toads." The majority of its species are native to the U.S.A.

The path that we were following rose through the upper plantations and eventually rejoined the road to the Silver Table about three or four kilometers from the Residence. The clicking of the cephalopods occupied in scything through the young shoots of the tea-plants, the coffee-bushes and the sugar-canes now filled the air to the right and left of the path, all along the green terraces arranged like an amphitheater around the rocky wall in which the little haven was inscribed. It was mingled there with an infernal mewling coming from the foot of the station, the intensity of which was multiplied tenfold by the exceptional sonority of the atmosphere and the lack of wind.

Monsieur Brillat-Dessaigne, very nervous, pursed his lips ironically. "That's probably our porter, amusing himself whipping up his menagerie instead of occupying himself usefully against a scourge of which his boarders might well be the first victims."

He was, however, slandering the worthy Alsatian. As we emerged from a clump of banana-trees, we saw him, in the center of a tea-field, perched in one of the aerial cages universally distributed throughout the island of Sunda: a simple lattice of reeds covered but not closed and supported by four sticks, from which a series of scarecrows designed to frighten birds is maneuvered with the aid of strings—scarecrows generally composed of a pole at the summit of which one or several palm-leaves rotates. The poor fellow was activating these devices with all the strength of his arms, while howling terribly, in spite of the mockery of a group of spectators among whom I recognized my wife and Moustier.

The group came to meet us, and I took advantage of the opportunity to introduce Yvonne to Monsieur Brillat-Dessaigne, who complimented her on her valor and good humor. At the same time, a strong contingent of coolies rushed through the plantations armed with flails normally used for threshing wheat, of which they made use to kill the cephalopods by the dozen. One might have thought, however, that some mysterious overflow was filling up the voids as soon as they appeared in their ranks, for neither the clicking nor the filthy squirming among the green shoots diminished.

In the new-denuded area around the foot of the aerial cage there was something like a prodigious gray tide undulating between the bamboo poles. At any moment the latter might be cut, and the unfortunate porter would then be precipitated to the ground—or, rather, on to the swarming, drooling mass of cephalopods, which would not hesitate to attack him and tattoo him in an extravagant fashion.

"Get down from there, you great poltroon," shouted Monsieur Brillat-Dessaigne, "or you'll be cooked!"

"All the more so," added Moustier, "as what you're doing is completely useless. All the young bushes are gone—there's not one left standing, and as for mastering these filthy creatures by terror, there's no possibility, especially with machines like those."

The learned chemist appeared to reflect. "It's obvious," he declared, "that only an energetic means is capable of ridding us of them…an energetic and radical means."

"Scalding them?" suggested Moustier.

"I've thought of that. We could direct one of our sources of hot water. At any rate, it would help us clear away the cadavers and flush them into the sea—but first we need to take away these crazed individuals' taste for tea, if I might risk that colorful expression."

"Sulfuric acid, then?" Moustier propose.

"All our crops would be doomed, and for a long time. No, if I recall the results of certain old experiments by Claude Bernard, ether will suffice…all the more so as sulfuric acid is too precious and constantly useful to waste."[22]

"Bah! We have a hundred carboys of vitriol in the cellars."

---

[22] The physiologist Claude Bernard (1813-1878) carried out extensive experiments with ether, primarily investigating its use as an anesthetic, but also its potency as a poison.

"We have as much ether—and ether doesn't destroy anything, and is, in consequence, less useful to us. Have a carboy of ether fetched, a bucket half-full of water and a hand-pump. I'll take charge of the rest."

The scientist's order were carried out with such rapidity that less than twenty minutes afterwards the hand-pump was functioning, projecting on the cephalopods a mixture of ether and water, the fan-like jet of which soon created a void within the area of its range.

All the cephalopods that were touched by the shower, or were even in its vicinity, immediately retracted their tentacles and were discolored, their ash-gray hue turning to an absinthe tint—which, in the majority of cases corresponded with death, or at least the complete anesthesia of the subject. The flails and shovels of the coolies finished the work. The survivors were driven back and tumbled down the slope. They were seen, a sticky mass of agglutinated clusters, almost inert, bouncing in a cascade from one terrace to the next, all the way to the foot of the cliff, where the torrent of a deflected hot spring dragged them away to the sea.

We went back into the Residence via the big portal opening on to the strand. Standing in the middle of his poultry-yard, the porter, who had run ahead of us was wringing his hands in despair.

Stumbling, half-blinded, their plumage bristling and soiled, his birds were wallowing in a tidal wave of ink, in the middle of which lay the cadaver of his pet marmoset.

"Fried, the poor beast!" he howled. "Fried, boiled—they've wrung his neck, the savages. And where's Maria? No more Maria, not the slightest trace. They've killed her, the poor innocent! Killed her, I tell you!! And he stamped his feet in rage, whirling like a dervish.

"But what? What has done this?" asked Monsieur Brillat-Dessaigne.

"How do I know? The squid, probably."

"That's impossible," Moustier declared. "For the marmoset, maybe, but Maria! They'd never have been able to reckon with something so big."

"Which doesn't make any difference to the fact that she's disappeared. Who knows? Perhaps there are other vermin here, more redoubtable than the squid. When I came in, I heard a kind of hum…and I thought I saw a big shadow disappearing over the wall."

Deeply upset, Yvonne took me to one side. "The situation is becoming too alarming for us not to put our hosts on their guard. I think the Unclean Ones have been following our trail since we left the Valley—and that they're the true instigators of all these depredations."

"That's quite possible. In any case, we'll know what's going on before long, since it's tomorrow that the Pure Ones are coming back to the Silver Table to find out the result of my mission. They'll surely give us the key to the puzzle."

My response did not seem to reassure my wife, all the more so as she had been convinced for some time of the inanity of the mission, and was anticipating a reversal of the good dispositions of our friends. As she insisted, I thought that I ought to defer to her desire, but the two scientists had just left, and I found that they had shut themselves up in their laboratory until the following day.

"Well, the die is cast," Yvonne declared, in a tone of the most extreme disappointment. "God only knows when we'll be able to get away from this accursed island."

In the evening, we went down to the shore, as usual, to enjoy the marvelous pyrotechnics of the sunset. But it chanced that the sky remained sullen, and what completed our dismal impression was seeing the epic porter go past as night fell, followed by a squad of coolies, which he was leading toward the yacht. Phantasmal, his hair blowing in the wind, pajama trousers floating over his thin legs, he was gesticulating and howling without interruption, and we heard fragments of phrases spun out by the sea breeze:

"It's with lead that this filth has to be killed...thunder of God...yes, it's lead that they must be given to drunk...but try to make these scientists understand...*scheissdreck und schmussbarieundess.*[23] Me, I'll show them what an old soldier can do...I'm going to fetch the machine gun and a good dozen guns...and we'll see who has the last laugh..."

"Do you hear that great fool?" I said, in jest, to my wife.

But her brow did not unfurrow, and she replied: "A fool whose inspiration, at the moment, might well have something Providential about it."

---

[23] Author's note: "Untranslatable into French." In English, it approximates to "Shit and sugarlumps."

X

"And now I'm listening to you," pronounced Monsieur Brillat-Dessaigne, when we met up again the following day, at the agreed time, sitting face to face at his desk.

"Do you know," I said, then, "what I thought when you told me about the fashion in which the Pure Ones were brought up? That, consciously or not, your botanist constructed a pastiche of the old Biblical theogony, enclosing the future of the Pure Ones in a kind of adaptation of *Genesis* based on that of the Bible, with a paradise devoid of Eve, in which the role of the tree of knowledge, the forbidden fruit, was represented by the Book—which is to say, by reading, the gift of reading, the faculty of self-education. With the result that they find themselves placed today, with regard to you, in the same situation as the first man of *Genesis* with regard to the Christian God."

"Of the first man before the fall, yes, and believe me, the analogy—the parallelism, if you like—of the two situations hasn't escaped me. It was in order not to modify an order of things whose sudden disturbance after the death of the botanist might have had the gravest consequences that I aped the Catholic God in my turn by rendering myself invisible, and as inaccessible as possible. As, in addition, faith is the correlative of the absence of intellectual culture, I maintained the Pure Ones in ignorance and superstition. Blessed are the poor in spirit, no? To remain happy, it was necessary that they didn't approach the tree of science—the book—and that they had no commerce with the divines; which is to say, with passionate humanity, from which their very physiology separates them. That took care of everything."

Monsieur Brillat-Dessaigne said that with a profound phlegm, proving that he didn't have the slightest idea where I was heading.

"No, not everything—for, suppose now that one of the Pure Ones, one of those men so securely bound in your fake genesis, the most intelligent of them, wanted, in spite of all prohibition, to sample the tree of science. Suppose that he succeeded, at the price of the most praiseworthy perseverance, in learning to read—what would become of him?

"That man, perhaps happy, according to the formula proposed by you, would cease to understand the purpose and utility of his existence. He would want to know amour, that prestigious word on which the entire life of other men reposes; he would want to taste the sacred joys and sadness attached to the manifestations of the sexual instinct, all the frissons of the flesh in joy, all the magic and all the alarms of Desire and Satisfaction.

"And then that man would come to you, his Father, his God, and, in his naïve and touching ignorance, mistaking you for an omnipotent Demiurge, he would ask you to give him the organs he lacks, which would make him the equal of the divines, the equal of the Adam of the Bible, who preferred to be damned and expelled from Paradise rather than not to taste the joys promised to him by Eve's lips."

This time, Monsieur Brillat-Dessaigne had followed me with an intense interest. My final words provoked an imperceptible shrug of the shoulders, while the flash of an emotion passed over his features. Then smiling and without malice, he said:

"Well, now we've arrived. If I've understood your apologue, a Pure One has learned to read, has revealed the veritable humanity—pitiful sexual humanity—to his brothers, and those unfortunates...because from then on, they were unfortunate...have charged you, who were passing through, to submit their complaints, to intercede with me, their Demiurge, as you put it, in order to persuade me to correct my work, and make them into beings similar to us. Take note that the most annoying aspect of the affair is that it appears to me to be impossible to make them understand that what they're asking of me is not in my power."

"That's exactly what I thought."

"How can it be explained to them, in fact, that they're simply chemical products, if I might put it like that—which is to say, the results of a series of exceedingly complicated reactions in which I played no part, for I was able to provoke those reactions and direct their progress, but my intervention was limited to that, and for good reason. The true creator of the Pure Ones is, therefore, Chemistry, not me. But Chemistry resembles nature in the sense that it cannot add anything to a living organism. Furthermore, if the Pure Ones were children of nature, if they represented, like us, the terminus of many thousands of intellectualized generations, they would understand everything themselves; but they're artificial beings, devoid of roots in the human past, with no mental heritage, no atavistic memory: beings as completely new as the symbolic Adam himself. So?"

"I recognize that the dilemma is embarrassing...for all sorts of reasons force you to continue to play the role of the inaccessible and inexorable Biblical God in whose guise you've been clad. You won't give them what they because you can't give them what they want, and you can't even—since they wouldn't understand—explain why you can't...which doesn't alter the fact that you're in the presence of a group of beings who are reproaching you for having rendered them unfortunate, by refusing them systematically the very thing by virtue of which we reproach the Biblical God for having damned us: amour."

"Hasn't it!" exclaimed Monsieur Brillat-Dessaigne, glad to underline an observation that absolved him.

There was a brief silence, and then he went on: "All this is ridiculous. This quest for sensations that they can't experience, sensations for which they don't even have the apparatus, is inexplicable! They're ignorant of the passionate tempests that agitate us. They're completely unaware of the obscure folly of embracing and swooning that has haunted humankind since the world's beginning. You know what sensuality is: a frisson delegated to us by creation—what am I saying, which is creation itself!—in the remotest ages, which lives again and dies again in us in the space of a lightning-flash, the narrow interval in which the frisson lasts.

"To be able to feel that, it's necessary to be the issue of nature, and not a vain chemical formula; it's necessary to be like us: impulsive—which is to say, beings incessantly dominated by the sexual instinct that summarizes impulsiveness in general. The Pure Ones, as you know, are liberated from that instinct; they're ignorant of its impetuous exigencies, its demented and sometimes bloody rages. How, then, can they estimate that they're unhappy—which is to say, troubled in the enjoyment of functions they scarcely suspect, and which don't correspond in them to any organ?"

"Perhaps the function can create the organ?" I remarked, smiling. But I added, immediately: "In truth, though, I believe that it isn't so much the quest for the genetic frisson that's tormenting the Pure Ones; perhaps, in fact, they scarcely suspect it, as you say, and only esteem it for its ultimate goal: procreation. I think that it's not so much that they deplore not being martyrs to the sexual instinct as the troubling mirage of *sentimental* amour that's haunting their minds, or at least their chief's mind, since reading an old copy of *Graziella* that he stole from our camp."

"One never profits from goods dishonestly acquired," sniggered the scientist, to mach my tone. "Oh, the poor fellows! They've become in their turn the victims of the old mirage of love that has dazzled generations of imbeciles. They're asking to bear the chains of the sentimental lie! But what prevents them? All things considered, then, it's necessary to suppose that, if they're asking for a surplus of male attributes, it's with the unique aim of perpetuating their ephemeral race!"

"Who can tell, in fact, whether the consciousness of annihilation—of imminent annihilation, since you're only giving them a few more months to live—isn't doubled for them by the terror of disappearing without having penetrated the meaning of life or left any traces upon the earth?"

Monsieur Brillat-Dessaigne made a broad gesture of compassion. "And what about us? Do we penetrate it—the meaning of life? Don't we disappear entirely, even those of us who leave great works of numerous descendants? No, believe me, these naïve individuals have simply perceived that they were too happy—which is to say, too tranquil; two homologous words, aren't they?—and they suddenly want to suffer a little pain, that's all. Amour! Oh, how can we tell them, how can we make them understand, that claiming the right to amour is claiming that of being the voluntary dupe of a vocal image, a word representative of a certain number of odious illusions and lies, from which many men like us have liberated themselves by murder or suicide?"

The great chemist fell silent. An inexpressible sadness veiled his blue eyes, which, wide open, seemed to stare for a few seconds at distant abolished images.

Then he looked at me, smiling again, bountifully.

"Don't tell them that. They wouldn't understand."

That conclusion brought us to the point of returning us to face the real problem to be solved: how to reply to the Pures...or, rather, how to send them away.

And it was thus that I was led to give the scientist the most detailed account of our skirmish with the Unclean Ones, and make him party to the various alarming indications on which my wife's apprehensions were based, and our near certainty that the zoological station would soon have to defend itself against aggressions even more redoubtable by their numbers than their strategic resources.

I was unable to convince him, however that it was a subject worthy of the slightest examination. He accepted responsibility for sweeping away the Unclean Ones as he had the cephalopods, their predecessors—and as for the Pure Ones, he gave me *carte blanche* to give them whatever rejection was best suited to their intelligence.

And we separated on that note, which had the appearance of having settled matters, while actually leaving everything in suspense.

"We can't count on Brillat-Dessaigne," I told my wife, when I got back. "Once beyond his chemical formulas, the man seems to be devoid of all practical intelligence."

And it was agreed that we would make an immediate approach to Moustier, in order to persuade him to take a few defensive precautions, just in case. At the same time, we would ask him to equip the yacht in such a way as to permit us to leave the island as soon as possible, a longer sojourn there being insufficiently attractive to us.

Unfortunately, we were unable to see the associate chemist, who was, we were told, supervising the taxidermic operations to which some of the cephalopod cadavers that had been picked up on the beach were being subjected.

That reminded me that I had promised myself, out of curiosity, to conserve one of the animals in question, which I had picked up in the poultry-yard. I had, for the time being, shut it in an empty box, where we found it dying in the middle of a sea of ink.

Examined closely, the monster differed visibly from the one we had seen at the peat-bog and the one that Brillat-Dessaigne had captured, from which I concluded that the scientists' "trials" had given rise to very various species. All it had of the cephalopod were the tentacles, four of which had been transformed into short legs with claws at the end; the other four, garnished with numerous suckers on the inner surface, were implanted in pairs on either side of the head, which resembled that of a *Bombyx*.[24] As for the skin, which was scaly and very shiny, it might, chemically prepared, have served some artistic purpose. Many times since I have regretted that the vertiginous pace of subsequent events did not permit me to preserve at least one specimen of those extraordinary creatures.

---

[24] The genus of silk-moths.

XI

The Pure Ones were punctual at the rendezvous. That same evening, toward sunset, I distinguished from afar, in the heights, the first flickers of the fires designed to signal their arrival at the Silver Table. I set forth immediately, accompanied by the two Pure Ones, who had solicited the favor of serving as my escort. That favor was an infraction of the regulations concerning them, but I thought that, given they were aware of the return of their brethren, they must also know many other things; doubtless they had made contact with them on the day of our arrival, when the porter had imprudently sent them for the luggage.

From then on, all regulation had become pointless, and it only remained for me to yield to the insistences of my precious Yvonne, who, with her habitual clarity of sight, decreed the utility of their departure, saying: "Better for them to be taken away; it's almost certain that they'll stay out there, and that will be two spies fewer in this place."

When we reached the encampment of the Pure Ones, the chief came toward me, without manifesting the slightest emotion, his features remaining impassive. Only his gaze, moist and shiny, betrayed the tumultuous sentiments of his infant soul. In order to conform to our customs, he offered me his hand; and as he looked at me without saying a word, I was struck by his fatigued complexion, the even more marked weakness of the essential muscles of the face, of a certain *crumpling*—something dull, heavy and weary—spread over and within his entire person, and which, among short-lived animals like dogs, is a characteristic sign of old age.

We went into the circle of the tents. I noticed at first glance that they were considerable in number, and I learned, not without surprise, that all the Pure Ones were present, all of them having demanded to join in a displacement that, this time, usurped the gravity of an expedition of war.

"I was sure of it," the chief said to me, having become bleak and somber, as soon as I had told him, briefly, about the complete failure of my mission. "I knew that he would refuse."

"He says that he cannot change the laws of creation."

"He lies, for whoever can do the most can do the least, as is said in your books. Why have we been extracted from nothing if we have to disappear completely, hardly having lived? For we are already reaching the end of our duration; our strength is diminishing day by day; our features are becoming hollow, our hair is turning white, like that of your old men. It is necessary that the Father intervene, that he recreate us in his image; we do not want to die like this; we do not want to die without having at least known all the joys of life. We demand a sex."

"The Father says that all of that is just a mirage—that what you mistake for the joys of life do not exist, and that true happiness consists in being unaware of them. As for sex, it is the damnation of humans and the source of their distress."

"If that were true, why would you live with a wife—a wife with whom you travel through the vast world, where millions of men travel with millions of other wives?"

"We all have our hidden distress, and we all regret only being children of nature."

"We have neither joys not distress, and what we regret is not being children of nature. But it is necessary that that changes, no matter what the cost. We want to be like you; we want to suffer; we want to love; we want to feel the world shuddering and palpitating in our veins—for to suffer is to live, to love is to live; even to die, as you die, is still to live, since living substance, that which has a soul and a sex, is imperishable."

"You're falling for the allure of words. The soul is only a metaphor serving to designate the most elevated manifestations of the personality. Death, for us as for you, is the total abolition of that personality; what does the rest matter?"

"That's precisely what we are demanding: a personality. It matters little to us that we disappear thereafter, since everything passes; the essential thing is to have existed. Furthermore, why does the Father never show himself to us? It is to have the right not to grant our prayers. Well, we shall constrain him to surrender his secrets to us, and then we shall be omnipotent, like him."

This time, the threat was too direct for me not to contrive a step backwards, at the risk of diminishing the Father's prestige.

"You're running to your doom, poor fellow! The Father can do nothing for you; his secrets are those that science steals from nature; they're within the range of everyone, of all those who combine great intelligence with a persevering an indefatigable determination."

"The secrets of nature are not within our range; the Father must surrender them to us, or we shall take them from him by force. Look over here!"

His gesture indicated the edge of the forest, where, between the scattered trees, gray shadows, strangely illuminated by the nearby fire, were capering, running, interlacing, sketching farandoles or delivering themselves to acrobatics that were reminiscent of the demons and witches of the Brocken. A shrill sound, like that of a child's bagpipe gave rhythm to those diabolical evolutions, and I ended up discerning, against a tree—as rigid and dull as him—the old fossil lemur, who was blowing into a little flaccid black bag that one might have imagined tailored in the skin of a vampire bat.

It even seemed to me at one moment that he perceived me, ceased blowing, and pointed his claws in my direction. Then the monsters that were dancing froze, and I saw the flames of the pyre scintillating in multitudes of vitreous lashless eyes. Then the bagpipe began to screech, and the entire band reentered into tumult, humming, with nightmarish contortions, brandished tentacles whirling, which seemed to be as many threats addressed to me.

"They have all come with us," the chief explained, in his uniformly sad and grave voice. "And it is the fossil-man over there who led them. We finally discovered his retreat. He has lived for years and years in an almost-impenetrable grotto, so he is almost blind. His eyes are those of night-birds, and he cannot talk, although he almost understands the language of signs. I believe that he does not know where he came from or what he is. No one knows him. I alone, who have read a great deal, divine in him one of our brethren from over there, doubtless paralyzed and cast into a lethargy by a quake of the earth or the sun, and whom another quake awakened when he was already beginning to take on the form and hue of the ones among which he had gone to sleep.

"Whatever he is, that man is far superior to the abject beings with which the Father has populated the island, so he has obtained an ascendancy over them; it is by his intermediation now that we can make the Unclean Ones carry out all our demands. Unity of command, is that not the expression? Always facilitate the movement of masses...

"In any case, you have already seen an example of what discipline can do with simple brutes. The Unclean Ones who, it appears, had already followed the trail during our first journey, preceded us here by two or three days, and, discovering the lush plantations on the cliff, they immediately released upon your rice-fields the army of cephalopods, which they normally employ for tasks of hygiene, but which they also use as nourishment when there is a dearth of snakes. The cephalopods only nourish themselves on green shoots. They received the mission to sack everything. You have seen them at work. Rather than disobey their orders, they were massacred to the last one. And the Unclean Ones will do the same if we launch them against the Residence—except that you might not be the stronger...

"Go, then, and tell the Father everything that you have seen. His fate is in his own hands. Let him grant our wishes, and we shall send all these monsters back to their lairs, even if we have to exterminate them to get rid of them."

"Once again, the father can do nothing for you. If you attack him, he will punish you."

"Who can tell? Our weapons are as good as his. But we do not desire his doom. Let him surrender his secret to us, and we will remain his respectful and grateful children. Tomorrow morning, at dawn, let him hoist a white flag over his wall, and the Unclean Ones will withdraw without committing the slightest depredation. I give you my word of honor."

The chief was now speaking with an increasing excitement, and I suddenly understood that no reasoning could overcome his demi-intellectual obstinacy. Then the vision of the catastrophes that he would draw down on his head and those of his fellows by his refusal to understand—and, alas, his incapacity to understand—appeared to me with a clarity so gripping that I was moved to the depths of my soul. The unfortunate fellow was, after all, a good and loyal individual, induced into error by ignorance alone. If he had read the book that was to cause his doom, was it not our fault—the fault of those he had saved from death spontaneously, out of simple humanity?

I took his hand, in an impulse of sincere pity.

"I beg you to reflect further," I said to him. "Remember that it is a friend who is speaking to you, a man who owes you his life, and also that of his wife. That man swears to you that the Father is telling the truth, that he can do nothing for you. Believe me; I have no reason to deceive you—on the contrary, I only wish you well."

"I also am your friend," replied the chief, while an emotion softened his voice, this time. "But I do not want to die yet, do you hear?—I do not want to die…and it is on our friendship that I am counting to make the Father understand that he ought not to let us age and die so quickly, so frightfully quickly"—a sudden terror shone in his pupils—"it is too sad, you see, and too stupid, to die without even having had the time to understand existence."

"The Father has given you life; he is not free alas, to prolong it."

A poignant silence greeted that confession. I looked at the chief, who lowered his head. His face had contracted, like that of a child about to burst into tears.

"It does not matter," he said. "I have read in the books that the majority of your people rebelled against their God because he could not give them immortality. We are only following their example. If, tomorrow, at midday, the white flag is not floating over the walls of the Residence, we shall commence the siege immediately. When the Father and his entourage have fallen into our hands, perhaps he will consent to negotiate. As for you, flee with your wife as soon as you can. Take refuge aboard the yacht that is moored in the harbor; recruit a summary crew, and quit this accursed island, never to return. That is the only advice that my friendship can give you."

"I can't follow it. You must sense yourself that it would be to betray my hosts to abandon them at such a critical moment."

"Adieu, then, and let destiny pronounce between us."

We shook hands one more time; then I headed for the exit from the encampment, searching my surroundings with my eyes for the two Pure Ones who had escorted me—but none of them came forward, and it would certainly have been impossible for me to recognize them among the exactly similar silhouettes arranged in a circle in almost complete obscurity, with nothing in their impassive, identical faces but the reflection of the protective fires--which, from time to time, splashed the dark underwood, where in Unclean Ones were continuing their Sabbat, with a more vivid flame.

My imagination tortured by the most sinister apprehensions, I went back down the florid slope alone, along the path that led to the foot of the wall behind which the zoological station was asleep, in its last night of repose.

XII

The magnificent dawn of the next day found Yvonne and me leaning on the balustrade of our veranda and calmly discussing the chances of our getting out of the deplorable situation in one piece. As the sun rose, gilding the prestigious equatorial décor in slices, reanimating the chirping life of the arbors, the impression of the previous evening's nightmare became more precise, doubtless by contrast, turning to physical malaise before the certain and increasingly imminent peril. If, at that moment, I was still able to talk calmly to my wife about the things I had seen at the Silver Table, and the threats suspended over our heads, it was uniquely because we were the only ones who knew, who were able to understand, who were attempting to do something.

I don't know whether you've noticed how much the absence or presence of others, of a host of others, of the mere fact of feeling that one is not alone in knowing that there is danger, modifies our attitude with regard to that danger. In Europe, where everybody feels the proximity of others at every hours of the day, and even the night, those who are threatened by any kind of danger immediately begun to agitate like poisoned rats, and that agitation spreads from neighbor to neighbor, extends and radiates, like a patch of oil, until the desired number of people are aware of it, and ready to give the episode all the appropriate noise and drama.

Such a resource was lacking here. We, who had seen the Unclean Ones at work, were the only ones who knew, the only ones who understood, the only ones to have a presentiment of the disaster that was in preparation. The bulk of the inhabitants of the Residence were uninformed, and the scientist didn't give a damn.

Yes, he *didn't give a damn*—that was the expression that Brillat-Dessaigne had used, the previous evening, when I had reported to my conversation with the chief him, word for word, and the considerations with which he had supported his ultimatum. Having never demanded anything of the Pure Ones, he did not admit that they were entitled to demand anything whatsoever of him. He had given them life and had furnished them with the means of subsistence. That that justified sufficiently in their eyes the ridiculous paternity that they attributed to him was of no importance to him; he did not intend to go any further along that path. Never, never, moreover, would he admit their claim to be unfortunate, when he was convinced—it was the bee in his bonnet—that they possessed the only true formula of happiness, that which resides in a life exempt from any passionate element.

As, in addition, he really could not give them what they were asking for, he did not even intend to communicate with them personally, appreciating very well that invisibility, inaccessibility and mystery, perhaps even inexorability, constitute the great strength of autocrats and potentates of divine right. Moustier, his assistant, would be charged with recording their vain grievances, for form's sake, if they presented themselves with a pacific attitude. In the contrary case, they would be met with rifle fire.

It was that final statement that my wife and I were discussing at that moment, with the anguished sensation that those words, pronounced too lightly, were sufficient to poison the regal décor that surrounded us, mingling I don't know what venomous tint with the green of the trees and the blue of the sea, and rendering the fiery breath of the equatorial sun more unbreathable and murderous than as reasonable. Not that rifle shots, fired, after all, in legitimate self-defense constituted an extraordinary and terrifying thing in themselves—but how and with what would they be fired, and by whom? Such was the question that, for the moment, was furrowing our brows and adding, perhaps ironically, to the hieratic attitude of our silhouettes, motionless within the florid frame of the veranda.

Rifles! Doubtless there were a few of them at the Residence now, thanks to the initiative of the porter, who had spent a good part of the night trailing weapons around beneath the arcades of the vestibule, where they produced fantastic sonorities that woke up the entire poultry-yard. But what state could those weapons, evidently coming from the yacht, be in? In any case, even if the rifles were usable, the cartridges must be defective, for we have just heard the Alsatian singing at the top of his extraordinary ventriloquial voice: "It's powder that we need now, powder and bullets, as the Victor Hugo's ballad says"—words from which he drew a special refrain a few minutes later, abridged and fitted to the tune of *C'est ta poire*.[25]

Thus, the rifle fire by means of which one could respond to eventual aggressors, whatever it was, remained for the moment in the realm of pure hypothesis. Leaving aside the hunting rifles possessed by the Europeans, one single carbine, for which I could answer, was ready to fire—mine—and that would never fire at people to whom both of us owed our lives, and whom I was determined, whatever happened, not to treat as enemies

As for the Unclean Ones, you will recall that they were immune to bullets, by virtue of their inconsistent skeleton—or, rather, their absence of a skeleton, the gelatinous substance if which their tissues and muscles were composed presenting no trace of vertebrae.

To these pessimistic observations—pessimistic in the sense that they demonstrated clearly the scant efficacious resistance that the people of the Residence could oppose to a general attack by the hostile forces in coalition against them—was added the obviousness of their numerical inferiority. There were only a dozen Europeans, Moustier had said, thirteen counting the porter—who did not count. And we commented in passing on the ironic lie given to that gibe by the astonishing porter himself, alone for the moment in organizing the defense. There remained the coolies, perhaps numbering

---

[25] A popular song from an 1887 revue of the same title by Julien Serment and Louis Bataille. The Victor Hugo poem to which the porter refers is "L'Enfant" from *Orientales* (1829).

two hundred, but apart from the fact that the majority were currently employed outside in repairing the damage to the plantations—they were all the multicolored patches that could be seen moving amid the distant green waves, like insects collecting pollen in the sun—it seemed to us quite plausible that they would take to their heels as soon as the Unclean Ones put in an appearance.

We were at that point in our reflections and conjectures when a note was brought to me from Monsieur Brillat-Dessaigne asking whether I wanted to accompany him and his collaborator to the reservoir, where unusual things were happening, as he had just observed with the aid of binoculars.

I replied affirmatively, and got ready to depart alone, but my wife made the observation that circumstances imposed a requirement upon us to remain together henceforth as much as possible. As she manifested the desire to accompany me, I had her put on knickerbockers, and I stuck the machete in my belt. Then we went up to the upper gardens, where a coolie on guard introduced us into a tower serving for various meteorological observations.

The two chemists were waiting for us there.

"Devil take me if I can understand what can be happening out there," Brillat-Dessaigne said to us, his binoculars aimed at the mountain. "No human form is distinguishable on the ridge of rock overlooking the reservoir, and yet the crowns of the trees are moving, and large stones are falling from time to time."

That was true; I had just seen one fall without the aid of binoculars.

It was not yet ten o'clock. According to their ultimatum, the Pure Ones would not commence their hostilities until the sun reached its maximum—which is to say, at noon. It could, therefore, only be some move on the part of their acolytes. The best thing was to go and see—and, if necessary, to inflict on the Unclean Ones a lesson that they would remember.

We departed immediately, accompanied by two coolies, all riding ponies. We took the spiral path that was familiar to us since our excursions with Moustier: a difficult route for our mounts, but which offered the advantage of being out of visual range of the Silver Table.

Twenty minutes later we were within sight of the little platform of the reservoir. At that place the path was almost level, and we were about to start galloping when an explosion of frightful cries immobilized the ponies. Using both spurs, I succeeded in making mine advance as far as a bed from which the entire masonry of the reservoir was visible.

I have said, I think, that a part of that masonry—about three-fifths of the cylinder—was adapted to the very wall of the mountain, which was almost vertical there and carpeted with an inextricable tangle of spiniferous plants. Now, there was a gaping hole in that thicket, from which a jet of steaming water was spurting—definitely sulfurous, as my hypersensitive nasal mucus attested—which was falling in spray into the reservoir, in the depths of which a human voice was howling mortally. Attached to a nearby banyan, three ponies from the Residence were bucking and whinnying in terror. I calmed the down by means of a few pats on the neck and looped the reins of my own pony over the branches of the same tree.

Meanwhile, the howling suddenly diminished in intensity. It had ceased completely when I reached the top of the heap of stones I had used a week before to hoist myself up to the rim of the reservoir.

Three human bodies were lying inanimate among the long grass at the bottom of the vat, whose steep sides were beginning to disappear under the water. I recognized the porter and two coolies. On the side where I was, the reservoir, very uneven in its level, was scarcely three meters deep. I let myself slide down the internal wall, and one bound took me to the bodies of the three men.

One of the coolies was lying face down, mortally struck by a boulder that had broken his neck. The other was still breathing, but losing blood from a wound that cut into his forehead from one temple to the other. The porter seemed simply to have fainted from terror; at the most, he might have been slightly scalded. He came to, in fact, as soon as I slapped his face with my handkerchief, dipped in the pool formed by the cascade that was falling at least four meters in front of us.

Immediately, he stated moaning: "They're boiling me, the dirty beasts, they're boiling me!"

"Get up quickly," I said. "You can explain outside."

He leapt to his feet. His eyes fell upon the two bodies lying at our feet.

"Ah! Ah!" he muttered. "They've killed my coolies...all right...all right...we'll have something to say about that..."

In the meantime, I tried to reanimate the wounded Hindu, who soon opened his eyes and thanked me with the sad smile typical of the indigenes of Ceylon. He might have been eighteen years old at the most. His wound wasn't serious; he quickly recovered full possession of his senses and his strength, and helped me to carry the corpse of his comrade to the foot of the wall, where we laid it down temporarily. The Alsatian watched us, sniggering and mumbling a kind of burlesque monologue which incessantly came back to the idiotic refrain of the previous evening: "It's powder, it's powder, it's powder that we need."

A breach permitted us to climb back up to the crest of the wall as footfalls announced the arrival of the little troop I had preceded.

Apprised of the situation, Brillat-Dessaigne shook his head, and did not say a word to begin with. Then, perceiving the porter, he scolded him harshly, not being able to tolerate, he said, employees or functionaries of the station leaving their post without authorization.

"I was fetching powder," was all the response that the Alsatian stammered—but he eventually explained that the previous evening, after the affair with the "squid," he had brought the revolving cannon and a quantity of rifles from the yacht, but as the munitions were defective, it had occurred to him to come and see whether the powder-store of the reservoir might contain any.

"You're nothing but an imbecile," thundered Brillat-Dessaigne. "Given the time you've been here, you ought to know that that storage-bunker only contains dynamite. Anyway, you haven't been authorized to go into it, and you wouldn't even have been able to get into it, since the lid bolted to the disk requires a special key to unscrew it."

The Alsatian objected timidly that he had found the key in the taxidermy laboratory, and that he had done it "for the best."

"Give me the key immediately," said the scientist, "get back to your spy-hole, and stay there until further notice."

His features convulsed, even paler than usual, and trembling from head to toe, the unfortunate porter rummaged in his pockets, mumbled a few oaths in his incomprehensible idiom, and then, with a discourage gesture, pointed at the reservoir. He had presumably dropped the key at the moment when the terrible jet of scalding water, mingled with stones, had descended upon his two companions.

"It's absolutely necessary to recover that key immediately," the scientist declared. "Show me where and how you lost it."

And as he scaled the wall with a thoroughly youthful ardor, we all followed him, including my wife, to whom her costume conferred gymnastic aptitudes that she had not previously manifested. I feared the shock to her sensibility of the sight of the Hindu's cadaver, but she was spared that sad spectacle, the coolies having already removed their unfortunate comrade, who was taken back to the Residence on a stretcher.

It was evident that the beings that had provoked, one way or another, the outflow of the sulfurous spring must have profited from the simultaneous debilitation of the three men to take possession of the key. Interrogated again, however, the porter affirmed that at no time had he perceived any animate form whatsoever in the vicinity of the reservoir. The accident had become abruptly manifest at the moment when he was trying to unfasten the screws of the disk. A few blocks of stone had fallen first, followed by an interval of a few minutes, and then a mass of water had gushed out in a jet, which, simply by virtue of the displacement of air, had knocked him down. That was when he had perceived the sad condition of the coolies and had fainted in fear.

The fact, rather grave, in sum, was the object of an argument between Brillat-Dessaigne and me. He declared his conviction that the criminal maneuver had to be attributed to the Pure Ones. My own opinion was directly contrary to his. To begin with, the Pure Ones would not have hidden in order to act; that was not their habit and they would never, in any case, have been able to dissimulate themselves so completely. The absence of any footprint or other revelatory indication, and the inductions drawn from the location itself, sheer and scarcely propitious to the gymnastic prowess of ordinary individuals all indicated, on the contrary, that we were in the presence of creatures more agile and able to displace themselves more rapidly than humans.

At that very moment, as if to support my arguments with palpable and irrefutable proof, a hum burst out in the thorny thicket that overlooked the enclosed part of the reservoir. Having searched that kind of suspended thicket with my eyes, I distinguished several gray patches agitating among the creepers about thirty meters above the crest of the wall, almost at the same level as the fissure from which the improvised cascade was spurting. I pointed out the suspect location to the scientist and his collaborator, who directed their binoculars upwards. Already, however, the porter, whom my gesture had not escaped, had precipitated himself outside the vat, with baroque roars.

"Ah! I'll winkle them out…what will it take…what will it take?"

"You're right," said Brillat-Dessaigne, lowering his binoculars. "They really are Unclean Ones, and the most dangerous species—if that adjective can be applied to such paltry and inconsistent beings."

"Don't you think," said Moustier, "that they have the rudiments of vertebrae?"

But Brillat-Dessaigne shook his head negatively. "I don't believe so. They're articulated brachiopods or cephalopods originating from the accidental fusion of a little of the vitellus of a human egg with the germinative plasma of a mollusk egg, doubtless the egg of the *Cuciotenthis unguiculatis*[26] that we had kept alive for such a long time in the layer of Bathybius vitalized by radium."

Their discussion was interrupted by hurrahs descending from the spiny thicket, and almost immediately the brushwood parted. The Alsatian appeared on the edge of a narrow ledge carved into the sheer wall, ten meters above our heads, clutching in his vigorous fist the two tentacular arms of an Unclean One, which was struggling like a rodent caught in a snare.

---

[26] Author's note: "During his last expedition to the Azores the Prince of Monaco captured a cephalopod of this species, whose ten arms bear more than a hundred claws sharper than those of a tiger. It also has thick armor. It was found in the stomach of a sperm whale that had just, when caught, eaten half a dozen of the monsters after having decapitated them with a single bite." The taxonomic appellation cited here was given by the Prince of Monaco's chief associate in his report of the expedition in question, but was never adopted generally; the Latin name by which the then-legendary species in question—the "giant squid"—is more usually known is *Architeuthis*. More than a hundred partial specimens were recovered from the stomachs of sperm whales before a live specimen was finally captured by Japanese fishermen in 2012. Rumors of its giantism, although a boon to writers of adventure fiction—who have always been more inclined to recast the species as a "giant octopus"—are much exaggerated, and actual specimens have never implied a total length much in excess of ten meters, although that can still be reckoned impressive.

"Got me the Olibrius!"[27] he cried. "It's as soft as a tobacco-plug and hums like a Dutch top... Wait, and I'll show you the thing at close range."

We saw him tumble down in two or three bounds, which resembled as many successive falls, through the thorny clumps, and then appear on the half-obliterated crest of the wall.

At the same moment, however, the prisoner braced its two free arms against the rocky wall, and imparted such a shock to the poor devil that he lost his balance. He tottered, and fell into the bottom of the vat, already covered at that point by two feet of sulfurous water. One of the tentacles remained in his hand, the Unclean One having preferred to have the limb torn away than to allow itself to be dragged into the abyss.

Scalded once again, more seriously this time than the first, the unfortunate porter uttered a terrible imprecation, while the monster, which did not appear to be suffering from its mutilation, got ready to rejoin its fellows by the most rapid route. One or two gyrations to build up its momentum, and a chromatic hum, and it was about to disappear when one of the coolies grabbed his machete and hurled it parabolically, in the fashion of a boomerang. It was struck laterally in the body and sectioned into two halves, a short distance apart.

And the habitual phenomenon occurred: the two fractional beings stretched themselves out, in order to meet up, so successfully that they were reconnected. They no longer offered anything to the eyes but a homogenous and diffluent

---

[27] The porter's "oliprius"—which corresponds in his eccentric eye-dialect to olibrius, might be a misrendering of "octopus," but French readers as well-read as Hoche would have recognized Olibrius as a legendary governor of Gaul, who became a stock character in Medieval mystery plays and whose name was adapted by Molière and others as a generic term for cruel braggarts. As the porter can quote Victor Hugo, there is no reason why he should not be able to reference Molière too.

150

gelatinous mass, which started moving in the direction of the declivity—a spectacle almost familiar to me, but which Brillat-Dessaigne followed with intense interest.

"You can clearly see," he said to Moustier, "that my conjectures relative to the evanescence of their form were absolutely correct; this one dissolved as soon as its movement—which is to say, life—ceased, but the molecular mass conserved the ameboid properties of the Bathybius."

The two chemists were doubtless about to mount their terrible biological hobby-horse, but the water, which was rising, and driving us into the last remaining corner of the reservoir, interrupted them. The flood was already licking our feet; it was time to climb back up the wall, and that was what we all did, including the porter, who continued to screech, as my wife put it "like a scalded cat," but without letting go of the tentacle removed from his victim, which he was brandishing in the fashion of a trophy.

The scientist tore it from his hands and ordered: "Go back and get your wounds dressed."

As the porter started to go away, moaning, with his head bowed, Brillat-Dessaigne called him back, saying: "In fact, what did you see up there?"

"It's a deflected spring." Immediately ready for further feats of prowess, he added: "I'll go block it if you want."

"Not on your life...go on, get back to the station." Turning toward us, the scientist added: "Since the key is lost, it's better that a few feet of water cover the disk until further notice."

Moustier had drawn nearer, and examined the tentacle curiously. It was visibly discoloring. One might have thought it the skin of a balloon formed into a miniature elephant's trunk.

"These monsters," he said, laughing, "could, if necessary, be classified among the proboscideans..."

"Not at all," riposted Brillat-Dessaigne. "It really is a true human arm in the process of perfection. Look—no trace of suckers from top to bottom, and that disappearance must be caused, as always, by atrophy due to lack of use. In consequence"—he turned toward my wife and me—"the qualification 'dangerous' that I used just now must be pure hyperbole; these monsters are all the more inoffensive because their arms have lost the properties of the arms of squids without having yet acquired all those of human limbs. Notice that they no longer have more than four tentacles out of eight[28]—two arms and two legs, evidently—a reduction that confirms another biological law, the one by virtue of which the number of organs diminishes as they become more advanced, quantity being inversely proportional to quality. From which I conclude that with a few jets of sulfuric acid diluted with water, this time propelled by a steam pump, we can annihilate them in a matter of minutes, even if there are several thousand.

At that moment a shrill, almost metallic whistle, like that of a large caliber bullet, passed over our heads. A coolie who had remained sitting astride the crest of the wall pointed his index-finger in a south-westerly direction, where the sharp ridge of the Silver Table stood out distinctly, and I only remembered then that the topography of the locations, at the same level and directly opposite, permitted a direct mutual view, while hiding the routes by which one reached them.

My watch, consulted, informed me that it was five past noon.

"Damn!" said Brillat-Dessaigne. "Is that the opening of hostilities?"

I replied that I did not believe so, the Pure Ones being too expert as marksmen for such a miss not to have been intentional. For me, it was a simple warning, or even a signal, addressed to the people on the mountain.

"Too bad!" murmured the scientist, and remained pensive for a moment. Then he added, more loudly: "No more

---

[28] His previous footnote confirms that the author was aware of the fact that squid have ten tentacles rather than the eight possessed by octopodes, but confusion of the two kinds of cephalopods was very common at the time.

hesitation, now; we'll all go back and arm ourselves; the station is about to be put in a state of siege."

We set forth, preceded by the coolies, whose proud allure I now admired, although I had previously had a low opinion of them. Brillat-Dessaigne rode alongside my wife, while I formed the rearguard with Moustier—who, since the rifle bullet, seemed even more perplexed than his boss.

Looking back at hazard, I perceived that the waterfall had just dried up, as if by magic.

XIII

Monsieur Brillat-Dessaigne invited us to lunch, but we were all too preoccupied for it to be permissible to linger long at table, so the service was expedited in less than half an hour. The call of a siren then gathered all the male personnel of the station in the central courtyard. The ten European employees formed a kind of exceptional platoon, consisting, as I think I've already mentioned, of a blacksmith, two mechanics, two electricians, two secretaries and three mariners, one of them a helmsman. The last three constituted the entirety of the yacht's crew. Those ten men were precious, in the circumstances, in that they each possessed a hunting rifle and a supply of cartridges. The two women, of course, did not count.

The coolies numbered exactly a hundred and ninety-five. Twenty of them were elected to form a permanent company of guards charged with the surveillance of the enclosing wall and its round-path. That company took up its service immediately, only armed with machetes and hatchets, because the dozen rifles brought from the yacht by the porter were not in a useable state, and in any case, the ammunition was still in the storage-locker. It was decided, moreover, that the unoccupied coolies would make several trips to the boat during the day in order to provide arms and cartridges to all the valid men and to bring back several boxes of projectiles for the machine-gun, which was placed on the south-west bastion, its muzzle aimed at the Silver Table.

The execution of that order had, unfortunately, to be postponed, because a coolie who had been on watch in the little meteorological observatory suddenly arrived, with terror in his eyes, to announce that the various paths extending through the plantations had been invaded by confused masses of shapeless and indescribable creatures, which seemed to be advancing—or, rather, rolling—in profound columns toward the southern wall of the Residence.

Brillat-Dessaigne aimed his binoculars at the enemy and said, smiling: "It's an entire army! And the Silver Table is still disgorging more. All the heights are swarming and seething with nameless creatures, some of which don't even have faces..." As Moustier approached he said: "Would you believe, Moustier, that they could be so prolific, these descendants of Zoé?"[29]

Already, on his orders, the steam pumps had been set up in a battery at the foot of the wall, in proximity to a number of vats almost full of water, into which the scientist had just finished emptying the contents of a carboy of sulfuric acid himself. He then invited us to climb up to the south-eastern bastion, from which we could follow all the incidents of the battle.

I have already mentioned the gymnastic qualities of certain species of Unclean Ones, whose rigid tongues permitted them to progress with an extraordinary rapidity by spinning vertically like clowns performing cartwheels. The entire advance guard of the attacking corps was formed by those speedy beings, some of which, carried away by their momentum, came to crash into the wall. Others, however, seeing the danger, succeeded in rising up in prodigious leaps, which carried them over the obstacle. Their fate was scarcely more enviable, however, for the coolies massed at the foot of the round-path, received them with the blades of their machetes. Several hundred of them were fatally slashed, and trampled underfoot with savage clamors. A general halt was effected in the files disseminated among the crops; then they rallied and concentrated into compact masses, at the hazard of clumps of

---

[29] Author's note: "Biologists call a zoé the creature that emerges from a crab's egg." The term—derived, of course, from the Greek word for "life," which provides the prefix of zoology—is indeed used in that specific form in French scientific terminology to denote the larval form of various crustaceans, and employed more widely to denote a particular phase of post-embryonic development, but Brillat-Dessaigne is also making a pun on the common Christian name.

trees that remained standing. Closer to us, toward the bottom of the slope, the sun suddenly struck micaceous carapaces, which began to scintillate like a river of precious stones, and then sank fugitively into the green waves of the rice-fields. For a few seconds, there was a formidable silence, which none of us cared to break. Only my wife, her forehead creased, who was also equipped with binoculars, whispered in my ear: "They're waiting for the signal of the gong."

She had hardly finished that sentence when a dull rumor burst out on the heights of the Silver Table. The rumor grew, amplified, and Yvonne and I recognized the precipitate strokes of the gong that had once saved us from the most horrible death.

Then a sadness descended upon us, and I felt my wife's shoulder shuddering against mine. The air was not vibrating as it had before, however, with an ample and placid rhythm. It was, on the contrary a rapid succession of abrupt strokes, which was sounding the charge. But nothing budged in the plantations, where the Unclean Ones were so well hidden that, at the most, only an abnormal palpitation of the bushes or stems revealed their presence.

The bellowing of the gongs suddenly fell silent and once again, absolute silence reigned. After a few minutes however, the shrill and whining song of the bagpipe rose up at the front of the nearest terrace.

Then we saw a strange, disconcerting spectacle, well designed to terrify the coolies, who had never heard of the marching forest of *Macbeth*. The entire mass of the bushes and stems that were still standing came forward, with a single slow, coordinated movement. One might have thought that all the crops on the cliff had come to life and were advancing to attack the Residence.

Moustier let slip an imprecation. "Whatever's going on, our crops are ruined!" He turned to Brillat-Dessaigne. "There's nothing else for it—I'll start up the pumps, and as soon as they're within range of the jet, I'll..."

The scientist interrupted him with a resounding exclamation: "Look at that!" And without taking the binoculars away from his eyes, he designate, slightly to the rear of the marching nursery, an isolated biped, human in form, with the face of a mummy and legs that look like corkscrews, by virtue of the thousand folds and disjunctures of their inconsistent substance: the bagpiper, the old lemur!

"A living specter, in truth," sniggered Moustier.

The scientist continued examining him through his binoculars. "Better than that," he said, "a living fossil, but which has nothing comparable in paleontology.[30] It's absolutely necessary that we capture it without damaging it. You're going to aim the hose yourself, my dear Moustier, be careful to spare it...spare that entire battalion if necessary...we can have it put to the sword by the coolies..."

Moustier shouted a brief command to the mechanic manning the pump. The machine went into operation, and the chemist, who had brought the hose up on to the round-path, directed the nozzle toward the nearest assailants, those in the rice-fields. But the latter were out of range and remained immobile, while the bagpiper's battalion continued to advance. Having come within forty meters of the wall it stopped in its turn, the wing pivoting about the center in a leftward movement, unmasking an entire field of tea, which rushed forward amid a concert of the most sinister ululations that we had ever heard in our lives.

At the same time, however, a noise of flowing water cut through the air; the pump began its work. A great liquid ser-

---

[30] As when the narrator used the term "fossil" with respect to this creature, this sentence does not necessarily imply that what Brillat-Dessaigne means by the term is a literal survivor from remote prehistory. The hypothesis emitted by the chief of the Pure Ones, which attributed the origin of the "lemur" to Brillat-Dessaigne's experiment, is surely much more plausible, and much more likely to have occurred to any observer in the circumstances.

pent leapt forward to meet the assailants, and its enormous head, darting this way and that, sowed death in their ranks.

Two entire ranks collapsed, half-buried under the bushes that their carriers dropped as soon as they were hit; other arriving ranks, hampered by the branches blocking their passage, stumbled and got up, only to be annihilated in their turn.

The bagpiper's battalion bore stoical witness, without moving, to that disaster, nightmarishly orchestrated by that most bewildering of tunes.

Pale fumes rose up above the field of the massacre, and a strong odor of burnt horn spread through the air. A disquiet began to freeze the wave of the surviving tree-bearers; it was communicated from rank to rank, degenerating into a panic. The majority of the newcomers hastened to drop their burdens in order to remain masters of their movements. The mass was still hesitating when a squadron of coolies came around a corner of the wall, machetes raised, charged with taking possession of the fossil man.

Then the rare bushes that were still upraised fell at a stroke, and the entire center of the attacking army flowed back toward the heights.

The pump having ceased its play, the coolies advanced, charging the immobile battalion, behind the ranks of which the bagpiper was shielded. They were already falling upon the monsters, blades high, when the creatures hidden in the rice-fields spread out over the green waves where they had been crouching. They were no longer micaceous now; they were rutilant in the sunlight, throwing off red, yellow, emerald and blue flames, the semblance of a maleficent crop germinated beneath the wand of some demon.

Brillat-Dessaigne clapped his hands, delighted and exultant.

"Marvelous mimics!" he cried. "What we mistook for grains of mica was simply the gleam of their chromoplasts at rest. While they were hidden in the rice-fields they took on a green coloration, and that's why we could no longer see them."

Disconcerted, the coolies had stopped, apparently wondering whether they ought to confront that new enemy or beat the retreat. Then the entire gemmed horde went into action, and charged them in unison, spinning and humming with a savage frenzy.

"The imperial guard going into the furnace," Moustier joked.[31]

"Have you seen those creatures before, out there?" Brillat-Dessaigne asked my wife, and on her negative response, he went on: "They must have been encysted, then, dormant in some crevice in the mountain, and the Unclean Ones, recently arrived, have revived them, God knows how…look at them lurching, though; they're surely blind, guided solely by smell. In any case, it's the most magnificent example of creatures that have remained adapted to the mollusk stage, while being elevated by certain quasi-human faculties. I absolutely must obtain a few living specimens."

He coolies had almost broken ranks and fled at the moment when the little rotating rainbows arrived. They rallied on seeing the first rank scythed down by a well-directed jet from the hose, and all the creatures composing it instantly slain, as many flaccid and tarnished corpses strewing the ground. Their dead bodies had the form of an oval sac in the center of which, beneath hoops of sticky filaments, was the sketch of an eyeless face.

The pump having suspended its intervention, the monsters resumed their fantastic charge, saluted by a resounding "*Ave Caesar!*" from Moustier, whose ostentatious irony, careless of chronology, evoked Waterloo and Byzantium by turns. A veritable hedge of sharp blades received them, on which their successive ranks came to impale themselves, until the moment when an eddy produced by the agglomeration of carapaces slithering over one another impelled them in a new

---

[31] Moustier is quoting Victor Hugo, describing the battle of Waterloo in "L'Expiation": "Tranquil, smiling at the English grapeshot, the Imperial Guard went into the furnace."

direction—that of the bastion on which we were standing. The pump then resumed its office, stretching on the ground all those that disdained to flee or did not succeed in doing so.

"We're going to undertake a mass sortie," said Brillat-Dessaigne, "and fire a few rifle-shots to complete the rout—at the same time, we'll bring back the prisoners."

In response to a curt order, the Alsatian opened both battens of the great portal, not without a hectic mime, seasoned with mutterings about "popguns" and "paupers" uttered between clenched teeth.

"You're going to come a cropper!" he called to me, personally, as we went out at the head of a hundred coolies—and his prognosis was almost exact, for we had scarcely taken a few steps along the southern face of the wall when a fusillade burst forth about five hundred meters to our left, half way up the cliff. It lasted for ten seconds at the most, and all the bullets passed over our heads.

It was, without a doubt, a second warning from the Pure Ones. The Europeans, all equipped, as I've said, with hunting rifles and cartridges, replied with a salvo devoid of conviction, the enemy remaining invisible.

Nevertheless, the detonations accelerated the retreat of the Unclean Ones, who folded up for good this time, abandoning three-quarters of their number on the battlefield. Even the chromatophores ended up turning tail, charging in the opposite direction over the bare soil, taking on the color of earth, instantly turning green as soon as they arrived in the rice-fields. Our coolies captured a few of them.

Only the bagpiper's battalion, composed of the most human species of the Unclean Ones—those of the aforementioned *vitellus-Cuciothentus unguiculatis* formula—held firm. The coolies massacred them, one after another, not without a certain terrified admiration for their heroism—which was, however, nothing more than an imbecile suggestion grafted on to the imitative and collective instinct of beings deprived of an individual soul.

Let it be said in passing that the military heroes in whom our kind of cannon-fodder is sometimes specialized are, at the moment when they kill heroically, the victims of an analogous suggestion.

Blind and deaf, however—literally—the old lemur continued to extract from his bagpipe all the whining, hiccuping and burping of the most Japanese of martial music. The sense of smell alone appeared to warn him of the gradual tightening of the enemy circle, for we saw him shiver suddenly, sniff forcefully, his nose in the air, like a questing dog, with little movements up and down, his head tilted backwards and his nostrils palpitating. And he seemed to be scrutinizing us with his dead, half-calcified visage, with its hollow, purulent, sightless eyes.

Suddenly, he ceased blowing into his instrument. Two sinister holes were hollowed out in his elongated prognathous muzzle, beneath his cheekbones; the dolorous face retreated into the hectic oakum of the mane, which he brought down over his forehead with a despairing gesture. Finally, his head slumped on to his latticed thorax, and he allowed himself, meekly, to be led away.

"You, old chap," sniggered Brillat-Dessaigne, as the prisoner passed in front of our group, "will soon be carrying our news to our colleagues at the Académie des Science in Paris." And Moustier guffawed.

Once again, I had the very clear impression that the two chemists, in order to be joking as they were, had not the slightest consciousness of the danger suspended over their heads. Their attitude too, with regard to those exterminated beings, participated to some extent in the ironic disdain implicit in the epithetic of "laboratory reaction" with which they stigmatized indistinctly all the creatures issued from their manipulations. They only displayed the entrails of manufacturers of chemical products, in fact, where Yvonne and I, sickened by the unanalyzable odor emanating from the coagulated heap of Unclean Ones, perceived in ourselves the depressing polarizations of what is conventionally called a response of the soul...

It was in virtue of that response of the soul that we ended up leaning over one of those dying creatures, a young one by all appearances, which the thrust of a machete had disemboweled and laid out, gasping, at the feet of one of its own kind, doubtless its father, for whom it had tried in vain to make its own body a rampart. Under the superficial gash through which its life was escaping in large drops of glaucous starch, its infantile mouth was stammering supplications—or, perhaps, blurting out anathemas—into the void, and it was, for us, a poignant thing to glimpse in passing, showing in the unfathomable gulf of its eyes, the dolorous gaze that renders similar the visages of all beings that are about to die, on every rung of the animal scale.

XIV

A lugubrious night soon succeeded that day of emotions, the sky as heavy as a leaden cope over the still sea, without a breath of wind, a furnace-like heat causing the flowers to wilt, and even the winged tenants of the arbors—a sky and a night that would have been, for superstitious imaginations, the most evil of omens in themselves. But we were not superstitious, Yvonne and I, and if our hearts were constricted by the thought of all the formidable unknown that threatened the residence, at least we still hoped that all might end well, in accordance with the benign mode adopted thus far by our personal adventures.

It was, however, impossible for us to sleep, and we stayed up, as usual, sitting on our veranda, commenting on the events of the day, regretting that the illustrious scientist who was giving us hospitality had disdained to enter into negotiations with the disinherited individuals that his genius had summoned to life—which might have smoothed out all the difficulties and permitted us to leave the island immediately, without being false to the elementary sentiments of gratitude and human solidarity.

It might have been eleven o'clock, and I had just drawn Yvonne's attention to the rather suspicious fact that no fire was burning in the camp on the Silver Table when a strident call of: "To Arms!" descended from the top of the wall, from a point not far away from our bungalow. Then the grave clanging of a bell tolled with all his might by the porter split the night. The central courtyard was filled almost immediately with tumult and animation. I was one of the first to arrive, not without having promised my wife that I would rejoin her if there was any danger.

I was told that one of the men on guard on the northeastern bastion—the one overlooking the harbor—had seen shadows gesticulating around the yacht by means of a flash of lightning.

Monsieur Brillat-Dessaigne, arriving in his turn, appeared to comprehend the full gravity of the circumstance this time. It was the Pure Ones, evidently, who were trying to take possession of the vessel in order to appropriate the munitions it contained, or to bombard the Residence with the cannons on board. Orders had certainly been given to transport all the materiel in question to a safe place, but the multiple incidents of the afternoon had caused their execution to be deferred.

Moustier, brought up to date, shrugged his shoulders. The powder-store did not contain any cartridges that could be of use to them; as for the cannons, they did not know how to use them, and perhaps not even what their use was.

How did he know? Had not the Pure chief assimilated matters far more profound than a treatise on artillery or ballistics? With such a stubborn autodidact, it was necessary to expect anything.

"Might as well expect see the rifles or the cannons fire on their own!" the incorrigible optimist joked.

But it was not a moment to cavil. It was a matter of regaining control of the yacht moored at the quay, whose sides would be far too easy for the Pure Ones to scale, if they decidedly to do so, there being no surveillance. Then a permanent watch could be installed, which would permit the transfer of arms and munitions—of which the station personnel might have need—to be accomplished when the time came, without encumbrance. Such, at any rate, was the sage opinion of Monsieur Brillat-Dessaigne.

The men of the European staff—armed, as I have said, with excellent hunting-rifles and whose sticks of ammunition were not exhausted—offered spontaneously to take the lead of the expedition, which they thought to be child's play. Brillat-Dessaigne would direct the beam of an electric searchlight installed in the observatory at the boat. He invited me to accompany him, but I declined the offer.

·   "I'm still young," I told him, "and my duty is to defend my hosts against everyone. I'll join those who are going out, and will even claim the honor of marching at their head, but without any weapon—for I was also the guest of the Pure Ones! I owe them my life twice over, and whatever happens, I don't want to shed a drop of their blood."

Brillat-Dessaigne inclined courteously before those arguments. As for Moustier, who insisted on coming with us, he took the opportunity to ask me to lend him my carbine, which I had brought with me just in case. I agreed to that without difficulty, and we set forth into the black night outside, while the chemist, intoxicated by the unexpectedness and abnormality of any adventure, whispered his impressions to me.

"I adore this little war, myself. It reminds me of the regiment, the great maneuvers...burning powder at sparrows, massacring chimerical enemies...which is perhaps not unlike what we're doing..."

A storm of detonations cut his speech short. A hundred and fifty meters ahead of us, above the waves of the harbor, brief flashes rent the darkness, indicating that the fire of the platoon was coming from the yacht. The Pure Ones had detected our movements; their eyes dark-adapted eyes were following our every step, discerning our actions as if in broad daylight.

"Those fellows seem to me to be numerous, and determined to sell their skins as dearly as possible," breathed Moustier, somewhat sobered up.

We soon found out. A beam of milky light swept through the air, seemed to hesitate momentarily, and then pause slightly above the surface of the water, and within the luminous orb, the yacht appeared, with the slightest details of its fitments, its dazzling white hull and its delicate rails. The deck seemed deserted.

"What does that signify?" Moustier murmured, as we continued to advance.

A further salvo replied to him, and the brief trail of gleams indicated that the shots were being fired through the vessel's bulwark ports. A deathly wind had whistled in our ears. We called a halt in order not to be shot at close range; then, by the feeble light radiated around its axis by the electric beam that passed above our heads, we looked at one another, more disturbed than fearful. Neither Moustier nor I had been hit, but one of the Europeans and four or five coolies were lying on the ground, seriously wounded. Immediately, there were numerous defections in the indigenous group.

"We're in a bad position," I said to Moustier. "It's futile to keep going forward in these conditions; we'd be massacred to the last man—and besides, the coolies wouldn't follow us. I'll go on alone and try to make them listen to reason. I know them; the chief is sentimental and chivalrous; a step made in these conditions can't leave him insensible."

"But that's crazy imprudence!" Moustier protested.

I was already on my way. I calculated that about a hundred meters separated me from the yacht, and went at the double in order to minimize the risk I was running.

Nothing troubled the profound silence of the night. The darkness gradually diminished as I approached the area of electric radiance. Ten meters from the yacht I went into the beam, properly speaking. Then, seeing several rifle barrels shining in the bulwark ports, I raised my arms and shouted: "Stop, wretches! Why shed the blood of innocents? You've already killed one divine and some of your Hindu brethren. Stop!"

"We know no brothers," riposted the chief, whose silhouette emerged from a porthole, "and we're glad to learn that divines can be killed as easily as us. The fear of death will force the Father to satisfy our legitimate demands."

"No one has the right to take anyone's life," I said, in a firm voice, "and whoever strikes will be struck. If you weren't demanding the impossible, the Father would have granted your wishes a long time ago."

While talking I continued to advance. The deck-ladder came down. I was invited to come up; I did not have to be begged. While I was climbing the rungs, the chief said in a softer tone: "The Father ought to explain that to us himself."

I set foot on the deck. "I promise on my honor," I said, "to try to obtain an audience for you. But you were wrong to employ violence; it's the most detestable means of persuasion. Look, I've come to you without weapons."

"Yes, but your troop over there is armed," the chief retorted, "and besides, your people carried out an unnecessary butchery of the Unclean Ones today. The divines are worse than us."

"That remains to be seen!" I said, a trifle ironically. "In the meantime, what are you going to do?"

"We're going to deliberate. I'll submit to my brothers, immediately, the offer you've made of an audience with the Father."

He clapped his hands, and the deck immediately filled up with a lot of astonishingly similar old men—as similar in senility as they had been in the prime of their short life. For they were definitely old this time, all white-haired; only their gaze and their skin remained astonishingly young, with wrinkles as artificial as the electric light, with an appearance of make-up, insignificance, even unreality.

All the chief's twins arranged themselves in a circle around him—but at the same moment, a discharge of rifle fire ravaged the air around us.

It was ours that were firing this time, either because they thought I had fallen into a trap, or simply because they thought the opportunity propitious for revenge. Two Pure Ones fell.

The chief looked at me with an indescribable nuance of scorn, and chagrin darkened his voice.

"You can see," he said, "that the divines are worse than us. We welcomed you in all confidence, and they took advantage of it to fire at us."

"It's a misunderstanding!" I exclaimed. "I'll give orders—let me do it."

I got ready to go back down the ladder, but the chief held me back.

"No," he said, "we are here to respond."

He made a sign. With a single automatic gesture, all the old men, like marvelously-drilled soldiers, raised their weapons.

"I'll share the fate of my own," I said simply—and I launched myself forward for a second time—but two Pure Ones blocked my way.

"You will remain our prisoner," the chief told me, "or rather, our hostage, until the Father has consented to receive me."

"That's a felony!" I said, indignantly. "I took you for a friend."

"We are not your enemies, and certainly will not do you any harm, but the grave turn of events does not permit us to act otherwise...especially if we want to avoid further bloodshed. We need a guarantee. Can you give us our word that you will not try to escape?"

"No, I can't," I said, adding, by way of an irrefutable argument, that my wife must be mortally anxious, and that my place was with her.

I saw a sad, soft gleam pass through the chief's eyes; for a few seconds, his face offered an indefinable expression. Then, as if mastering himself, he articulated, almost harshly: "Since that is the case, I shall have you guarded by these two men." He designated the two who had interrupted me with a gesture. "As for us, we shall pursue the divines until..."

He was unable to say any more.

The din of a hundred pieces of artillery burst forth above the Residence. The entire island caught fire, vomiting a column of flame toward the heavens. Then it appeared to sink into the night that closed upon it. At the same time, we were hurled pell-mell across the deck, which bucked as if it had been lifted up by a big wave. I had the sensation that the world had just fallen apart.

Strangely enough, in that total collapse, above the chaos divined in the distance, in the place where the Residence had been, the little tower remained motionless, and also motionless was the spectral beam of light that linked it to our deck.

A few seconds went by...perhaps a few minutes...centuries...at any rate, then the night lit up again.

Flames were now rising above the bungalows that were still standing. Two or three more explosions rent the air, followed by a brief but torrential downpour of shards of glass and stone, doubtless the reserves of the laboratories, which had exploded.

And then something even more tragic augmented the horror and terror of the scene: something that I had expected, in fact, and trembled at not having seen it produced: the cry of human distress, the appeals of anguish, folly and agony of those who had survived the catastrophe but who did not know, who could no longer know, how to get out of that inferno. Croaks, howls and demented vociferations, overlapping in the air, and plaints too, and cries of supreme despair....among which I thought I suddenly recognized the voice of my wife: of my wife, whose memory invaded me, as suddenly as if it were surging from the void of an entire year of forgetfulness.

In fact, during the frightful minute that had just gone by, I must have been struck by a total amnesia, incapable of thinking about anyone or anything. A new fact suddenly made the image of my poor Yvonne more precise: the bell of the central courtyard started ringing: the same bell that had sounded the alarm a little while ago, at the moment when I had left our lodgings, with neither an explanation nor an adieu, for fear that Yvonne might try to hold me back.

I raised my eyes, and saw a cloud of vapor, doubtless mortal, slowly descending the slope of the cliff.

With one bound I was on my feet, and only then did I notice that the Pure chief was still there, motionless, clinging to the mainmast, his eyes widened by an immense astonishment exempt from any fear. But he perceived my movement, and once again, he put his hand on my shoulder, and ordered, briefly: "You must stay."

I wanted to go past him, to employ brutal force, but the others had stood up too, and at a sign from the chief I found myself surrounded by menacing figures, which I divined to be inexorable.

Then, suddenly, an idea struck me, arousing my indignation and fury against those soulless beings.

"You're executioners," I said to the chief. "It's you who have provoked this horrible catastrophe and heaped up all those ruins. You've blown up the powder-store in the reservoir."

"That's true," he said, in a calm tone, "but we are not the criminals that you say, for we did not know exactly what the powder-store contained."

"It was dynamite, wretch."

He appeared to search his memory, and then he said: "I did not know the terrible effects of dynamite, and I believed that the cellar contained ordinary powder. My intention was simply to destroy the reservoir—our cradle, I have heard it said—in order that it could never again be used to fabricate a false humanity. At the same time, I was counting on the salutary effect that the energetic and violent action would produce on the imagination of the Father and his entourage."

In any other circumstances, I could have admired the fact that the false faith of the Pure Ones, the imbecile faith that a conceited teacher had fabricated with crumbs of the Bible, had ended, like dying Christianity, in anarchism and propaganda by action, but the moment was not one for philosophical speculations.

Before my thunderous gaze, which was not without a hint of theatricality, the chief lowered his head.

"I've already told you," I burst out, "that violence is always inimical and criminal."

"Our ignorance alone is culpable, and we are the first to deplore it."

"And if my wife is dead?"

He appeared to awaken from a dream, and suddenly, agitated by a nervous tremor. He cried: "Your wife! Oh, the poor woman! We had nothing against her! We all loved her..."

He stopped, his forehead and his eyes rejuvenated, as if by a miracle, his entire visage haloed by tenderness and bounty, by an ardent desire for redemption, for self-sacrifice—and then, straight away, with a contagious exaltation, he exclaimed: "But I shall save her! To me, my bothers! Follow me! We must save the wife of the divine. It's necessary to save her, or die with her."

"I'll put myself at your head," I said.

But he refused, and this time put me in the hands of the two men wounded by the discharge of our men. They took the precaution, in response to his order, of binding my wrists and ankles.

"But you won't find the person you're trying to save!" I shouted, exasperated.

He pointed to two of his companions. "They will find her," he said, "for they are the ones who were held in the Residence."

And he reiterated the assurance that no harm would come to me, but that it was necessary that they had a hostage. Ready to depart, the little troop took a count; they were only twenty-six, the two who were missing having been blown up, I subsequently learned, with the powder-store.

A minute later, they left the deck and disappeared into the night that had fallen once again on the shore. But almost immediately, a terrible fusillade burst forth, and a nearby bush that had just caught fire illuminated a scene of carnage that I do not have the courage to depict for you.

The horror that rose up within me, combined with the distress of my personal situation, was such that I fainted under the atonal gaze of the two wounded Pure Ones, sitting motionless in a flood of electric light that gave them the faces of dying men.

XV

I shall summarize now, in accordance with what the principal actor told me, the events that occurred while I was unconscious.

At the moment of the explosion, the men of our troop, obedient either to a command or merely to instinct, threw themselves flat on the ground. They remained in that position throughout the time that the partial explosions lasted. The burning bush having suddenly dissipated the darkness, they were getting to their feet when they saw the Pure Ones, who were coming among the shore at a run. They believed that they were being attacked. A voice—doubtless Moustier's—commanded: "Fire!"

The Pure Ones received the volley almost at point blank range. Fifteen fell, struck dead. The others riposted, and killed all the Europeans, plus a few indigenes. Moustier, who was at the head of the troop, had his skull cleaved by the stroke of a machete.

Terrified, the surviving coolies fled toward the Residence. The portal was still wide open. They plunged into it and, believing that they were still pursued, rushed across the courtyard toward the furnace of the arbors, while the Pure Ones paused on the threshold, rallied by the forceful voice of their chief.

"Let our two brothers guide us now," he ordered, "and let no one shed any more blood needlessly. We have no other mission here but to save the wife of the divine."

The two former prisoners of the station emerged from the ranks and took the head of the little troop, which penetrated cautiously into the central courtyard. The tocsin as still making itself heard at intervals, but slowly and softly, as if the bell-rope were being pulled by the hand of a child. The paving-stones were strewn with the wounded, dead and dying, some of them hideously disfigured, their limbs torn away, their bodies lying in pools of black blood. Others had contracted features, blue-tinted or blackened masks, but presented no evidence of any wound.

Doubtless a column of hot asphyxiating gas had finished the work of the dynamite. That, at least, is the way that I have reconstituted the drama. In disemboweling the small crater, the explosion had not only determined the collapse of the interior lake, but a partial eruption of lava and incandescent gas. Then, all the survivors among the station personnel—all those who had not been thrown into the flames or hurled into the distance, or crushed under the rubble of collapsed buildings, took refuge in the courtyard, where they perished, victims of the successive explosions of the reserves of fuel.

An even more horrible spectacle chilled the Pure Ones as they were about to run into the gardens. The sinister glare of the fires illuminated the courtyard now. In a corner of the vault, immediately in front of the menagerie, the cages of which were no longer emitting anything but faint moans, a body was swinging in mid-air, attached by the neck to the rope of the bell. Another human form, crouching on the ground in the oriental style, was pulling the hanged man by the feet, allowing itself to be lifted off the ground by the ascensional force of the bell and falling back again into a sitting position thereafter, puffing and groaning with pleasure at the sound of the knell produced by that feeble traction.

The hanged man was the porter, who, doubtless in a paroxysm of madness, had found that means of reconciling his grim ex-military respect for orders with God only knows what point of demented honor forbidding him to go on living among so many cadavers.

That way, he could continue sounding the tocsin, even dead.

He was hideous to behold, his eyes bulging out of their sockets, his nose half-carbonized, sarcastic laughter on his lips, his forehead cut by a red gash from which blood was escaping in a sheet, making his hair sticky and tattooing his face with ocher-red stripes.

The other was the fossil-man, doubtless escaped from the niche where he had been imprisoned after his capture. The Unclean Ones, his co-detainees, were lying inanimate around him, apparently killed by the asphyxiant gases.

Stiffening themselves against an increasing terror, and without perceiving that the fossil-man was following them, the Pure Ones ran over the lawn to the intersection, partly reddened by a flow of lava. There they were forced to stop. The fire had taken hold in all the arbors. A vast wall of flame barred their way.

The chief looked at his brothers, and understood that they would not go any further.

"Where is the dwelling of the two divines?" he asked, curtly.

With their hands, the two guides designated the white arches of our bungalow, rose-tinted by the glare of the flames.

"Good," he said. "Wait for me here."

And he launched himself into the furnace.

Meanwhile, the storm that had been threatening for several hours finally burst. Large raindrops fell, bloodily reflecting the conflagration. A dull rumble filled the air, from one horizon to the other. One might have thought that the violence of the earth was being belatedly echoed in the sky. The flames were, however, so bright that they prevented the sight of the lightning.

The chief had reached the sandy pathway leading to the bungalow. A torrent of sulfurous water had devastated it. Thick, suffocating smoke formed a vault above his head. He was walking slowly, half-blinded by the burning flakes falling from the trees, which were blazing like torches. One of them set fire to his white waistcoat. He tore it away from his breast, burning his hands. Then, sensing that his hair was on fire, he unfastened his belt and wound it around his head.

He finally arrived at the peristyle of the bungalow. His courage almost failed. Three cadavers were lying on the steps. One was Monsieur Brillat-Dessaigne, his face violet and tumefied, but the features nevertheless calm and the eyes closed, as if he were asleep. The other two cadavers were those of two European female employees of the station. Doubtless the scientist, spared by the explosion, had encountered the two women fleeing from the cataclysm; they had clung on to him, considering his mere presence as a safeguard, a talisman against death, and they had followed him when the idea had occurred to him of coming to save my wife. The whirlwind of hot gases had overtaken them on the way, and all three of them had fallen just outside the house, where they might have found salvation if they had only reached it a few seconds earlier.

A frightful anguish had seized the chief by the throat. The Father was dead, taking his secret away into annihilation. Nothing more remained except for him either—but first, he intended to keep his word. He would save my wife.

Oh, let her be alive, her, at least, for if he arrived too late, he would pass for a murderer in my eyes, and what was worse, the murderer of a woman in whom he loved, in his own fashion, all women.

For he loved, he felt that intensely now. He loved her for her grace and her weakness, for the troubling mystery that her sex brought into the universe, a mystery of which he had a presentiment—he, the disinherited of an entire sweet world of unexperienced tenderness and incorruptible felicities, everything that might spring from the divine spark that presides over the birth and maintains the life of beings of true flesh.

Oh, to hug her, alive or dead, against his breast!

Head down, he rushed into the house, already aureoled by flames. The electricity had held firm; it radiated soft and joyful light over the scene of tragedy—but the rooms were empty. Not all of them though, for in the last one he visited, which seemed to him to be the bedroom, half a dozen Unclean Ones were gyrating frantically, like rats caught in a trap.

As soon as they perceived him they precipitated themselves toward him, brandishing their tentacles in a hostile fashion. He scythed down three or four with machete-thrusts, leapt over their quivering stumps and discovered the bay to the veranda open. As he was crossing the threshold he stumbled over a body lying on the ground.

Her! It was her! And she was still breathing, although she was unconscious.

She had survived, the one for whom he would willingly have given ten thousand lives like his own. He wanted to pick her up but his strength betrayed him. Then, inflating his voice, which was breaking, he called for help,

No one responded. No one came.

It was, for her and for him, certain and frightful death, which every passing second rendered more inevitable.

He ran to the balustrade, leaned over the sea of fire of the burning trees, a sea over which enormous waves of black smoke were rolling, above which the sky was no more than an immense sheet of blinding lightning flashes.

He was about to launch a supreme appeal to his brothers, whose confused silhouettes were immobilized beyond the curtain of fire when a dazzling furrow cut through the clouds, uniting the sky with the earth, darting its mortal beam into the very center of the distant group. A formidable explosion ravaged the world. He saw bodies hurled to the ground, and others precipitated of their own accord into the flames; then there was nothing more, save for the frightful tumult of thunder that continued to fill space with its din.

He turned round, sensing that he was going mad. Standing in the frame of the bay, the fossil-man was staring at him from the depths of his purulent orbits, his head nodding to the rhythm of inaudible music, his muzzle wedged on the mouthpiece of an imaginary bagpipe.

It would not have taken much for the chief to leap upon the macabre phantom and strike him dead, but four brachiopod Unclean Ones surged forth in their turn, tentacles his, only waiting for their favorite tune to go into action. And the chief suddenly understood that those grotesque beings were unwittingly bringing him salvation. Recovering the gestures with which he had once domesticated them and trained them to carry out all kinds of tasks, he ordered them to help him to carry away the body extended on the ground.

They obeyed instantly, uniting their efforts. The chief carried the upper body in order to protect the head against the assault of the flames. Faithful to his role, the old lemur opened the march, nodding his head, his metacarpals swinging, agitated by an isochronic movement, as if he were beating time.

As soon as they were outside and past the steps where the Father and the two European women were sleeping their final slumber, the chief clapped his hands to make them accelerate their pace. They bounded through the flames.

The air was so fiery that their backs smoked and swelled, like boiling glue. The chief felt the skin of his face and hands cracking in the furnace. All the cadavers that could be seen, Pure Ones or coolies, were demi-carbonized.

Soon, having passed through the vault of fire and smoke, they saw the sky again, where the electric discharges were succeeding one another without interruption. One might have thought that a battle was raging in the atmosphere between invisible and colossal artilleries—or, better still, a formidable firing exercise whose target was the earth.

In the central courtyard death had finished its work. Nothing was moving any longer: neither the animals in their cages nor the bodies extended on the paving-stones; not even the porter hanged by his bell-rope. Everything, nightmarishly illuminated by the fire or the lightning, gave the illusion of a monstrous wax museum.

As the danger was reduced here, the chief called a halt for a few seconds: the time to lean over the woman whose life he had saved at the price of his own—for he sensed that it was all over for him, and that the end would soon arrive. He had surpassed the limit of the sensations permitted to his artificial species, and in any case, his hour had sounded, his paltry role was complete. The chemical fluid to which he owed his fragile human form, which had permitted him to agitate on the earth for a few brief and miserable years, was now seeping away through his every pore, curdling along his hardened fibers, in an imminent stagnation for the frail cardiac mechanism that provided the rhythm of his respiration.

But what did dying matter to him, since the death of the Father decreed him irreparable, since he was sure henceforth that he could neither love nor be loved?

Having made sure that her heart was still beating, he made a sign, and the porters resumed their march.

At a pace so rapid that even the chief, out of breath and panting, was lurching unsteadily, they went through the portal and on across the strand, toward the shore. Strangely enough, they were no longer obedient either to the voice of the chief or to the direction in which he tried to point them, and although he had arranged himself at their head in order to steer them, and in spite of all their efforts, they deviated from the line they had to follow to reach the yacht, and headed straight for the sea.

Then, a frightful certainty suddenly rose up within him; either by virtue of a concerted vengeance against the race to which the stricken woman belonged, or the stubborn superstition of beings doubtless issued from the ocean, and who were returning to it in death as humans returned to the earth, the monsters had decided that the body must be cast into the sea.

And they would cast her into it, no matter what; for he no longer had the physical strength necessary to resist them. All that he could do, in the final extremity, was to kill them all. But then, how could he carry the body to the ship on his own?

In the meantime, that final extremity was approaching with frightful rapidity. Scarcely fifty meters away, the surf was roaring, increasingly deafening. And they were almost running.

Behind them were the crackling flames, the immense conflagration of the island, which the fire was devouring alive; in front of them, the profound darkness of the waters. They were going toward the night.

An instant later, the distance had diminished to twenty meters. The chief had the sensation that the entire immense ocean was hurling itself toward them in order to engulf them.

Already, they were enveloped by its fresh and intoxicating breath, and perhaps such a death would have had a welcoming smile, for him—but for her, it was necessary that she live; it was necessary that she be saved.

He made a superhuman effort, and succeeded in immobilizing the porters for a few seconds, in order to show them once again the luminous halo in which the silhouette of the yacht was inscribed. Then he grabbed the old lemur by the shoulder and shoved him in that direction.

After a few strides, however, the latter stopped dead, seemed to jib, and then threw himself sideways again, his gestures inviting the porters to do likewise.

By the glare of a lightning flash the chief saw tangled forms lying on the ground in pools of blood. He recognized the outlines, and realized that they had reached the place where the terrible fusillade had occurred. While he hesitated, searching for a way through, the porters set off again with their burden, this time resuming their slanting course without him. He had to precipitate himself in their pursuit, but the sea was only two strides away, and he understood that there was no longer any hope of overtaking or mastering the brutes.

He unsheathed his blade, and launched a strident appeal. The old one turned round, and his cranium was slit by a terrible blow. He collapsed, howling in the most horrible fashion.

Terrorized, the porters stopped, dropped their prey and vanished into the darkness.

A few minutes went by, during which the chief wondered what he ought to do.

The freshness of the sea was gradually reanimating the woman he had saved; her respiration was more ample and more regular, but her lips were still contorted, her eyes closed, her face the pale and rigid mask of beings brushed by the wing of death.

He tried to pick her up and carry her in his arms. Alas, he did not even have the strength to raise her from the ground, and soon observed that the rising tide was licking the hem of her dress.

At that point, however, the shore had a narrow band of fine dry sand over which a body might be dragged gently, without shocks or impacts. He tried, and succeeded in taking a few strides like that. Everything was, therefore, still possible.

At the very moment when he made that reflection, however, he perceived that everything was, on the contrary, definitively lost—for now the shadows around him were filling up with crawling or hoping forms, the number of which seemed to be augmenting with every flash of lightning.

The last survivors of the Valley, attracted by the osprey-like cries of the old one, and doubtless guided by their comrades, the turncoat porters, were about to avenge on the chief everything that their race had had to suffer at the behest of the Pure Ones. A further flash of lightning, and he saw that he was surrounded by grimacing beings who had not waited to be able to see clearly to rush him.

He set down the upper body that he was sustaining in his arms and set about executing circular sweeps with his blade, in such a manner as to trace an uncrossable zone around the body lying at his feet. But nothing could any longer stop the overexcited monsters. A certain number allowed themselves to be mutilated, hacked and cut to pieces in order to permit the others to tighten the circle.

Then, sensing that he was doomed, he gathered what remained of his strength, and uttered a supreme appeal toward the yacht, moored less than a hundred meters away.

"To me, Divine! Help!"

XVI

It was that cry, repeated several times, that ended up extracting me from unconsciousness. I understood immediately that the situation must be terribly grave.

"Do you hear?" I said, to the two wounded men lying nearby.

They raised their heads painfully, and fixed me with distant, haggard gazes in which the mists of death were already rising.

"Quickly, quickly!" I shouted at them. "Cut my bonds; the chief is in peril."

But they looked at one another, and their impersonal visages only expressed incredulity and painful bewilderment. My God! Did they not have the strength any longer to understand?

In the end, however, one last cry from the chief, echoed by the harbor wall, caused them to shiver. One of them dragged himself toward me, and cut the cord that bound my wrists, seeming to exhale in that effort the little life that remained to him. He fell inert alongside me. I seized the machete, and with a single blow I cut the rope securing my legs. I was free. Then I bounded outside the vessel.

It was with blows of a hatchet that I had to fray a passage through the Unclean Ones; there were at least sixty, of which I had to cleave or strike down more than half in order to reach the chief. The joy of finding my dear Yvonne alive multiplied my strength tenfold.

I lifted her up in my arms, and in a single surge I carried her all the way to the ship, while the chief contented himself with holding at bay the screeching mob that was obstinate in following us.

Finally, we arrived safe and sound on the deck, and while the chief narrated the Homeric epic of which he was the hero, I made every effort to bring my wife round. She did not take long to open her eyes. We were only able to exchange a few words; the universal tragedy that surrounded us forbade us to yield to the egotism of effusions, of intimate joys.

The two wounded men were dying. Having approached them with the chief to collect their last sighs, I noticed that the blood flowing from their wounds—they had refused forcefully to allow them to be bandaged—was not like ours, liquid and deep carmine; it was more akin to pale vermilion, of a thick and syrupy consistency. I also noticed that the unfortunate chief was gazing fearfully into their vitreous pupils, as their faces abruptly oxidized, while retaining in their effigy the image of his own, at the increasingly clear vision of the mysterious black gulf into which he felt himself falling. To die, to cease to live—that must have had a frightful meaning for him, who had lived so little.

Meanwhile, the Unclean Ones who had pursued us all the way to the hull of the vessel were resuming a threatening attitude. A few tried to climb on to the deck. I repelled them with blows of the hatchet. There were no more than twenty now. Abruptly, they changed tactics, climbing on to one another's shoulders in order to form a kind of pyramid supported at the base by three of them, which surpassed the level of the stern rail by several feet. The pyramid suddenly oscillated, leaning over the poop; its summit broke up, letting half a dozen attackers fall on to the deck.

Weary of wielding the machete and the hatchet, I herded them toward a gap in the rail and tumbled them into the waves. But the purely impulsive brutes, which the two chemists had justly termed "laboratory reactions" had not the slightest consciousness of death. Doubtless they perceived it as a simple transformation, the passage from one material state to another. And perhaps death, for them—as for us—was, in reality, just that. At any rate, without any concern for the fate of their comrades, those who remained immediately prepared to repeat their endeavor.

This time, it was the heavens that came to my aid. Yes, the heavens!

A bolide—which is to say, a globe of fire—several centimeters in apparent diameter suddenly emerged from the fuliginous clouds suspended over the island.[32] I saw it descending slowly, following an oblique trajectory that was bringing it straight toward the ship, so that for an instant, I dreaded the worst of catastrophes—but it was interrupted in flight by the reconstituted pyramid. It brushed them and burst with an infernal bang, and an eruption of light that left Yvonne and myself blind for several seconds.

When we opened our eyes again, the pyramid no longer existed. In the place where it had risen up a moment before, two or three gelatinous, seemingly phosphorescent puddles were distributed over the gravel of the dock. We saw them extend, elongate, converge on a central point and complete their fusion. And of all the fauna that had once haunted the tenebrous ravines of the island, nothing any longer remained but that enigmatic pool of Bathybius, an imperishable living jelly, which slowly and invincibly orientated itself in the direction of the sea, the primordial womb of all animate beings.

The electricity that had presided over the birth of the Unclean Ones had returned at a given moment to disaggregate their temporary forms, to restore to the Ocean the drops of immortality that science had stolen.

We remained in contemplation of that spectacle for some time, prey to the imprecise anguish awakened in every thinking being by the eternal mystery of creation, and also with a vague pity for those abolished forms, which would never again appear on the earth, and for which we now reproached ourselves for not having shown a little of the clemency and

---

[32] Information regarding the phenomenon that is now known as "ball lightning" had been collated and popularized in France by Wilfrid de Fonvielle, a prolific scientific journalist with whom Hoche might well have been acquainted, initially in *Éclairs et tonnerre* (1866; tr. as *Thunder and Lightning*) and subsequently in numerous articles in newspapers and magazines.

shame that humans owe to everything that breathes under the sun, and from which they are only separated by a few rungs, more or less conquered, on the scale of life.

It was the same sentiment, merely pierced with a greater intensity, that gripped our hearts when we returned to the chief, now extended alongside his brothers. We saw his face oxydize and hollow out, as the other two had, and understood that his hour had come.

My wife knelt beside him, and kissed his forehead, and then took his hand in hers for as long as his agony lasted. And I thought I read in his features that dying thus seemed finer to him than living as he had lived. At any rate, he did not pronounce another word. Only my wife moved her lips, as if in mute prayer. Doubtless she was recommending to her God that orphan of human science, and asking him to assume the paternity—to which he could, moreover, have consented without any loss of face.

In my turn I squeezed the hand of our unfortunate friend, but I could not find anything to say to him. His wide open eyes reflected a black sky, hermetic and inexorable, the only sky admitted by reason that has quarreled irredeemably with the gilded chimera of a second life—and I preferred to keep quiet rather than lull his agony with a pious lie.

His features gradually faded, as if diffused in the withered skin of the face. He must certainly have reached the extreme limit of his old age, and only a miracle of will-power had been able to sustain him in the heroic and generous adventure that had crowned his life.

A heart-rending "adieu" suddenly escaped his discolored lips; the flame of life flickered in the corners of his eyes, and then sank into the black depths of the slowly extinguished gaze.

We were alone henceforth on an unusable vessel, facing the devastated island, its soil strewn with ruins and cadavers: alone in that nightmare world, between a sky of terror and an earth of malediction. But something worse still awaited us. The electric searchlight suddenly went out, and there was black night aboard, hideous and terrifying, while on land, the blazing, spectral Residence, seemed to be wrapped in a bloody shroud.

Then we perceived that we were so wretched that it was impossible to be any more so.

XVII

Toward morning, the sea paled, gradually illuminated. Increasingly numerous waves, running from the far horizon, laid siege to the shore. The sky remained dark; a sinister daylight rose over the apocalyptic scene.

The island was still burning, but the conflagration had made ground in the last few hours; it was the forest that was ablaze now: the immense virgin forest that covered almost all of the areas between the southern ravines and the northern volcanic massif. Already the nearest heights seemed to be crowned with flames; spirals of black smoke were trailing half way up the volcanoes, and if the breeze had not been bowing from the sea, our position would have become untenable; the yacht itself would have caught fire. I'm certain that the temperature, at that moment, was over sixty degrees.

Toward noon, especially, the situation got worse, to the point that, after having immersed our dead, we had to remain shut up between decks, and we stayed there until dusk, with all the hatches closed. Fortunately, we found numerous tins of food, and some vegetables, which permitted us to restore our strength and reassure us with regard to the days to come. That was as much a mental as a material relief, for several times during the terrible night, while other dangers progressively diminished, the prospect of dying of hunger—since we were then unaware that there was food aboard—had racked our imagination.

The next day, the heat of the fire having eased as the flames had moved away, we risked going ashore, urged by the fact that the tossing of the waves was beginning to make us sick, the waters of the harbor experiencing the repercussions of a tempest raging at sea. We made a detour in order not to have to step over too many cadavers.

The distant forest was still burning. A terrible silence weighed upon the cliff, but in the distance we could hear trees

186

splitting, moaning and exploding, the wild cries of creatures at bay, and he desperate roars of predators driven mad by terror. The enclosure of the station was nothing but ruins and rubble; we walked there on a bed of warm ashes.

The three volcanoes had resumed their customary physiognomy. The smallest one, however, had an immense excavation at its base from which a steamy cascade was flowing, reminiscent at a distance to liquid fog. The central spray described a curve above the rim of the cliff and fell on to calcined stones and the skeletons of trees indicating the place where the scientist's residence had stood two days before. The searchlight tower was still upright, isolated in the midst of the ruins, a blind lighthouse now, but one that had valiantly done its duty during the terrible drama, and whose vigilant eye had been the last to be extinguished.

A flock of eagles and pelicans was circling above our bungalow, one of the rare houses that had remained intact. Toward evening, I risked going into the central courtyard, which was nothing but a vast charnel-house, and fired a few rifle-shots at them through an embrasure—the sole means of protecting the corpses that they coveted from their rapacity.

As I turned round, my head bumped into a rope hanging down from the vault, which ended two feet from the ground. It was obviously the bell-rope, but the body of the porter, which the chief had told me he had seen hanging from it by the neck, had disappeared, and I ought to add that it remained undiscoverable.

When I was finally able to approach our bungalow, a human creature emerged from an air-vent. I nearly fainted with terror, so overwrought we my nerves, but I quickly recognized one of the Europeans of the station: the helmsman of the yacht. He was in a lamentable state, his face covered with wounds, his hair singed, dragging himself along in charred shoes and having difficulty gathering the shreds of his clothing around his body.

He had been part of Moustier's troop, and had run away when the explosion rang out. He had spent the night and the following day in a fissure in the rock near the northern reefs. Half-dead of hunger, however, and believing that the yacht was in the hands of the Pure Ones, he had ended up deciding to return to the station, thinking that perhaps he would find some nourishment in the bungalows that had been spared, and that perhaps he might even find survivors of the catastrophe ready to join him in facing the thousand dangers that threatened. But he had not take long to acquire the conviction that all the inhabitants of the station were dead; no one, in fact, had showed himself anywhere, nor was anyone occupied with the numerous cadavers strewn around.

In our bungalow he had found the remains of a meal, with which to calm his hunger and aliment him summarily for a few days. Then he had decided to stay there and had accommodated himself in the cellar for fear of further seismic shocks—he really believed that there had been an earthquake followed by a volcanic eruption.

I had one question burning on my lips—a capital question, since our fate might perhaps depend on it. Did the mariner think that the two of us could maneuver the yacht and travel by means of its sails? Obviously, there was no question of making use of its engine.

The response was affirmative.

We were saved, and I can still remember the delirious joy with which Yvonne and I hugged one another when, a few hours later, having hoisted the mainsail and raised anchor, cutting the moorings with strokes of an ax, we sensed the yacht began to move slowly away. It hesitated at first, its nose saluting a squadron of bounding waves, jibbing before the swell that seemed to be more inclined to engulf us than carry us, and then made its decision, and proudly launched itself forward toward the exit from the harbor.

The helmsman had found some comfortable clothes aboard, and enough food to keep our strength up. The liquor store even contained a few bottles of old wine fabricated by the chemists, of which we did not hesitate to make use, for want of water, no matter how suspect its taste seemed.

Our final moment on land had been devoted to the immersion of all the European cadavers. Only those of the two scientists were carried aboard in order to be buried at sea. We rendered them that supreme duty as soon as the yacht had reached open water, and I meditated for some time upon the ferocious destiny that had caused a man like Monsieur Brillat-Dessaigne—a genius such as only surges at rare intervals from the banal bosom of pullulating humankind—to disappear so wretchedly. Who could tell how many years, and how many coincident and extraordinary hazards, it would require for an intelligence of similar scope to appear on the earth and rediscover the marvelous secrets that he had carried with him into the abyss?

The night threatened to be very bad. We could not steer in a determined direction; it was necessary to content ourselves with traveling westwards at the behest of the wind, away from the little island that soon no longer seemed to be anything but an immense beacon fire illuminated on the rim of the sky, illuminating the darkness of the sea for a dozen leagues around. We could only reckon ourselves fortunate now because of the extent assumed by that terrible conflagration, for it was impossible that such a blaze would not attract the attention of some ship, which would come close enough to see our signals.

Toward midnight, the mainmast broke, and we lost the only sail we had. The situation then seemed desperate. Furious waves were sweeping the deck, which had become impracticable. Abysms opened up beneath the prow, from which the frail vessel only emerged by virtue of a miracle, and not without leaving behind each time, some fragments of its flesh: spars, a hawser, the frame of a bunk, glass from the portholes or a section of rail. The tempest also rid us of the two cannons; needless to say, their loss did not cause us any regret. A loss that was much more sensible to us, for good reason, was that of our only lifeboat, doubtless poorly secured.

The most serious matter was that, deprived of charts and a compass, we had no idea where we were going through that

189

black darkness; we only knew that in the strait strewn with islands, great and small, we might run into a rocky bank at any moment, a reef on which our hull would be spitted, capsized or broken like glass.

In the morning, however, the wind dropped, as if by magic. The wind put a muffler ion its furies; the waves lost their white manes, stretched themselves out, and eventually mutated into a gentle cradling swell. We were able to go up on deck again, at last, and breathe.

We had been sitting on the poop deck for several minutes when Yvonne uttered a cry of joy. On the extreme horizon, in a gap in the sky, three matchsticks were discernible, planted obliquely: the tips of the masts of a steamer. So far as we could judge at that distance, the funnel not being visible as yet, it appeared to be traveling in the same direction as us.

We sent up distress signals, although they were surely invisible at such a long distance, and after half an hour we had the heart-rending disappointment of observing that the two lines marking our respective routes seemed to be visibly drawing apart.

Suddenly, our helmsman, who had gone below decks at my request to look for powder in order to send up a further signal, appeared at one of the hatches, his face distraught. "To the pumps quickly!" he shouted. "Water in the powder locker!"

As I pressed him with questions he replied: "Three feet of water already...and impossible to block the hole...can't see it...but I found one of those accursed squids with a bird's beak floating in the water...a beak that it must have used as an auger...I broke its head against the trap..."

We searched in vain for pumps; there no longer were any. The helmsman ended up remembering that they had been taken to the Residence, one of them having played its role in the battle against the army of cephalopods—perhaps a further lesson in destiny. A single one of those infimal monsters was about to avenge all of its kind, all the monsters that we had taken back by violence from the life that a flash of genius had granted them—for, since we no longer had a lifeboat, we were doomed, barring a miracle. Soon, the ship would begin to list, and a few hours later, having become the plaything of the waves, it would heel over to port, and finally sink.

That, in fact, is what happened. Less than three hours later, we were in perdition, the hull of the vessel inclined at a forty-five degree angle and the poop no longer showing above the waves.

Only one hope of salvation remained. It seemed that the distant steamer had finally perceived our signals, because it had been coming closer, the dot growing, for more than an hour.

Soon, we were able to distinguish with the naked eye that it was heading toward us, and the helmsman assured us that it was traveling at full steam. Would it arrive in time? That was the only question that Yvonne and I could ask one another now as we clasped hands, ready to confront death courageously if it were finally about to take us, after having spared us so miraculously and so stubbornly.

Suddenly, running out of strength, her nerves overwhelmed, all her prophetic energy adrift, convinced that salvation would arrive too late and that it really was death this time, Yvonne collapsed on my shoulder, and I heard her murmur, through her sobs: "Forgive me! Please forgive me!"

I did not have time to reply. The screech of a siren cut through the air. A gigantic shadow leaned over us. A few minutes later, all three of us were safe on the deck of the savior vessel, a mail-boat, while the yacht sank with a tragic, whistling death-rattle that faded away into the splashing of the victorious waves.

Thus concludes the story of our nuptial voyage, a story that you might perhaps think implausible, even as a lover of the unreal—a story increasingly improbable in the eyes of my wife, who was congratulating herself only yesterday for never having had anything for which to reproach herself, or for which to require forgiveness, since the day of our marriage.

DOCTOR QUID

*All human actions are the fatal products
of the cerebral substance*
Taine[33]

I

Omnia in mensura, in numero, et pondera disposuisti![34]

And Doctor Quid paced back and forth in his laboratory, his gaze somber and his head bowed, his upper body buckling under the weight of the enormous problem of which his cerebral lobes had just taken hold.

Here, a description would be *de rigueur*, in order to impress the reader suitably and not to be neglectful with regard to the constitutional elements of my story, but the task is beyond the scope of my pen, I humbly confess. There are mysterious bonds between Dr. Quid and his laboratory that I do not have the strength to disentangle. Both of them, although bristling with a thousand tangible or intangible asperities, encapsulated and completed one another so well that the abstract reasoning necessary to introduce them separately to the reader would destroy that secret harmony by its very essence.

The laboratory, in all respects similar to that of Wagner in *Faust*, the complex fluids saturating its atmosphere, the sticky, viscous floor furrowed here and there with grooves

---

[33] The positivist sociologist Hippolyte Taine (1828-1893). The quotation is from *L'Intelligence* (1870).

[34] The quotation, more accurately rendered as *omnia in mensura et numero et pondere disposuisiti* is from the Vulgate Bible version of *Wisdom* 11:21: "Thou has ordered all things in measure, and number, and weight."

carrying crystalline residues toward nether regions, the bottles, flasks, retorts and alembics with disparate and uneven forms, the whitewashed walls covered with cabalistic symbols testifying that coarse charcoal was sometimes placed at the disposal of the scientist's lucubrations, and finally, the scientist himself, the tenebrous Dr. Quid, who wears on his face and throughout his appearance the accusatory imprints of the chaos in whose bosom he consumes his existence, all form a single whole, utterly heterogeneous but perfectly indissoluble into its elements.

That isn't sufficient for you? So be it; I shall enter into a few details with regard to Dr. Quid. He is a scientist, as I have said. I will add that he is a modern scientist, for he is married.

Nowadays, scientists are divided into two classes: the ancient and the modern. Those two classes are completely different from one another in their manner of comprehending the usage of the natural attributes that Providence has granted them. The ancient scientist is celibate; the modern scientist is married. Between the two categories there is an abyss, which the former can only cross by means of the hymeneal tightrope. The ancient is still somewhat stained by alchemy; the modern has harnessed his chariot to the triumphal march symbolic of the rapid progress of chemistry.

Let no one be in doubt; it is marriage that has created modern science; it is matrimonial contracts that have extract chemistry from the bosom of alchemy, and the latter will only disappear completely when the last bachelor among scientists, or the last scientist among bachelors, ties the knot.

How can the influence of marriage on the progress of science be explained? I shall leave the care of that problem to those who cultivate the arid terrain of social physiology.

Dr. Quid had the fine and delicate features, the accentuated profile and the neat bone structure that characterize nervous temperaments. A wan pallor was spread over his entire face, the bloodless flesh denoting, in addition, an unfortunate predisposition to encephalic neuroses.

Thanks to those physical particularities, Dr. Quid could easily be taken into the possession of environments. His laboratory had gradually become indentified with him, and vice versa. His eyes had taken on a hyaline transparency; the proportions of his body had been slowly transformed. The slightest preoccupations were translated externally by implausible attitudes; his limbs were then grouped in accordance with certain geometrical shapes, borrowed from his bizarre instruments, and all his movements appeared to be the result of forces elaborated in his retorts.

Dr. Quid had been pacing back and forth in his laboratory for half an hour when he suddenly stopped and folded his arms—which indicated, in him, a violent nervous crisis.

"Well," he said, "this can't go on; either I emerge from this question victorious, or I consent to lose forever the faculty of solving problems. The spectacle of nature is sufficient in itself to demonstrate that everything in the organic realm, as in the inorganic realm, is submissive to the laws of number.

"Number is the first link that intelligence conceives between the phenomena of sound, light, heat, electricity, etc., when it studies them and seeks the common relationships that might unite them. Definite quantities intervene in every propagation, transmission or exchange of substance. The harmony that reigns in the world is, in consequence, immediate.

"Number is, moreover, an indispensable condition for the production of any harmony whatsoever. To take account of that, it's sufficient to consider audigible phenomena such as music. All sounds are linked together by numerical relationships; such and such a note corresponds to such and such a number of vibrations, and consonances between chords can only take place if the numbers of vibrations in the notes have a simple ratio.

"Furthermore, phrenology informs us that there are such intimate relationships between the relationships of sounds and those of numbers that the organ of numbers in the brain is like a continuation of that of music, a sort of prolongation of the nethermost convolution of that organ. In all the branches of art, in its most varied forms, harmony is submissive to the same laws. A combination of colors, or an arrangement of lines forming a drawing, can only please if they're chosen or disposed in such a fashion as to emit vibrations whose numbers have a simple ratio.

"One thing is, therefore, to be posited in principle: number plays a supreme role in everything that is in movement; now, movement is the source of all like, so number plays an essential and preponderant role in life.

"Given that, if we pass from the physical domain to the mental by the insensible gradation that leads from physical events to psychic events, we will always find number playing the same role in actions attributed to the human soul. If we analyze sensations, the initial origins of ideas, we will find logarithmic relationships between their intensities and those of sentiments derived from them.

"Thus, certain psychological phenomena whose intensities increase in a geometrical progression correspond point by point with certain physiological phenomena whose intensities increase in an arithmetical progression. Number therefore links all the sensitive phenomena and ought to serve as the point of departure of a new way of envisaging them and studying them.

"People have often sought to explain why accord cannot be obtained between two people who have been brought together by an absolute conformity of character and seem to be made to understand one another. With the theory of number that is easily explained. It is known that a series of identical numbers of sonorous vibrations cannot constitute a perfect chord. In the same way, two characters represented by identical numbers cannot concord; to produce the desired accord it is indispensable that their respective elements are in a given relationship. 'Those who resemble one another assemble,' says popular wisdom. It is true, but it is necessary not to conclude from it that any confraternity can reign between peoples. Human attractions obey the same laws as electrical and magnetic attractions; contrary elements attract one another and similar elements repel one another. As soon as to similar numbers are in proximity a repulsion makes itself felt. That is why people who resemble one another can assemble as much as they like, but will never reach an understanding.

"In my opinion, these general considerations ought to permit the founding of a unique, clear and simple theory, which applies mathematics to the moral sciences, and in particular to psychology. Metaphysics, squeezed tightly by geometric reasoning and algebraic demonstrations, will then beat a retreat; all dubious questions will be formulated as equations, all the unknowns will soon be determined, and a new era will begin for human intelligence: the glorious era of number.

"Yes, but how can we assign to so many various and complex phenomena the same cause? How can we explain by one unique law all the anomalies of thought and sensibility, of human will? That's what I've been seeking for a long time, and will perhaps never find. There would be nothing new under the sun thereafter, because science could cross the eternal limits of the unknown!"

At this point, Dr. Quid's lower lip was elongated by bitterness, and he passed his hand over the anxious creases in his forehead. While his absent mind struggled in the grip of the problem that was obsessing it, his haggard eyes wandered over the immobile retorts that extended their curved necks into the air as if to listen to some silent sound or grasp something intangible. One of the gas lamps, which was burning almost above his head, with a shrill hiss, cast soft and vacillating gleams over his polished cranium.

Suddenly, he shivered.

His gaze had just fallen upon the opposite wall. A few hours earlier, at grips with his problem, he had despairingly scribbled in charcoal the famous dictum: *Nihil novi sub sole.*[35]

---

[35] Nothing new under the sun; the substitution is a trifle ambiguous, it seems to be construed, in the context of the story, as "what [is]," although it could also be interpreted as "something."

Now—he could not believed his eyes—the *Nihil* had been transformed into a majestic *Quid*, and above the vigorous period that he had placed behind the four words, as if by magic, an enormous question mark now floated.

Had the charcoal betrayed the internal preoccupations of the scientist when the latter had exhaled his despair and made it take form on the wall? No—he was sure that he had written *Nihil*. And then again, where had that question mark come from, which was trembling—for it could definitely be seen moving—as if it were afraid of being suspended over such a big question?

A slight smile now stayed over the scientist's lips. A part of the mystery was explained. The question mark was the shadow of a big hook curved in the form of an S and suspended from a curtain-rod in front of the gas lamp. The heat radiated by the flame was imparting an oscillation to it, very slight in reality but whose amplitude was significantly augmented in the shadow. Nevertheless, the transformation of the *Nihil* into *Quid* remained a mystery.

After convincing himself that he could not account for that anomaly, the scientist ceased to worry about it, let himself fall into a chair and resumed his algebraic meditations.

Then a small, tenuous, crystalline sound, similar to the silvery plaint of a dropped pin, burst forth in the torpid sonorities of the laboratory. Unfortunately for him, the scientist did not hear it. If he had heard it, he would have darted a glance at the round-bottomed glass flask placed not far from his nose and would have recoiled swiftly. The flask contained nitrous oxide, and it had just cracked.

Slowly, the gas filtered through the fissure in the wall and spread out as far as Dr. Quid's nasal fossas.

The latter did not take long to feel its anesthetic virtues. His eyebrows fell heavily, like unbolted chassis, his head slumped forward on to this collar and he lapsed into a soporific state that affected the form of the most profound lethargy.

He might perhaps have remained like that for a long time but for the solicitude of his wife. Having become impatient with a wait that seemed to be extending indefinitely, and seeing that the time for dinner was long past, she decided to penetrate into the sanctuary of science. Her surprise was great when she perceived the god asleep in the midst of his retorts.

"Well, my love, you've forgotten dinner, then?"

The doctor did not budge.

His wife's anguished hands required a quarter of an hour to bring him round.

Finally, it was as if the scientist emerged from a dream, and his first words were: "What is it? What's happening? What's new?"

II

While Dr. Quid was asleep a strange phenomenon had occurred in his brain. The intellectual tension that existed there beforehand had become localized or fixed in his head, and now remained there in a permanent state.

That phenomenon, however, presented an additional grave complication. Dr. Quid was afflicted by a partial amnesia, which created within him an entirely new mode of existence. He had lost all memory of the solutions to problems that he had previously solved, and all the questions that he now wanted to resolve escaped him the moment he thought that he had the solution. Thus, having arrived at the end of a perfectly reasoned equation, he found that he could no longer find the value of the unknown. Furthermore, all the objects that struck his eyes immediately became, for him, insoluble problems. Everything was translated in his brain into figures, which he ornamented with all the signs invented by calculation, or in more or less regular lines between which he sought to establish trigonometric calculations. Sometimes, his mind hovered between a sine and a cosine, sometimes it oscillated at the end of a tangent...and yet, he never found what he was looking for.

On the night of the day when his fatal accident had occurred, he had gone to bed with painful apprehensions. Immediately, he had seen himself assailed by a sea of figures bristling with fateful gleams and escorted by question marks that swirled in the curtains of the bed like a host of hobgoblins. Then he had wanted to read in order to distract himself—to which his wife had only consented in very grudgingly.

He had opened the first book that came to hand, which was *La Peau de chagrin*[36]—but he had closed it again immediately, because, on the page into which his thumb had just plunged he had read these words traced in flamboyant characters:

"The leader of all the sciences is undoubtedly the question mark; we owe the greatest of our discoveries to How? and the wisdom of life perhaps consists of asking of every proposition: Why?"

His neck plunged back under the bedclothes, Dr. Quid had been seized by an interrogatory erethism that is impossible to describe. His entire body twisted and gradually took on the elegantly curved form that distinguishes the question mark. Even his the groans of his wife, into whose back he was digging, and who, her patience exhausted, ended up telling him vulgarly that he was sleeping "like the hammer of a gun," could not restore him to a plausible attitude.

The following day, while he was pacing back and forth in his laboratory, it seemed to him that the retorts were standing up around him like so many question marks, and distilling through their sides a vague anxiety, a feverish spirit of perquisition.

Then, to escape the exploratory rays that his flasks were emitting, he went out into the street. The walls were covered with multicolored posters on which flagrant appeals to public curiosity stood out in capital letters: WHAT'S NEW? WHAT'S NEW?—followed by an advertisement. It was enough to drive one mad.

After a few days, Dr. Quid was the victim of a repulsive obsession. The field of his investigations had ended up extend-

---

[36] The 1831 novel by Honoré de Balzac.

ing beyond all limits. The smallest details of material life pre-occupied him, and cause him terrible insomnias. He exerted himself most furiously on things that were reputed to be inexplicable.

If his wife made one of those abrupt, involuntary, nervous movement that sometimes accompany the regular action of a muscle and which physiologists call 'concomitant movements,' he asked her for the reason for it. If a dog barked in the street, he asked himself why. Everything that walked, crawled or scuttled appeared to him to have an account to render, and to owe science a solution to the problem contained in its bosom.

Music, above all, had the ability to impassion him sharply, although he had once execrated it. The most banal and insignificant motif had, for him, a well-determined language. Incisive notes, sequenced sounds, the *stretti* of fugues all represented regiments of figures that married harmoniously and signified a heap of things of which it was indispensable to take account.

Then Dr. Quid accumulated mountains of signs, pursued his solutions through an ocean of xs and ys, searching, always searching…and never finding.

III

It was a month, to the day, that Dr. Quid's brain had been drowning in mysteries of numbers.

As on the evening when we saw him attacking that terrible problem for the first time, the scientist was standing upright in the center of his laboratory, concentrating all his living forces in the crossing of his arms. The fatal *Quid novi sub sole?* was still diabolically radiant in the diffuse light of the wall, and the gigantic question mark was still swaying before him, as if to mock him.

The more the scientist considered the *Quid*, the more the mysterious vocable took on a real existence in his head, a significance of its own beyond the mind that conceived it. That

Quid was no longer, for him, a simple assemblage of dead letters; it was saying something to him, speaking vibrantly with its entire being. For a start, did not the *Q* itself already have the form of a question mark? The letter began with a graceful curve condensing in its folds something incisive and sovereignly interrogative. Then, stretching like a swan's neck, it reared up with a loose stroke and finally, after having completed itself with a loop affecting the agreeable form of an ellipse, it was terminated by a curved flourish of the proudest allure.

Decidedly, it was only the Latin tongues that enjoyed the privilege of being translated by signs having some relationship with the idea they represent. The English, who translated *Quid* as *What* and the Germans, who translated it as *Was*, were very unfortunate in being deprived of that immense advantage. A heavy and graceless W could never have any interrogatory intention.

While the scientist was making these reflections he composed his attitude unconsciously on the model of the *Quid*, filling out his head, contorting his upper body, rounding his legs and gradually talking on the crouched and meditative posture of the Sphinx, an animal that effectively enjoyed, with the question mark and the seventeenth letter of the alphabet, the privilege of stereotyping, after a fashion, a divinatory idea, a mute and constant problem. In that attitude, Dr. Quid, with his huge head emerging anxiously from his false collar and the enigmatic tails of his coat projecting behind him, seemed to be a mysterious incarnation of the question mark.

Suddenly, as if gripped by frenzy, he bounded toward the wall and struck the vacillating shadow of the hook a mighty blow with his fist.

Then he tottered.

His neurosis had been suddenly aggravated; a lesion had just developed in the cerebral substance.

Choreic movements immediately became manifest, shaking his head and all his abductor muscles.

Slowly, as if dominated by an occult power, he drew closer to the hypnotic hook, now hopping. Having arrived there, he tore off his cravat, knotted the two ends and suspended it solidly from the iron hook.

He struck his forehead as if to try to make one supreme spark spring forth, and at the same time, he darted one last glance at the wall.

Nothing had changed. Strangely, the cravat did not project any shadow!

That was too much. He brought up a chair, climbed on to it and put his head through the batiste ellipse. Immediately, the chair fell, as if tipped over by an invisible hand, and the unfortunate scientist remained suspended beneath the hook.

Then, as a rapid congestion dilated his brain, he recovered all his lucidity. He had it now, the solution to the great problem that had disturbed his faculties; it stood out clearly in his mind.

Dr. Quid struggled, in a supreme gasp. He was too late. Already, blue and green tints of tumescence were invading his entire face. His knees buckled; his body writhed like a worm impaled on a fishing-hook.

Over there on the wall, a question mark was swaying, now, even more gigantic than that of the hook: it was his own shadow.

And his bloodshot eyes read, clearly:

Nihil novi sub sole!

Alas, there was no longer any *Quid* but him, suspended under the curtain-rod in the laboratory.

MEISTER FULT

*The mind depends so strongly on temperament
and the disposition of the organs of the body
that if it is possible to find a means to render
humans in general wiser and cleverer than they
have been thus far, I believe that it is in medicine
that it must be sought...*
Descartes

I

I beg the reader's pardon, but I have never been able to discover in exactly which era the story that I am about to tell transpired. One day, I had been devoting myself for an hour to violent gymnastic exercises on my grandfather's right knee. War-weary, and fearing that my evolutions might eventually cause some damage to the fabric of his trousers, he decided to tell me this story, which he said he got from his own grandfather, who got it from his grandfather, who got it from his, etc.

Later, I searched the archives of Strasbourg with an ardor worthy of a better fate, and observed dolorously that the history of the most remote times—"backward" seems more apt to me than "remote," for time always advances and never turns back—makes no mention of any such prodigious event.

After that confession, almost humiliating for me, it only remains for me to beg the reader to pass on, and to forgive me for that chronological lacuna in view of my good faith.

I shall suppose, therefore, in order to fix the ideas, that the story happened in the year 40, certain that no one will attack any significance to that date, about which people generally do not care at all.

In that epoch, a man lived in Strasbourg who wore no wig, and had, moreover, an indecent head of hair, unkempt and bristling, and a beard like a river, as yellow s parchment, stained, ragged and dirty—disgusting, in a word: all the external features that characterize a great scientist.

The place where he lived was something akin to a cave, a lair, or a den, but surely had nothing that even remotely resembled the honest houses that nowadays shelter the majority of mortals.

Behind the lair in question, an immense workplace extended, which no human eye except those of its master had ever penetrated. The palisades that surrounded it scarcely allowed its existence to be suspected.

Meister Fult had long been the scientist's official name, before a worthy corporation of old women, whom a similar evangelical zeal brought together four times a day at the cathedral, and in whom the equivocal appearance of the scientist provoked insomnias, took audacity so far as to call him "*Der Deifel*"—the Devil.[37]

In the year 40, alas, devotion had its victims, exactly as in our day, and those poor housewives, who "took the devil by the tail" all the year round, were finding another reason for going to church, in order to have the assurance that they would only ever see his heels—the devil's, that is—but that is a simple reflection that I owe to my grandfather.

Meister Fult, whom we are going to know as intimately as tradition permits, was indeed a great scientist and also—which might appear almost antithetical—a great philanthropist. He dreamed for Strasbourg of nothing less than a complete renovation in all the domains of social life, and it was science that was to furnish the means for it. Bearing little resemblance in that regard to ideological dreamers, intransigent moralists, ferocious socialists and all the other scatterbrains

---

[37] The German for Devil is actually *Teufel*; all the German terms employed in the story are deliberately mangled, presumably reflecting the idiosyncrasies of the Alsatian accent.

who are the modern products of a more advanced civilization, he did not draw up chimerical plans or nourish vain utopias. The project he pursued was colossal.

What did he want to attack? Social life. In order to do that, it was necessary for him to render himself the absolute master of one of the principal elements of physical life, and force it to submit to an immense and radical modification. Meister Fult took on and solved that dangerous problem, and that fact alone, stripped of all the bizarre phenomena that marked the social revolution of which he was the author, ought to have sufficed to cover his name with an immortal glory. But history is ingrate and I shudder at the idea that without my grandfather and your humble servant, the memory of Fult would have been lost to posterity.

After fifty years of monstrous, hyperbolic toil, of which no one has any idea nowadays, fifty years during which Meister Fult was seen wandering the streets of Strasbourg every day, as in a dream, nibbling a *subredel*, his gaze lost in vagueness, the great scientist found what he was looking for.

Just as he convinced himself that he had got a grip on the great problem to which he had dedicated his life, he turned the corner of the Rue des Hallebardes. He lengthened his stride, and having reached his lair, he locked the door. There, after having made sure that no one could see or hear him, he murmured very quietly, with a quavering vocal inflection, sticking his fleshless arms to his sides as if to contain himself: "Eureka!" And then again, as tears ran down the parchment of his face: "Eureka! Eureka!"

Then, ever more loudly—and now he was laughing, weeping and jumping: "Eureka! Eureka! Eureka! Eureka!"

And his philanthropic expansibility, repressed for fifty years, burst forth in a veritable flood, which the four walls of his lair had difficulty containing.

However, Meister Fult remained prudently at home in order that the devout old women of Strasbourg could not accuse him of having stolen the soul of Archimedes.

What, then, had the illustrious scientist found?

He had found—and it is certainly regrettable for science that Meister Fult carried his secret to the tomb—a means of augmenting atmospheric pressure, and, in consequence, the density of the air.

II

Once he had mastered his problem, Meister Fult went to see the burgomeister the very next day. The latter was secretly his friend, because of the great services the scientist had rendered him and the good advice he had always given him.

When Meister Fult had revealed his project, the burgomeister leapt up in an enormous bound, with the effect of gravely compromising the existence of his Dutch pipe, which never quit his teeth.

"But, God in Heaven," he said, after having shaken his head and the bowl of his pipe, "why do you want to do all that?"

Then Meister Fult talked, and he talked for a long time. As he talked, his voice became more forceful and more enthusiastic; his dull complexion became animated; his eyes shone for the first time with an almost divine gleam. The beautiful soul of the scientist and philanthropist was finally expanding. He trembled with emotion, utterly confused by the beautiful ideas that he was about to set forth. In the city, people slandered him, accusing him of having signed a pact with the devil. To his fellow citizens he was a scarecrow. My God, he knew that! But he forgave them. He wanted nothing but the good of the people: to regenerate the mores and customs of his compatriots, which had always been too *steckelburier*;[38] to endow the city with a constitution of which neither Solon or Lycurgus had ever dreamed.

Then he set out the detailed plan of all his vast calculations. The reform that he was going to bring about was radical.

---

[38] An improvised and slightly garbled bilingual term implying "stuck in the mud."

It omitted nothing. It touched the most intimate features of life. A general upheaval was necessary in order to undermine everything and uproot everything and leave no trace of the old regime.

"And you see, my dear Burgomeister," said Meister Fult, in an inspired tone, "I've now arrived at the capital point. The phenomenon has happened. The density of the air is augmenting in considerable proportions. Calculate the formidable consequences that will result from it."

The poor burgomeister was sweating in large drops. With the particular instinct that characterizes nullity and impotence, he sensed that he was in the presence of a frightful chaos, which the most heroic efforts of his intelligence could not succeed in disentangling. The man of science was crushing him. He tossed back three tankards of beer while Meister Fult continued.

"You're familiar with Archimedes' principle, aren't you?"

The burgomeister made a problematic gesture.

"You know that a body plunged into a heavy fluid experiences a diminution of weight equal to the weight of the fluid that it displaces. You know, for example, that when you take a bath in the Ill, Burgomeister, you float because the volume of water that you displace is superior to your own weight."

The burgomeister moved his chair back slightly, and darted a furtive and anxious glance behind him, as if to make sure that there was a way out in case of danger. It is necessary to say that the poor man, with the aid of age and beer, had taken on almost implausible dimensions. It was said that his abdomen attained more than a meter in circumference.

"Well," Meister Fult continued, "suppose that our atmosphere became even denser than the water in which you float. What would happen? You'd experience within that atmosphere an upward vertical pressure, which would transport you directly into the celestial regions."

"Holy Virgin Mary, have pity on us!" howled the unfortunate burgomeister, while his pale head slumped on to his face.

"Don't worry," said the scientist, taking him by the hand, "If I said 'you' that was only to focus your ideas by means of an example. In reality, you'll doubtless be the one man on whom the phenomenon will have no purchase, for your own weight, acting as a downward vertical force, will be considerable enough to cancel out the pressure in the opposite direction and leave you in a state of indifferent equilibrium."

"How do you expect the misfortunate of my administratees to leave me indifferent?" said the burgomeister, tearfully.

"Once again, don't worry, and listen to me. I have no intention of sending my fellow citizens to the Moon or making them participate in the perilous and uncertain life of the birds. The objection that you're making constitutes the very basis of my reforms. It's indispensable—mark me well, *indispensable*, I say—that no citizen should ever leave the streets of Strasbourg, because the floating life would throw disarray into all the functions of social life and would not take long to bring about the most disastrous consequences. To begin with, the family would be destroyed forever. No more commerce and no more industry; peace and law would no longer be possible if everyone could fly like a sparrow at whim. How could you expect to regulate by legislation the mores of a people soaring continuously several thousand meters above sea level? Would you dare to talk about your superiority over people who had such a considerable elevation above you? People would laugh at you, Burgomeister."

The idea of such audacity covered the worthy burgomeister's face with an anticipatory sweat. He drank a fourth beer in order to collect himself.

"And then, you see," Meister Fulk continued, "Strasbourgians are too positive, too down to earth, for that aerial life to suit them. Not everyone has a taste for the clouds. It's necessary to have a contemplative, poetic soul—that of a madman, in a word—and our good fellow citizens are too well-equilibrated for that. The invasion of poetry into the heads of Strasbourgians would be a public calamity: adieu gilded sauerkraut, adieu knockwurst, adieu beer, adieu the pipe!

"Oh! Oh!" gurgled the burgomeister, pitiably, clinging to his pipe as if it were about to fly away.

"So, this is what it will be necessary to do,"

And Meister Fult took from his overcoat pocket a wad of papers of various sizes. One by one, he showed them to the burgomeister.

"Here," he said, "are the new Codes that you must bring into force, and the laws that will apply throughout the territory of Strasbourg and the suburbs. Here are the documents of civil estate. This is the Code of conventional contracts. This is the procedural Code. This is the penal Code, etc. Here, in addition, is the text of the posters that you will put up all over the city on the day that I indicate to you. You see that I haven't forgotten anything. Reading all that very carefully, and the few preliminary instructions that I'll give you, will be sufficient for you to understand everything. The entire new Constitution rests on a system of weight. Every citizen, in order not to rise into the clouds, will be required to carry on their person a complementary or additional weight that will figure in the Codes under the title of 'dead weight.' The Council of Arbiters will confer the dead weight on a child on the day the birth is registered. That dead weight will be, from then on, an integral part of the citizen, and will be carried to the tomb. Every first of January, a new allocation of dead weight will be allocated to all those whose volume had increased in the course of the year, and whose social equilibrium is thus disturbed.

"The system of standard weights for each age will be deposited in the city archives. A citizen who wishes to contract a marriage will be required to rivet his weight to his wife's by means of a chain, in accordance with a standard deposited in the archives. That chain, the symbol of an indissoluble union, will be blessed by the priest and unbreakable, under pain of the most severe punishments. It will only be unfastened temporarily in urgent cases. Furthermore, the couple will be required to have the chain inspected once a month by a civil officer. Thanks to that chain, the wife will be held to strict obedience of the article in the Civil Code that requires her to follow her spouse wherever he cares to go. She will also be forced to exercise the same profession as her husband. We shall thus realize the emancipation of women and banish adultery forever.

"But that's not all. When a man commits a crime against society, what does society do? It takes revenge by excluding him permanently from its bosom, and to do that it cuts off his head. Obviously, that is its right, since it's the only way of getting rid of great criminals. But I have a better one. With my system, the death penalty is abolished. A citizen, momentarily going astray, commits a crime liable to capital punishment. I leave him his life, but I remove him from society by taking away his dead weight. The guilty party goes to expiate his sin in the clouds. In that fashion, society is rid of the criminal, but does not commit a second crime to avenge the first."

The suffocating burgomeister was now contemplating Meister Fult with an almost superstitious admiration and respect. In his eyes, the man was taking on the proportions of a demigod. Assuredly, if his pipe had not been so dear to him, he would have unclenched his teeth, and an opening gaping like a gulf surging forth between his thick lips would have given a just measure of his amazement. In the meantime, the various sentiments that were agitating him were translated in his visage by an unaccustomed relaxation of all the facial muscles and a dilation of the naïve, almost stupid pupils.

Pleased with the impression that he had produced, Meister Fult took his leave of the burgomeister in order to give him time to collect himself. Back home, the scientist threw himself into a chair, took his head between his hands and exhaled a deep sigh.

"O Science," he murmured, "I have given you my youth, I have given you all that I had of what is most precious in the world, I have sacrificed the best years of my life to you, and the gilded dreams of the imagination, and the illusions of the heart, and the ardent passions of the soul. When I went astray, feeble and devoid of support, in the immense fields of your tenebrous domain, no light guided me, no human voice affirmed my courage, so often shaken. No tender affection down here has ever consoled my pains. Only the hope of finding a path in that profound darkness that would lead me to happiness sustained me."

Here the scientist's voice became quieter and more tremulous. A secret dolor was visibly oppressing him.

After a long sigh, he went on: "And now that I have attained my life's goal, now that my fellow citizens are going to enjoy the fruits of my labor and I might hope to reanimate my own withered years with the spectacle of their happiness, which will be due to me, now you are demanding that sacrifice as well! You will not permit me to be happy too! You will not permit that I inhabit the promised land to which I have led my people. Oh, how have I offended you, in what respect have I disobeyed you, that you should inflict that frightful torture upon me? But I am your slave, and I shall submit...yes, I shall submit..."

A single tear rolled down from the scientist's wrinkled eyelid. He wiped it away, and that was all.

He was calm now. He was resigned. He was great.

III

A few notes of explanation for the scientific reader, whom Meister Fult's projects might have plunged into an understandable astonishment. In the epoch in which my story happened, science was still very backward. The formidable progress that it would realize later did not even exist as a seed in the minds of the scientists of old. Today, when we know the composition of the air and the preponderant role that it plays in organic life, we can grasp at a glance the ensemble of the deplorable consequences that the phenomenon of which Meister Fult dreamed would bring in its wake—consequences that the latter was unable to foresee.

In fact, Meister Fult, although he was the greatest scientist of his era, did not know that air is composed of oxygen and nitrogen, that life is a phenomenon of slow combustion, that a human being is a hearth that burns 250 grams of carbon per day and a little hydrogen, and, in sum, that the human race removes from the air by respiration 160 trillion cubic meters of oxygen per year, and replaces it by as much carbon dioxide. If Meister Fult had known that, either he would have tried to modify the air after the fashion of Dr. Ox[39] or he would have left Nature in repose, agreeing with Leibnitz that all is for the best in the best of all possible worlds.

But the illustrious scientist only had one idea, one unique dream: to regenerate the physical life of his fellow citizens, and, in consequence, their social life.

The people, he had said to himself, *are slack and slow; the excessive quantity of beer they ingest, and the tobacco smoke that they breathe in have softened their fibers and distended their brains. Strasbourgians are strong only in terms of physical force; the energy with which they are endowed in only translated into corporeal activity. By plunging them into a thicker atmosphere, respiration will be facilitated while physical movement will be hindered. Then the superabundance of bodily forces will perhaps be diverted to the brain; the diminution of corporeal activity will correspond to an augmentation of cerebral activity, and Strasbourgians will become elite human beings.*

As you can see, Meister Fult had a completely mistaken idea of vital dynamism, of assimilation and dissimilation., but

---

[39] The protagonist of Jules Verne's novella "Une Fantaisie du docteur Ox" (1872; tr. as "Doctor Ox" or "Dr. Ox's Experiment")—the obvious inspiration for the present story—in which a scientist attempts to improve the life of his village in Flanders by installing oxy-hydric gas lighting, but an oxygen leak intoxicates the villagers and causes chaos.

History will forgive him, in view of the elevated goal that he was pursuing.

IV

On the fourth of December of year 40, when the citizens of Strasbourg awoke they saw, to their amazement, al the walls covered with striking posters summoning them all to the Gemeindehaus, where the burgomeister was to prepare them for the grave events that were about to occur.

Strasbourg Observatory had signaled in advance for the night of the tenth and the eleventh a phenomenon unique in the annals of meteorology, the duration of which was completely unknown. In the presence of such a grave occurrence, the authorities of the city had taken measures to prepare for the most urgent needs of the new life that the phenomenon in question was about to create for the inhabitants.

When the Strasbourgians learned from the mouth of the burgomeister what was involved there was a momentary concert of exclamations, tears, vociferations, and a frightful confusion. The burgomeister, pressed, harassed and overwhelmed by questions, let it all pass over him, although visibly disturbed, and retrenched himself in an obstinate silence—which was, in any case, imposed on him by his ignorance.

That silence was nearly fatal for him. For a moment, there was a danger of revolution. Habitually, however one only revolts against human laws, never those of Nature. The Strasbourgians were forced to fall into line. The next few days went by without any major incident. The authorities proceeded rapidly with the distribution of dead weights. In order to inform the citizens of the new duties that they would be called upon to fulfill, they had recourse to all means to facilitate the propagation of the new laws.

A week after the convocation, order and peace reigned once again among the population. By virtue of one of those turnabouts typical of the human mind, the heads overexcited by the anticipation of the phenomenon now wanted it to arrive as soon as possible. A few were even dreaming of an immediate denouement and promising to please themselves enormously in a life that would contrast so singularly with their past existence. Souls were tormented by a need for change that they had never known before. The new, the artificial and the unknown exercised a powerful attraction on those simple and naïve organisms.

Only the battalion of devout old women, reinforced by a few men whose bigotry was proof against anything, resisted the enthusiasm that took possession of hearts, and made novenas in order to bend the will of heaven and deflect the cataclysm. The altar of the Virgin Mary in the Cathedral did not take long to disappear beneath ex-votos.

V

In the meantime, what was Meister Fult doing?

According to the residents of his neighborhood, the scientist was now devoting himself to nocturnal labors very alarming for public repose. It was affirmed that every evening, a long file of phantoms slipped into his workyard by means of an invisible door; confused rumors were then heard rising from that deserted location, the muffled sound of hammering and the grating of saws, all in the most profound obscurity.

The truth is that Meister Fult, obedient to an internal voice that forbade him to enjoy the fruits of his labor himself, and preparing a means of effecting his departure. His decision had been rapidly made. He would make arrangements so that the manifestation of the phenomenon that he would provoke would lift him forever from the soil of his natal city and remove him in a sure fashion from the gratitude of his fellow citizens. For that purpose, he constructed a vast vessel in his workyard destined to rise into the air when the atmospheric pressure attained a sufficient level. It was an ark similar to the one whose form is conserved for us by the Bible and which, it is said, carried Noah and his pigeons. It was fitted with a profound keel that was hermetically sealed and armored with sheet metal. Three safety-valves had been fitted into the ceiling.

Meister Fult's idea was quite simple. When the ambient pressure increased, the pressure inside the keel would become considerably inferior; the ark would therefore rise up by virtue of the difference between the two pressures.

There was, however, one thing to be feared. It is known that the density of the atmospheric layers increases as one rises up into the superior regions because the sun warms and dilates those that are in immediate contact with it. The ark would therefore rise up into the air with an increasing velocity. In consequence, by virtue of a particular phenomenon, operating independently of the one due to Meister Fulk, the keel might end floating on a layer of air dense enough to bear it, while the house that it supported might be plunged into an atmosphere that was too rarefied, and, in consequence, unbreathable. The safety valves were designed to overcome that inconvenience. It was sufficient to open one of those valves to augment the pressure in the hull; the ark would then descend slowly and could be maintained at a constant height. The ascensional force would, in any case, have been calculated in advance.

The tenth of December finally arrived. Everything was ready.

That evening, Meister Fult climbed into the ark and went to his cabin, which he locked.

One of those profound calms then spread though the atmosphere in which one thinks one can hear, through the eternal exchange of elements that constitutes vital dynamism, the bated breath of matter at work.

The great mystery was about to commence.

The powerful will of the scientist was about to project beyond the circle of its evolution one of the thousand latent forces of the organic world. Subjugated Nature slowly loosened the mysterious bonds that still held it captive.

VI

By four o'clock in the afternoon, the streets of Strasbourg were deserted and silent. Carriages abandoned by their masters were stationary in various locations.

By virtue of superior orders, circulation had been prohibited from sunset onwards. Everyone was confined to their homes, with painful apprehensions. Since the morning, the pitch of the general enthusiasm had diminished considerably, to the extent that when the shadows began to cover the earth, the level had become almost negative. Every family constituted a nucleus of intimate effervescence, of which I renounce the attempt to give any idea. Sometimes, everyone was talking at the same time; people communicated to one another their fears, their hopes and their plans for the future, in the case of a favorable outcome to the mystery; sometimes one strong mind demanded to speak alone, and emitted a reassuring opinion in a firm, peremptory, irresistible voice, scolding the cowards, encouraging the timid and pouring balm on timorous souls; then there were long pauses, long silences in which everyone trued to retreat into their own consciousness, in search of a spiritual refuge in order to retemper the soul.

No one ate that evening.

The burgomeister was at table, along with his maidservant and a bottle of beer, both destined—without prejudice to his pipe—to keep him company. The maid was as mute and motionless as a log; the burgomeister did not say a word. He had found a means of banishing the terror that had laid siege to him since dusk by persistently exploring an insignificant object: his right slipper. It was a gift from his late wife. The design represented a Turk in a gold-spangled costume, smoking a fantastic pipe. That incomprehensible pipe was his nightmare; it haunted him on his nights of insomnia. He had never been able to take an exact account of its forms, its dimensions or its dispositions. He was, however a connoisseur.

That evening, the Turkish pipe presented to him, as always, the problematic fissure of its bowl, like a great black eye. He clung on to it, like a saving branch, stuffed his reverie of brutalized smoker into the relit bowl, brought it out again through the end of the stem, followed the capricious spirals of the band that ornamented it, always searching for the vulnerable point where the imperfection was nested that shocked him so much.

That mental concentration ended up giving birth in the burgomeister's brain to one of those banal, vulgar but persistent ideas that claw you obstinately and surge forth in the midst of the gravest events, when the intelligence is absorbed in the keenest preoccupations.

From one moment to the next, that idea became increasingly clear in its accentuation, corresponding physically in the burgomeister to an every-increasing forced inclination. His eyes were fixed on the slipper with a fearful fixity.

He suddenly realized that the Turkish pipe was not a pipe.

"Oh my God! And to think that it took thirty years!" he murmured, mopping his brow.

The burgomeister was heartbroken.

At that moment, the clock chimed eight. A formidable detonation, which echoed for a long time, like a rumble of thunder, caused the entire mountain chain enveloping the valley of the Rhine to tremble. In the room where the burgomeister was, a dry metallic click was audible, and a barometric tube suspended on the wall shattered into little pieces.

While the burgomeister observed his singular mistake, the mysterious phenomenon caused by Meister Fult developed slowly. The ever-faithful mercury had indicated by a rapid ascension the almost-instantaneous increase in atmospheric pressure. Having reached the summit of the barometric chamber it had broken the glass and was now falling to the floor in a supple gleaming jet.

At the same minute of the same hour all the barometers in the city suffered the same fate. All the movements and pendulums of the clocks stopped at the same time, because of the excessive resistance of the air. The immobility of those faithful pendulums, which marked the regular and silent march of time so well and served, so to speak, as the piston of the various silences characteristic of a room, was to hollow out henceforth a fatal emptiness, impossible to fill, in all those existences made of habit and routine.

When the first moment of his double surprise had passed, the burgomeister tried to pull himself together. He got up and took a few steps around the room. It soon seemed as if he were moving through a thick fluid, which penetrated his entire body through his mouth, nostrils, ears and all his pores, causing him a rather disagreeable sensation. In the depths of the room the fluid, by virtue of its considerable density, took on a bluish tint; the room did not take long to resemble a vast aquarium. To complete the illusion, the maidservant, who had been making vain efforts to resist the increased pressure for several minutes, suddenly took flight, involuntarily but majestically, and slowly rose up to the ceiling. There she presented the burgomeister with the provocative spectacle of a skirt in disarray, revealing the slightest details of the beauties it sheltered.

The chair had preceded her in her aerial voyage, and was drifting tranquilly in the gaps between the joists. The poor girl clung on to it with the energy of desperation. Immediately—O prodigy!—she came back down slowly, and soon found herself on a level with her master, a level that she strove from then on not to surpass again.

Inside every home in the city analogous events were taking place, with slight variations.

Children, mad with joy, where delighting in foolish peregrinations in the space enclosed between the floor and ceiling, vaguely reminiscent of those enamel figurines which story-tellers cause to move at will through the water of ludions. Poorly attached wigs suddenly took flight slyly, discovering ridiculous craniums and unsuspected bald spots. Consumptives who were thought to be in a parlous state offered the spectacle of an instantaneous resurrection, the augmentation of pressure compensating in their lungs for the harmful effects of some organic lesion.

Outside, more or less grave events signaled the appearance of the phenomenon. On various roofs cats disappeared from various gutters, plunging their owners—mostly recruited from the battalion of devout old women—into unconsolable mourning.

Several hundred dogs scattered about the city lost their footing in the streets and rose up into the sky, all at once, in the midst of a concert of lamentable howling.

A hermetically sealed kiosk forgotten in the Place du Broglie also attempted to reach the region of the clouds, but a young scamp—that age is pitiless—having perceived it at the moment when it was furtively quitting the ground, threw a stone through one of its windows. The kiosk filled up with condensed air and fell like a ship in distress.

In the Grand-Rue—that quarter had, it appears, then as now, the monopoly on indecent desiccations—a multitude of dank items of lingerie drying out all over the place quit their lines and spread out in the air. Some people reported that there were so many of them the sky was darkened, and for several days there was a kind of cloud floating over the city, intercepting a significant quantity of light and heat...

VII

Meister Fult alone, calm in the midst of the perturbations of which he was the author, sure that no one now—except perhaps for the burgomeister—was thinking about him, waited tranquilly in his cabin for the waves of the air to acquire the force necessary to lift his ark. At about half past eight it began to move. Then the scientist went out on deck.

He was a little paler than usual. For a moment, he considered the ark, which was swaying above the workyard as if rocked by the waves of the Ocean. At his feet, deserted, silent and somber, his natal city was asleep. The glare of the streetlights was drowned, almost extinct.

Meister Fult uncovered his pale forehead. Sidereal light outlined his bony scholarly silhouette in a mysterious, almost supernatural light.

Slowly, he extended his hand and let these words fall into the darkness:

"Adieu, my homeland! I sense that I ought not to savor the happiness of which I have dreamed for my fellows. That happiness, which is dearer to me than my life, I am abandoning without bitterness. O people of Strasbourg, may you enjoy for a long time the glorious future that I have prepared for you!"

And Meister Fult went back into his cabin, with a firm and stoical tread.

A deathly silence descended over the ark.

A large black cloud had just enveloped it with thick darkness, and the enormous vessel placidly pursued its course toward the heavens.

VIII

As the reader will already have realized, Meister Fult's scheme, like all human things, enclosed in its very bosom the fatal germ that would lead to its destruction.

Grave inconveniences, obstacles that the scientist had been unable to anticipate, were about to surge forth at any moment in the new life that he had created for his fellow citizens and would eventually lead them, after a series of disheartening disillusionments, to a formidable revolution.

As always happens, however, with things that have the privilege of striking the imagination and flattering certain positive aspects of humanity, the majority of people closed their eyes to the petty snags that cropped up here and there, and only wanted to see, at first, the singular advantages that resulted from it.

They were ecstatic because all outdoor forms of work and those necessitating uncomfortable positions, such as the endeavors of masons, roofers, galvanizers, etc. were considerably simplified. Ladders and scaffolding were suppressed along with the angers attached to their usage. The various classes of workers once obliged to make use of them now had light hearts. In the exercise of their functions they removed their dead weight, enabling them to perform all possible acrobatics; it was sufficient to attach themselves in order that they did not fly away.

It is necessary to say here that Meister Fult's paternal laws stipulated the express prohibition of removing one's dead weight in the open, except in the circumstances just cited. Every citizen, however, gladly contracted the moral obligation of never infringing that law, not wishing to expose themselves to the peril of an aerial voyage without any hope of return, in which one would, in consequence, be in danger of dying of starvation.

In the bosom of families, distractions of an entirely new kind saw the light of day, all founded on Archimedes' principle.

Every evening, in intimate gatherings, people took off their dead weights and indulged themselves in highly original exercises in domestic natation.

Barbaric parents even ended up abusing the atmospheric pressure by making it serve correctional purposes, justly reproved by pedagogues. For the first time, Archimedes' principle was seen functioning as a means of repression and classified among objects of mortification. Thus, young Henri, the son of a cobbler in the Rue Brûlée, was condemned to spend the night in a corner of the ceiling, where he was almost devoured by the spiders.

That infatuation of the Strasbourgians with their new life—an infatuation that pushed them to deplorable excesses—did not take long to pass.

One of the gravest faults inherent in Meister Fult's creation, and of which the burgomeister was to have the harsh experience before anyone else, delivered the first blow to the enthusiasm of the masses.

IX

That day, the burgomeister had got out of bed on the wrong side.

He had dreamed once again about his enigmatic slipper. The satanic Moor had mocked him for hours in succession by presenting him with the mysterious and indecipherable object that he had so long mistaken for a pipe.

It was absolutely necessary for him to clarify the matter.

"Gretel!" he shouted, as soon as he was on his feet. "Fetch me some boiling water."

(I ought to warn the reader right away that my grandfather never told me exactly why the burgomeister had asked for boiling water. By stretching my intelligence to the most audacious conjectures, I have since acquired the semi-certainty that the vindictive Strasbourgian had founded on that liquid basis some infernal plan hatched against his slipper, but I only make that suggestion with all reservations.)

The burgomeister waited for his boiling water for ten minutes. It did not arrive.

"*Potz Himinel!* What are you doing, Gretel?" he cried, in an imperious and acerbic tone with which the maid was unfamiliar.

"It's not boiling yet," replied Gretel's voice, from the kitchen. "It's not my fault."

Another ten minutes went by. This time, it was the burgomeister who was boiling.

"Damnation!" he muttered, under his breath, matching his syllables to the steps he was taking toward the kitchen. "What have I done to deserve such a girl? Have you sworn to be the death of me today, Gretel?"

He stopped dead at the sight of his maid's distressed face. The latter was not even looking at him. Crouched before the terrible fire that was roaring in the range, she was watching her cast-iron stove, and her physiognomy expressed bewilderment pushed to its utmost limits.

Subjugated by that scene, and perhaps sensing vaguely that a superior power was in play, the burgomeister crouched down beside the maid without saying a word, and like her, widened his gross eyes.

In any other circumstances, the mere fire of his ferocious gaze might have sufficed to make the water boil, but it was written that the burgomeister would not put his subversive plans into action.

The water was holding firm. Not only was it not boiling, but it was not emitting the slightest vapor.

"That's prodigious," he said. And, standing up, he plunged his finger into the water. He withdrew it immediately, uttering a frightful howl.

The temperature of the water must have been considerable, for his finger was literally cooked.

"Water boils at a hundred degrees," he stammered, in the midst of groans that afflicted Gretel's sensibility rudely. "Water boils at a hundred degrees, but that must be at least three hundred. The devil's mixed up in this, Gretel, believe me. We're the victims of sorcery."

But the water was still not boiling.

The burgomeister now saw two somber mysteries looming up in his life: the slipper and the water. No longer knowing which saint to appeal to, he ended up taking refuge in his superstitions and his dolor, and contented himself with uttering intermittent moans punctuated with obsecrations in which Satan played a preponderant role.

Readers who possess some notion of physics will already have interpreted the phenomenon that upset the burgomeister so much, knowing that boiling is subject to well-defined laws, and that a liquid cannot boil until the elastic force of its vapor in equal to the pressure exerted by the atmosphere.

In the situation in which the burgomaster was placed, it would have been necessary, in order for the water to boil, for that liquid to obtain a much higher temperature—a condition that the magistrate's kitchen range could not produce.

X

The rumor of the cruel accident that had happened to the burgomeister did not take long to spread through the city.

Water did not boil, and not only did it not boil, but it did not emit any vapor. Evaporation was abolished. That discovery did not worry the majority of the citizens much, whose optimism was systematic. In reality, it was a scourge more terrible than the plague, because without evaporation, life on the surface of the earth is impossible. In fact, the slow evaporation of water from the earth's surface forms the clouds. One can judge from that the disastrous influence that the suppression of the phenomenon would exercise on animal life.

Meister Fult, however, had not been sufficiently aware of the verity that in the system of the world, considered in the smallest detail, everything is immutable. If humans could, by the force of will, cause a grain of sand falling by virtue of the law of gravity to deviate from its course, the world would be doomed. Life is a complex mechanism; it only requires a speck of dust in its gears for all movement to cease. The slightest perturbation introduced into the incessant exchange of substances that constitutes vita dynamism is sufficient to lead to stagnation—which is to say, to death. If the Strasbourgians of the year 40 had known that, they would have cut Meister Fult in quarters rather than let him put his science into action. But the Strasbourgians were to be punished for the sin they had committed, which was ignorance.

Once suspicions, doubt and anxiety had penetrated into hearts by the multiple doors that were opened every day by further incidents, the female sex was the first to raise the standard of revolt openly.

Woman, that delicate and sensitive being *par excellence*, always submits first and most cruelly to the repercussions of the faults that surge forth in the domain of civilization. She suffers doubly therefrom because of the weakness of her temperament and the precarious rank that she holds in social life.

Meister Fult ought to have realized that the chain he had introduced so brutally into the holy institution of marriage would shock every feminine soul; that the mere idea of enchainment—an idea that is always humiliating because it implies slavery and corporeal subordination—would end up inspiring in women an invincible disgust and repugnance for marriage. It was, to say the least, an original idea, if not ridiculous, to realize by a chain of forged metal what poetic language then referred to as "the sweet bonds of matrimony."

But Meister Fult was a scientist, and, by virtue of that title, dispensed with any delicacy with regard to women,

At any rate, that new fashion of union, because of the disagreeable reflections it suggested, and for other reasons that we are about to identify, soon fell into the most profound discredit and was booed by the entire feminine corporation.

I am not entirely sure how to explain honestly the other motives that I just mentioned. There is...well, there is a certain category of married women—meaning no offense to those of my adorable female readers who are married, all of whom I except from that category—who have enjoyed at all times the privilege of having gallant adventures. I will add, timidly, that it is doubtless because those ladies have also had, at all times, a strong propensity to throw their bonnets over the windmill.[40]

In the year of grace 40—you can see that it has already been a long time since then, and that mores have not changed—the corporation of Strasbourgian women, enrolled under the banners of *conjugo*, counted in its bosom several of these privileged ladies who liked to cast their bonnets over the Finkwiller's windmills.

Throwing a bonnet over a windmill is a very easy thing to do, is it not, Mesdames? But a chain of wrought iron complicates matters diabolically. The most valiant would think

---

[40] I have translated this French metaphor literally in order to protect its subsequent modification to refer to the mills of a particular quarter of Strasbourg, rather than substituting the less colorful "throw propriety to the winds."

twice about it. Now, it is precisely because it was necessary to think twice about it that the Strasbourgian women were discontented. If it had only been that...but their discontentment, it appears, was translated externally in a thousand ways. In the physiognomy, those charming faces, once fresh and plump, visibly paled, the eyes burning with a somber and taciturn fire that did not bode anything good. In matters of action, certain gestures became rare, symptomatic of depression and dissimulation. In the voice, intonations extended over all the diapasons of the passionate scale, from the most melodramatic note to the most shrill and grating.

Here is one fragment of wreckage among a thousand that history has collected and transmitted to us through the successive shipwrecks that engulfed people and things in that unfortunate epoch. It will give the reader an accurate idea of the unusual complication of the scenes that burst forth then in the purest matrimonial existences.

The room in which the action unfolds is modestly furnished, as is appropriate to a household income of three thousand francs a year.

Nature, dormant or dead, has no silence more profound than that which reigns between these four walls. No clock is ticking, for reasons we know, nor any fly buzzing—for it goes without saying that flies and a host of other more or less harmful insects had all gone to exercise their maleficence in the starry regions of the firmament.

One can get a clear idea of the thick and blue-tinted atmosphere that fills the room by reading certain lines of Byron in which the great poet speaks of the "blue depths" of Lake Geneva.[41] But in that seemingly calm and bleak element, a leaven of hatred and sly dissolution is fermenting, whose oppressive effect, augmented by the full weight of the atmospheric pressure, is acting painfully on conscious minds.

At the moment when we introduce the couple to our readers it is nine o'clock in the evening. The husband is sleep-

---

[41] In *Manfred* (1816-17).

ing in an armchair with a book open on his knees; the woman is pensive. Those two different psychological states draw their reason for being from the quotidian habits of the two individuals.

Every evening, at eight o'clock precisely, they devote themselves regularly, under the pale radiance of a suspended lamp, to the strategic furies of a game of dominoes. Needless to say, the pieces in the game are made of lead, to neutralize the effects of Archimedes' principle. After spending the regulation half-hour devoted to that genre of excitement, each of them is free to devote themselves to their preferred occupations.

This evening, the husband, who has a hint of eccentricity, has indulged himself in acrobatic exercises, all founded in the atmospheric pressure. To amuse his wife—or so he says, at least—he climbed the walls like a hydrophobic cat, and then, imitating flies, walked across the ceiling on all fours. The whole performance had been crowned by audacious vaulting exercises. Hence the fatigue that is now nailing him to his armchair.

The wife, far from rendering justice to her husband's corporeal talents, considered them all with a disdainful eye. She has begun to realize that the man was cut from the cloth of an acrobat, and has missed his vocation, and thus embarks on an ocean of reflections in which her self esteem suffers various tempests. In the end, overtaken by impatience and perhaps irritated by the striking contrast that exists between her husband's mental state and her own, she stands up and taps him lightly on the shoulder.

With that occurrence, the sleeper, abruptly woken up, has the fatal inspiration of risking a joke suggested to him by his recent acrobatics.

"Why wake a sleeping cat? You know the proverb."

Cruelly misinterpreting the scope of that remark, she replies in a bitter tone: "Well, that's fine. One dare not budge near Monsieur, now, when Monsieur is somnolent. Between us, it seems to me that you've been taking things very easy for some time."

The husband is momentarily nonplussed, alarmed by that angry sally.

Anxious, finally, about the turn that the conversation is taking, and knowing from experience the fatal outcome that it might have, he makes his decision. He opposes to his wife's recriminations a wounding silence, which only contributes to her further exasperation. She raises her voice, gradually becoming bolder, and heaps abuse upon him. The thick layer of air surrounding them enters into vibration, and radiates the flood of her blind rage in all directions.

The husband finally feels himself getting warmed up; in Strasbourg, people are fairly quick to lose their heads. He wants to avoid too violent an altercation. He tells his wife that he is going to the tavern to give her time to calm down, and goes into the next room to get his dead weight and his hat. He comes back with the hat alone. The dead weight has disappeared. He believes, however, that he put it on a chair that was manifesting violent tendencies to get closer to the ceiling.

Suddenly, a terrible idea strikes him. He considers his wife. Her triumphant expression leaves no doubt: she has hidden his dead weight to prevent him from going out. He masters his anger momentarily and says, in a seemingly calm voice: "Where have you put my dead weight? You know very well that..."

"Your dead weight is locked up. You shan't have it. That's just like you, like all of you. You sacrifice everything to the tavern. For her, you forget the most sacred duties, even your wife. Every evening you go out to drown yourself in beer and tobacco smoke, instead of staying quietly at home and savoring placid joys in the bosom of the family."

That last expression, in the wife's mouth, was, I must say, deeply steeped in exaggeration. Indeed, take a mahogany table and put it in the center of a dining room. Around the circumference, place two people, a man and a woman, devoting themselves on the table-top in the savant strategies of a game of dominoes. Even add to that luxurious picture a suspension lamp and an alabaster globe—that would never be sufficient to constitute a "bosom of a family," even reduced to its simplest expression.

No, a "bosom of the family"—the reader will grant me that abridged expression—cannot be circumscribed by such narrow limits.

Our Strasbourgian wife was therefore wrong to make use of phrases whose meaning she misunderstood so greatly. To that incontestable error she added the even graver one of needlessly provoking her husband. The denouement was easy to foresee.

"You're quite determined not to give me my dead weight?" said the husband, with a frightful calmness.

"You shan't go out this evening, I swear."

"That's all right. I'll say adieu, then, and forever." So saying, he headed for the window and opened it wide.

"You can go to Hell—I shan't come to look for you!" cried the wife, delighted by such an unexpected outcome.

"Hell will be for you; I'm going to Heaven. Adieu."

With those prophetic words, he stepped over the window sill and took off.

Palpitating with joy and triumphant intoxication, his wife followed him with her eyes. As he was passably voluminous, his body, twirling, rose into the night with a prodigious rapidity.

Soon, a beautiful white cloud, similar to those which once bore the gods of mythology, hid him from the eyes of his spouse. Legend reports that in the air, two thousand meters above sea level, he encountered a band of malefactors of the worst species, whom the Strasbourgian courts had sent to expiate their crimes in interplanetary space. He joined them.

It is said that every night, the group of excommunicates in question, descends to earth again—no one knows exactly how—with a pack of dogs collected here and there in the clouds, and carries out terrible reprisals on the society that had shown them mercy.

XI

Here is another story of a very different character. I repeat it only to give the reader a glimpse of the thousand anomalies and bizarreries that arose from the strange existence that Meister Fult had created for his fellow citizens. A poet by the name of Shakespeare, who came into the world a few centuries later, has transported the touching idyll in question to the English stage, while modifying it considerably and, of course, adapting it to the mores and atmospheric conditions of his own time.

If my own tale—the only authentic one, after all, the sole original—will not be to the taste of the majority of readers of have read Shakespeare, I can at least console myself with the thought that it will remain a document precious for the history of the theater.[42]

The scene represents a country house with a garden outside the gate of the Hospital. A road passes by. It is night.

Romeo arrives "heavily" (we know why). Looking at the garden wall: "Can I go any further, since my heart is here? Back, terrestrial mass, and find your center." He throws his dead weight over the wall, which the atmospheric pressure allows him to scale easily. Then, picking up his dead weight again, he advances as far as the windows of Juliet's apartment.

Juliet appears at the window: "How cam'st thou hither? The orchard walls are high and difficult to climb. Oh, if any of my kinsmen find thee here!"

Romeo: "With the light wings of atmospheric pressure did I o'erperch these walls. A nail seeks another nail. What Archimedes' principle can do, amour dares to attempt."

Juliet: "I am afraid, dear Romeo. I hear a noise in the kennels. 'Tis Medor waking up. Since his brother, in a mo-

---

[42] Author's note: "Those of my readers who find some obscurity in this scene are requested to reread their Shakespeare. Perhaps, by meditation thereon...."

ment of merriment, broke his chain and was carried into the sky, the wicked animal no longer sleeps. I would have thee gone, Romeo, and yet no further than a wanton's bird, who lets it hop little from her hand, like a poor prisoner in his twisted gyves, and with a silk thread plucks it back again. Oh, if thou couldst be my bird! But your dead weight!"

Romeo, excitedly: "Let that not hold. I shall throw it up. Seize it in flight." He throws his dead weight. His body rises slowly into the air, and he is soon in Juliet's arms.

Romeo: "Oh, my dear Juliet, how glad I am. We shall be married, shall we not? Tell me where and when thou want'st the ceremony accomplished; I shall lay my dead weight at your feet, and a brand new chain, which I have made myself and with which I counted on surprising thee."

(We have forgotten to mention that Romeo was a lock-smith.)

Juliet, whose expression has darkened at her lover's words: "Our parents will never consent to our marriage. Thou knowest that I am promised to another. And then, that chain does not smile at me; it is so unpoetic. Listen: if thou canst, like me, renounce this fatal earth forever, before this hand seals another contract, before my loyal heart, become perfidious and treacherous, is given to another, the atmospheric pressure will have reckoned with us both. The clouds will be our nuptial bed, and our dead weights, abandoned down here, will inform our parents of the fate that we have chosen."

Romeo, enthusiastically: "Oh, yes, Juliet, let us quit this Hell. Let us rise above the rest of mortals, even if we must perish. Let us breathe on high a rarer, purer air. Our love will soar triumphant over the gilded crests of the clouds. Then we shall go ever higher, ever higher, and we shall spend our honeymoon in the star itself..."

Juliet, interrupting: "Oh, no, let us not go to the moon, the inconstant moon, whose disk changes every month, for fear that thy love might become as variable. But here comes the day; I hear the lark uttering its raucous notes. Let's depart, let's flee, the dawn will guide us in the heavens. Go, window, let the daylight enter and our lives emerge."

Romeo and Juliet have climbed on to the window-ledge. Their silhouettes, confused in a kiss, are gracefully outline in the embrasure. After bidding one last adieu to the earth, they launch themselves smoothly into space. For a long time, one sees them bathed in the blonde light, swayed by the whim of the wind beneath the blue firmament. The rise, further and further, and end up disappearing into the heavens.

XII

The Fult Constitution functioned for two months, gradually undermined by the successive discovery of its faults. The most brilliant epoch of its reign scarcely lasted a fortnight. Decadence then set in, rapid, profound and irremediable. Those who had been the first to exalt and laud its advantages were also the first to identify its inconveniences, to take possession of the slightest quibbles in order to magnify them into monstrous grievances.

Bossuet has said, in speaking of the Constitution of the Egyptians: "Among such good laws, the best things of all is that everyone was nourished in the spirit of their observation." It is quite probable that that statement escaped the illustrious writer in a moment of distraction and that he never took a very exact account of what it meant. For, considered from that point of view, the Fult Constitution, which a two month trial was sufficient to overturn, might pass for the sovereign of Constitutions. Indeed, not only was everyone nourished in the spirit of its laws, but imbued, penetrated and saturated by the fundamental element of the Constitution. And yet, it was precisely that fact that killed it. Slowly, gradually, people came to doubt its virtues—until, finally, the boldest dared to complain out loud, waving their fists at the sky…and the storm burst.

It is necessary not to forget, moreover, that we are here in the presence of an important question of pathological physiology.

The atmospheric conditions had introduced profound modifications into the temperament of the entire population. The condensed air, in being introduced into the organs of respiration, disturbed the regular functioning of the lungs. Plants too had infinite difficulty in aspiring the carbon dioxide distributed in the air by animal combustion, and the atmosphere was gradually vitiated. The miasmas and all the fetid exhalation that condensed there with varying degrees of rapidity ended up engendering cruel epidemics, not to mention that the suppression of evaporation and cutaneous transpiration were already causing grave maladies.

The Strasbourgians, therefore, were floating in a nauseating atmosphere, which slowly soured them, mentally as well as physically. Nutrition deteriorated, sensitivity increased—as one can judge from the scene involving Romeo and Juliet. A few brains incapable of supporting the excessive air pressure gradually relaxed; mental illnesses became manifest.

To the physical causes that were acting upon organisms directly were added mental causes drawn from the unexpected, in the strangeness of the phenomena of which the Strasbourgians were victims. A great physician has said in a thesis on *Névrosisme*: "In every century, as soon as an idea is sown in the human species, and becomes a general passion, a new life for a society, nervous states multiply in a frightening manner. It is the time when philosophers play the game of praising by opposition the virtues, the calm and placid health of the man of the fields—or, even better, the uncivilized man. It is the time when physicians see convulsive epidemic appearing, the kinds of monomania that carry away entire nations, which produce the same dreads, the same hallucinations and the same follies in a thousand places."[43]

It was something absolutely analogous that was happening in Strasbourg.

---

[43] The obsolete French medical term *névrosisme* referred to a tendency to negative emotions that would nowadays be called "depression." The "quotation" is a fake.

In spite of Fult's sage prescriptions, the city, after two months, had become a veritable pandemonium. Religious beliefs had collapsed, dragging morality down in their fall. And then, the devout old women, in order to gladden their hearts, predicted all the scourges of which God is accustomed to make use in negotiating with his creatures: plague, famine, deluge, and the abomination of desolation. There were ecstatics, hallucinated individuals, convulsionaries, stigmatics—in brief, the entire series of visionaries surged forth as if by enchantment from the bosom of oblivion. Miracles burst forth and multiplied with an amazing rapidity, to the great amazement of the Strasbourgian female population, which had never seen such a feast.

That state of affairs could not last, however. Life had become Hellish. Change was necessary, at all costs. The notables of the city assembled. After a brief deliberation, a deputation was sent to the burgomeister with a mission to discuss with him the measures to take the remedy the evil.

Since the accident that had befallen him, the poor burgomeister no longer left his room, for fear of running head first into the thousand complications that the atmospheric pressure generated every day. He spent his life in alternative states of somnolence and pandiculation.

The notables found him sprawled in his armchair in front of the hearth, where a formidable fire was blazing. The room was as hot as a Turkish bath. They sat down around him and the debate began—but the frightful heat that reigned in the room seemed to have afflicted all brains with sterility.

After an hour consumed in fruitless deliberations, the burgomeister declared that he was falling asleep, and the discussion was adjourned until the following day. The notables stood up and were about to withdraw when one of them, considering the chairs that they had just quit, uttered an exclamation.

"Look!" he said. "Has the burgomeister put lead in his chairs in order to keep them tranquil? At home, it's sufficient to abandon one without additional weight to see it float up to the ceiling."

"In our homes too," exclaimed his colleagues—and they approached the chairs in order to examine them more carefully. They were no heavier than ordinary chairs, and the burgomeister affirmed that he had not subjected them to any special preparation.

There was a scientist among the notables. He walked around the chairs for a few moments, scratched his head, and suddenly shouted: "We're saved!"

"What? How?" said his colleagues, surrounding him solicitously.

Then the scientist, wanting to augment his importance and keep his secret, addressed the burgomeister in a solemn tone. "Burgomeister," he said, "great evils require great remedies. Cut down all the trees in the suburbs and make an immense heap of them—the bigger the better. Strip the hills of wood, depopulate the forests if necessary, and when everything is ready, let me know."

With those words, the scientist went out majestically, leaving all his colleagues in the most profound perplexity.

XIII

The scientist's instructions were carried out with an extraordinary promptitude. In less than a week, a prodigious quantity of felled trees was gathered into immense pyres in all the public squares in the city.

The scientist had them transported into the vast plains outside the fortifications and divided into four heaps, which were deposited at the four cardinal points.

Finally, when everything was ready, he summoned the entire population to the Place d'Armes at six o'clock in the evening.

"My dear citizens," he shouted, in the midst of the most profound silence, "I promised to deliver you from the scourge that has been weighing upon your existence for two months.

Today, I shall keep my promise. My means are quite simple. The phenomenon of which we are suffering the sad consequences is due to a mechanical compression that science cannot explain.

"The accumulation of vital forces that has condensed our atmosphere doubtless corresponds to a diminution in some other part of the globe. Fortunately, there is a powerful, energetic remedy that I have ended up discovering. Air dilates under the effect of heat. So, set fire to the four pyres that I have had built outside the city. The enormous heat that will be developed will doubtless be sufficient to triumph over the resistance of the phenomenon, and in an hour, we shall return to the normal conditions of pressure. I have spoken."

A formidable hurrah greeted the scientist's welcome speech, and the entire people, like an angry sea, ran to the pyres. Half an hour later, the city seemed to be surrounded by a vast ring of flames. An immense glare illuminated the Valley of Munster and colored the sky with ruddy reflections.[44]

Throughout the city and in the suburbs the temperature rose to fifty degrees.

The people waited, palpitating with emotion.

The dilated layers of air finally yielded. Soon, the sky seemed to be constellated with black dots, which grew visibly. The cadavers of dogs and cats, dank laundry and a heap of other objects were not long delayed in raining down on Strasbourg, greeted by the triumphant cries of the population.

A black cloud that had been floating above the place for some time suddenly burst. From its turn flanks the bewildered crowd saw an opaque mass suddenly emerge, shaped like a ship. The somber vessel descended slowly to the ground. When it was no more than two hundred meters away, a lightning-bolt departed from its bosom, outlining it clearly in the

---

[44] Author's note: "This was the origin of the famous aurora borealis recorded at that date in the archives of the Paris Observatory."

night. A man was seen standing on the deck, raising his arms to the heavens.

A frightful detonation rent the air.

Where the vessel had been there was no longer anything but a vaporous cloud which rose tranquilly back into the sky.

Only the burgomeister understood

He made the sign of the cross and whispered: "May God have mercy on his soul!"

XIV

A few months after these events, strange rumors circulated in Strasbourg. The disappearance of Meister Fult had finally been noticed; no one knew how to explain it. A few vague words let slip by the burgomeister, left inconsolable by the cooking of his finger, put the searchers on the track. After wandering for a long time in the field of conjectures, they arrived at clearly define conclusions: it really was Meister Fult who had governed them for two months, by means of Archimedes' principle; and it was really him, too, who had been standing on the deck of the vessel at the moment when it exploded.

At that time, there was a scholar living in Strasbourg by the name of Lese, of whom it was perfidiously insinuated one day that his name was an anagram of the word "Esel," which means "donkey." From then on the unfortunate man spent his life scrutinizing the names of his fellows, with the sole purpose of discovering ridiculous and humiliating anagrams.

The name of Fult was on all lips. The scholar took possession of it, and ended up discovering that the name was simply an anagram of the word "luft," which signifies "air."

237

A MECHANICAL COUPLE

A Neurodynamic Study

> *Human actions are always comprised, logically,*
> *by their own energy and that of other individuals*
> *acting upon it and modifying it.*
> Holbach

> *Man is the muscular part of humankind,*
> *woman is the nervous part.*
> Dr. Halley[45]

I

Monsieur Plombart, the good Monsieur Plombart—he was never called anything else in the neighborhood—with his strange build, his white face with icteric reflections, and his jerky gait, was quite simply a maniac of the worst kind.

There was a spring, a mechanism, in that plump fellow who skipped lightly along the Rue Montorgueil every morning on the way to his office. Always on the move, always agitated, his body was obedient to an unknown motive force that originated within his thoracic walls, from which it radiated outwards to all his extremities.

It is understandable, in consequence, that mania, tics and all manner of nervous bizarreries would find in him a marvelously predisposed subject.

---

[45] It seems unlikely that Edmond Halley ever made such an observation, and none of the French writers named Halley featured in the Bibliothèque Nationale catalogue seems a plausible candidate. The quote from the Baron d'Holbach, however, is fully in tune with his writings and probable genuine.

In the fifty years that Monsieur Plombart had been in the world, however, that tendency to automatism had remained latent in him and had not manifested itself in any external disorder. Thus, it could easily be anticipated, that when circumstances lent themselves to it, it would burst forth one day abruptly, unexpectedly, and all the more terrible because of the accumulation of the subject's pernicious energies during those long years of persistent concentration.

That is, in fact, what happened, and this is how.

That day, Monsieur Plombart, having dined copiously, as usual, had slumped into the arms of his dear armchair, lit his dear pipe and plunged into the smoke and dreams while gazing fondly at his dear little wife, who was leaning over beneath the lamp, reading a novel.

Everything was, in fact, "dear" to the good Monsieur Plombart, and that tender vocable, with which he saturated his speech, was scarcely sufficient to the outflow of his exuberant affectivity. The diminutive epithet with which he gratified his wife did not displease her, moreover, for she was at least twenty years younger than him, and that notable disproportion of age lent the husband in all their relations, a semi-paternal character, which—I hasten to add—only contributed to sweeten them and embellish existence.

In consequence, the Plombarts' was a model household, and could serve as an example to the whole neighborhood.

So, they were both sitting there, very tranquil and perfectly silent, the wife reading and the husband watching her read.

She was truly charming thus, with her little fingers buried in the icy pages, her expression serious, her eyes moving feverishly from left to right and from right to left in order to follow the sinuosity of the lines, and her lips sometimes sketching an intelligent smile.

And as Monsieur Plombart was contemplating all that, an idea occurred to him: a strange idea, which was to be permanently disastrous for him. For poor Monsieur Plombart to have an idea was a significant event, for his brain was made up in such a fashion that ideas were immediately transformed there into willful resolutions, and resolutions into fatal and stubborn determinations, and if it was a desire that came to him in that form, it was necessary for it to be immediately followed by the object of the desire.

Now, the idea that had occurred to Monsieur Plombart was indeed, a desire—and guess what it was.

Seeing that reading rendered his wife so gracious, he wondered if it might not suit him as well as it befit her.

That idea has no sooner seen the light in his mind than, in conformity with its principles, he formulated it aloud.

"Tell me, my dear little wife, what if I were to read too?"

His dear little wife, whom he had disturbed in the middle of the most beautiful passage—a scabrous passage, no doubt—first formed a very precise pout, and then, with a feverish twitch, elevated her nose.

I must admit that Monsieur Plombart possessed none of the fabric of a reader of novels; he had neither the qualities not the defects of one. As the defects are always acquired more easily than the qualities, however, Monsieur Plombart's abrupt resolution ought to have inspired serious anxieties in his wife.

It is not with impunity that, at the age of fifty, after having spent half one's existence dreaming and smoking in an armchair, one can constrain one's brain to assimilate on a daily basis several kilograms of intensive and truculent prose invented by Messieurs Monpépin & Co.[46] I am quite certain, for my own count, that unless one has a privileged organism, the quotidian consumption of such productions is bound to have fatal repercussions on the intellectual faculties.

---

[46] Xavier de Montépin was, along with Ponson du Terrail, one of the most prolific feuilletonistes of the Second Empire; the deliberate transformation of his name into "Monpépin" is a joke, *pépin* signifying, literally, a pip, and metaphorically, a snag or a whim (or an umbrella, although that is presumably irrelevant in this instance.).

But that day, destiny was to be accomplished, and Madame Plombart did not make all these reflections.

A slight cloud, however, passed over her face.

She thought that during those long evenings of reading and silence that had nailed Monsieur Plombart to his armchair, she alone had filled the mind of the dear man; she instinctively felt him fixing his eyes upon her, watching out for the slightest quiver of her physiognomy, and involuntarily reproducing in his own features the various expressions that reading gave hers. And as Madame Plombart was as much of a coquette as a woman can be at thirty, the thought of henceforth being deprived of that petty worship was painful. Nevertheless, that small egotistical impulse did not last long before the determined expression of Monsieur Plombart, who had already stood up and was running his feverish hands over the shelves of hr bookcase.

"Do as you like, my love," she said, in a deliberate voice. And she lowered her eyes with the air of a woman for whom every one of her husband's caprices was proof of an infallible genius and an irrevocable decision.

After a few minutes of searching, Monsieur Plombart came to sit down at the table beside his wife, and opened before her the voluminous works of Ponson du Terrail.

There followed one of those solemn silences which, in nature, precede great catastrophes, important transformations of matter, or secret evolutions of vital fluid—in before, the spontaneous explosion of some force that has thus far remained occult and unknown.

The muse of fiction had just seized Monsieur Plombart by the hair and dragged him, terrified, palpitating and sweating through the hair-raising adventures of Rocambole. His temples were beating feverishly, his skin was dry and warm, and he was holding himself rigid in his chair as if to concentrate his strength and combat the emotion that had taken possession of him.

It was at that moment that the mysterious organic process occurred within his body whose consequences were to be so deadly for the happiness of the household. To begin with he felt singular pricking sensations in his limbs, doubtless due to a titillation of the nervous papillae; then all the molecules of his being were subject to an intense vibratory movement, and the potential energy[47] developed by that change of state was translated by a slight trepidation of his lower limbs.

Finally, the active calorific forces that had sought to localize or burst forth at some point in the body suddenly passed into the state of sensible energy, and…a strange phenomenon was seen to manifest itself under the table.

Monsieur Plombart, who was utterly adrift in the twists and turns of his novel, drew his right leg back toward him, mechanically, and slowly lifted the heel; his metatarsus remained motionless momentarily, supported on the extremity of the toes. Then the neurosis that had been fermenting for years in that bilious body was suddenly unleashed with an incredible violence. Something like an electric shock passed through his motor nerves; a regular tremor progressively took hold of the heel, and then the entire foot—and in less than a second, isochronic oscillations of a frightening rapidity invaded the entire crural region.

The mechanical element had just irrupted into the household.

Five minutes passed thus, and then Madame Plombart suddenly raised an anxious and tormented forehead. For some moments already, it had seemed to her, regular taps succeeding one another rapidly had been audible under the table.

Without seeming to be doing anything, she had darted an oblique glance at her husband, seated to her left. O terror! She had seen his right leg moving dementedly, like the piston-rod of a steam engine. Recovering from her consternation, she had resumed reading, thinking that it was only a temporary crisis,

---

[47] Author's note: "Consult for this passage recent works on the *Théorie mécanique de la chaleur.*" The mechanical theory of heat was developed in France by Sadi Carnot in the 1820s

but the minutes had passed without bringing any change to the condition of the unfortunate limb.

An explanation was absolutely necessary.

"What's happening to you, my dear," she said, in a compassionate voice pierced by a hint of irony. "You're quivering under the chair like a wobbly grindstone."

"What?" said Monsieur Plombart, whose knee immediately ceased to function. "I think you're dreaming."

"It's you who's dreaming…with your leg."

"Eh? My leg! What's wrong with it?"

"Good! Now you're pretending that you don't know what it's about."

"May I be skinned alive if I know what you want me to say."

And that St. Vitus' dance that seized you just now—that was nothing?"

"Bah! You're frightening me. Have I been afflicted without knowing it by St. Vitus' dance?"

"Come on! I can see that reading troubles your imagination. I hope this warning will be sufficient for you, and that you won't start again."

Monsieur Plombart uttered a sigh accompanied by a slight shrug of the shoulders and plunged back into his gripping reading.

A minute later, the mechanical current was reestablished, and the leg recommenced its horrific movement.

This time, Madame Plombart darted a gaze charged with the most wrathful flames at her husband, and rapped her little hand on the table.

"Decidedly, you're becoming intolerable. Is it an illness that you've contracted?"

"Calm down, darling; I don't know what can have provoked your ill humor to that extent, but we'll talk about it in a moment. There's a chapter here that I absolutely must finish. In two minutes, I'll be yours."

"But this can't go on; there's no means of reading two words in succession, let alone comprehending them: your continual trembling is giving me vertigo."

"Vertigo!" repeated Monsieur Plombart, as if from the depths of a dream—for he had already picked up the thread of his story and given free rein to the disorderly frolics of his leg.

Madame Plombart, seeing that there was no means of making him listen to reason, slammed her book shut and got ready to go into the bedroom.

That abrupt action had more effect on our man than all the remonstrations in the world, for, similar in that respect to other mortals, he was a humble slave of habit. He hastened to finish his chapter and went to join his wife.

That evening, the Plombarts went to bed without saying goodnight to one another and went to sleep after having reciprocally opposed their dorsal regions. A worthy prologue to a drama that was to have such a lugubrious denouement!

II

The next morning, Madame Plombart was very sullen, and her bad mood became gradually worse as the day went by. One could easily have believed that her nervous susceptibility increased in inverse proportion to the height of the sun above the horizon. The development of that agitation was, however, merely due to the multiple worries that were gnawing at her.

First of all, she had had a frightful nightmare during the night.

She had seen her husband's pale leg swinging majestically in the void, and God knows what a hideous appearance it was! One might have taken it for an artificial leg escaped from a museum of anatomy. Through the transparent skin she perceived brown nerves as thick as the strings of a double bass, horrible dilated red veins, tensed and bloody muscles. All of that confused entanglement was writhing, prey to frightful spasms. The leg was subject to galvanic twitches, and independently of its own movement, another force was making it go up and down in mid-sir, with enormous bounds. Suddenly—a horrible thing to say—it assumed a horizontal position and came down with lightning rapidity on Madame Plombart's knees. Suffocated, she seized the rigid limb and desperately hurled it into the abyss.

It was at that moment that Monsieur Plombart, who was having less spicy dreams, detached a vigorous kick at a little dog that had launched itself at his legs with evident maleficent intentions.

Furthermore, Madame Plombart had recently read a popular medical textbook, and during the day the blackest ideas had been running through her head. She wondered whether the pernicious tic that her husband had just contracted might be the commencement of a terrible malady called locomotive ataxia, which is characterized by the incoherence and uncoordination of movements.

Evening finally arrived.

Dinner was scarcely concluded when Monsieur Plombart went in quest of his dear Rocambole—for he was already dearer than anything in the world—and, having opened it with tender precaution, he started on a new chapter.

Madame Plombart had sat down at the table with a painful apprehension, and, her mind concentrated in dolorous anticipation, she saw the lines filing before her eyes without understanding a word.

She did not have to wait for long.

A scarcely appreciable time had gone by when the limb was already going at full tilt. This time, however, to complete the desolation, it was not only the leg that as on the move, but also the table; the mechanical force had just found a point of application.

The table, it must be said, was excessively mobile; the slightest pressure was sufficient to imprint a sensible movement on it, and its castors lent themselves with a remarkable facility to the most capricious evolutions.

The room that had once been so calm and peaceful then offered a curious spectacle. Under the action of Monsieur

Plombart's muscular trepidation and the weight of his body, the table was slowly displaced, drawing with it the lamp and the two books, to the great despair of Madame Plombart, who made vain efforts to neutralize her husband's mechanical effects. The later, when he sensed the vision of the lines becoming confused, and could not incline his body any further, stopped, and instinctively drew his armchair closer. Then, when he had reestablished a normal distance between the table and himself, the same performance recommenced. In that fashion they circled the room several times, the table always fleeing before them and, so to speak, escaping from their hands.

After an hour of that promenade, Madame Plombart, exhausted, renounced reading once again and got up to go to bed, followed by Monsieur Plombart, ever faithful to his habits.

The game was not won, however.

It is now an oft-repeated commonplace to say that weak souls are more easily excited than others on great occasions, and that they are capable of drawing from difficult circumstances a courage and an energy directly proportional to the situations that give birth to them.

Madame Plombart was endowed with exactly that kind of eminently inflammable temperament. Desperation inspired her, and she went to sleep on one of the greatest resolutions that the mind of a woman has ever embraced.

The rising sun found her, the next morning, bent over a large book. It was a treatise on Mechanics, in which she hoped, not without reason, to find a means of combating her husband's deplorable passion, or at least of attenuating its effects.

So there she was, launched into the study of resultants and components. It was an occasion, if ever there was one, to say that misfortune is sometimes good, since Monsieur Plombart's baneful monomania was worth one more fervent adept to science. Sustained by the ardent desire she had to be able soon to oppose her knowledge to the poor maniac's insensate aberrations, Madame Plombart made rapid progress in a matter of days. Nevertheless, a blunder very pardonable in a woman of thirty venturing for the first time on to the arid terrain of science immediately caused her to commit a singular error.

One of the fundamental principles of statics had had an impact on her, and she had resolved to base her system of resistance upon it. That principle was formulated, approximately, in these terms: *Two equal and opposite forces applied to an invariable straight line maintain equilibrium.*

After having elaborated the meaning of those words, she thought that she would be able to apply that law in her own case, considering as the invariable straight line a diameter passing on a horizontal plane through the table, the two extremities of which were occupied by herself and her adversary. As his pressure caused the table to deviate to the left, she, facing him, would cause it to deviate to the right, thus restoring equilibrium.

Believing that all the conditions of the theorem were adequately fulfilled, and proud in advance of her success, she was only occupied thereafter with putting her plan into execution. In truth, that was not easy.

Until now, in fact, they had always remained at the table sitting beside one another. What would Monsieur Plombart say when she wanted to sit down facing him? She dared not begin the struggle so overtly.

It was, therefore, necessary to temporize and arrive slowly, by insensible degrees, at the desired change of position.

In all the little combats that she had to deliver in order to occupy that place, Madame Plombart showed her utter superiority. No general ever deployed more talent and skill in the presence of the enemy. All her slight retreats were cleverly planned, artfully executed and masked by the most delicate maneuvers.

Her entire feminine intelligence was absorbed by the solemn goal that she was pursing. So, for a long time, she had no

longer been reading, even though her book—a strategic resource—always remained open in front of her. Her mind had
changed direction, and her immense passion for reading had
easily ceded before considerations more closely related to the
cold realities of life. Sometimes, when she thought about her
former happiness and insouciance, hot tears rose to her eyes;
the memory of the irrevocable past, which, for so many years,
had brought her every evening beneath the radiant lamp and
framed her husband in the armchair made her heart ache, but,
with a view to a better future, she immediately suppressed
those heart-rending and egotistical emotions.

Madame Plombart devoted twelve days—or, rather,
twelve evenings—to the demi-circumnavigation of the table.
On the twelfth evening she was enthroned, replete with innocent impassivity, facing her husband, whose leg did not take
long to give the signal for the battle. Under the action of the
latter, the table, at first, deviated to the left. Madame Plombart
immediately set to work. But, O prestige, the mysterious item
of furniture, solicited by those two forces, only turned more
easily, and Monsieur Plombart's leg seemed to relish the
game, redoubling its velocity and fury.

Madame Plombart, completely at a loss, bewildered and
sweating copiously from the efforts she had made, was forced
once again to beat a retreat.

The next day, she realized that her precipitation had
caused her to commit a gross error. The most important part of
the theorem had escaped her: the two forces, in order to come
into equilibrium, had to operate in the same direction as the
straight line by which they were linked. The principle, given
that, was no longer applicable to the case in hand.

In order better to take account of her error she drew a
circle on the table with a horizontal diameter, and then represented the two forces as tangents commencing at the two ex-
tremes of the diameter and orientated in opposite directions.
She understood immediately what had happened the previous
evening. Having, in addition, consulted a book in order to ver-
ify her observations, she perceived that the forces, such as

they had been applied, constituted a "couple," which, by its very nature could only have the unique resultant and effect of rotating about its axis the straight line to which it was applied.

All these considerations, in combination, convinced Madame Plombart not to attempt anything else until she had read the treatise in its entirety. She thought, with reason, that the complete possession of all the secrets of science would enable her to avoid henceforth fruitless attempts that might be fatal.

That long and arid study lasted three whole months, during which Monsieur Plombart's mania put down profound roots.

As the poor man's neurosis was accentuated, and the tic seemed to be grafted on to his existence, his character soured, his habitual joviality diminishing. His gestures became more frequent and more angular; in brief, a new element seemed to have been introduced into his organism, gradually mingling its functions with the others and disturbing them sensibly.

While he was reading, gusts of warmth were suddenly manifest in his brain; he saw the fugitive images of the characters in his novel surged forth between the pages of the book. All of that moved, agitated and twitched before him, leaping into his head and disturbing his intellect horribly. Then his leg twitched too, tetanic convulsions seizing him; it was necessary to give them free rein.

The poor fellow, his head fixed between his two meta-carpals, the entire weight of his body borne on his cubital extremities, cased his knee to vibrate, gently pushing the table before him, thus forgetting himself in the vague bewilderment of his mechanical ardor. There was even, perhaps, in that apparent brutalization, a certain sensation of veiled sensuality, originating from the unconscious comparison that he made between his relative repose with the slow and smooth movement of the table, which glided beneath him.

O sensation! Where will you take refuge?

The great day arrived, however, when Monsieur Plombart's quietude was to receive a terrible blow.

Madame Plombart was now strong enough to give pointers to the most eminent mathematician. Statics no longer had any secrets from her. She no longer dreamed about anything but moments, intensities and centers of gravity, and nothing equaled, in her eyes, the virtues of the parallelepiped of forces and the parallelogram of rotations.

This time, it was with an art and a science verging on the prodigious that Madame Plombart organized her plan. Having measured the table and all the distances that were relevant to her problem, she drew a diagram on a piece of paper, with the aid of a ruler, representing the forces and their resultants. In brief, Madame Plombart's plan was based on the theorem that two parallel forces acting in the same direction and linked by an invariable straight line have a resultant equal to their sum, which is parallel to them, acting in the same direction, and dividing the straight line into two parts inversely proportional to their intensities.

Now, Monsieur Plombart pushing the table at one point in one direction, Madame Plombart pushing it at an opposite point in a parallel direction, the two forces acted in the same direction, and, if they could be considered equal, ought to divide the diameter into two equal parts. The table would then move in that direction. Then, it only remained to cancel out the resultant by the imposition of some resistance at a fixed point in that trajectory.

But what?

It was at this point that Madame Plombino gave evident proof of her genius. She arranged the table in such a way that one of its legs would follow the direction of its displacement. At a certain distance from the table she nailed a little piece of wood ten centimeters long and three centimeters high to the floor. It was obvious then that, when the table-leg arrived at that point, it would be stopped by the obstacle, and the table would no longer move.

It was all the more marvelous because, in giving the piece of wood a width of ten centimeters, Madame Plombart was simply playing the part of errors in calculation; thanks to that precaution, in fact, an error of less than nine or ten centimeters could not compromise the success of her enterprise.

Sure in advance of success this time, Madame Plombart manifested a hectic cheerfulness at diner, which Monsieur Plombart dared not criticize aloud, but nevertheless thought slightly out of place, not knowing to what to attribute it.

When the meal was over, Madame Plombart placed the armchair herself in the respective positions they were to occupy.

The struggle commenced.

The table, ceding initially to Monsieur Plombart's efforts, started moving. Immediately, Madame Plombart pushed in the same direction, and the docile item of furniture made its way gently toward the point at which it was to run aground.

The action thus commenced in perfect conditions, and Madame Plombart, full of self-confidence, carefully refrained from raising her nose above her book, in order not to give anything away.

The table had already traveled a meter when its foot encountered the piece of wood, without the slightest appreciable noise, and stopped dead.

Madame Plombart had difficulty suppressing a cry of triumph, but she contained herself, and observed her husband.

Although the poor fellow's head was still inclined over his book, he was no longer reading. His forehead furrowed, eyebrows twitching, nostril quivering, he was in the attitude of a man prey to an intense interior conflict. An attentive observer would have divined a dull and confused anger seething in his bosom.

Suddenly, without having turned his head, without having looked at his wife, he stood up, very pale, and with a calmness that denoted a stubborn and irrevocable resolution, he said:

"Either we cut this table in two and each of us can do with their own half whatever they like, or we separate his evening forever."

Then he stuck his hat on his head and went out.

Consternated, Madame Plombart had not said a word or made a gesture to retain him.

III

Early the next morning Monsieur Plombart came in carrying a saw and a plane borrowed from the carpenter who lived opposite. The table was sawn into two symmetrically equal parts, and each of the demi-circumferences retained three legs, thanks to which it maintained a perfect equilibrium.

That new mode of installation succeeded marvelously, and when evening came, it all worked out for the best. Monsieur Plombart, whose evolutions were considerably facilitated by virtue of the loss of weight that his vehicle had undergone, now traveled in all directions, amorously leaning over his demi-table, and not missing a single syllable of his novel in consequence.

Madame Plombart, retired into a corner with the segment that remained to her, watched her husband with an envious and almost sad gaze.

Something strange was happening within her.

Insensible to the powerful attractions that books had once offered her, she no longer saw anything but the contentment that blossomed on her husband's face, and one might have thought that she almost regretted remaining immobile now. It had had a powerful charm, that silent glide, when they had brought it about voluntarily, in order that Monsieur Plombart could take so much pleasure in it. Why should she not try to do the same, instead of condemning herself to a soporific idleness in her corner?

But no—that would render her ridiculous; perhaps Monsieur Plombart would even make fun of her.

And yet she had the right to act as she wished; her husband had explicitly conferred that privilege in the words he had pronounced the previous evening, to wit "each of us can do with their own half whatever they like."

What if she were to try? Whatever her husband might think or say to her, too bad! She had a whim to move a little, to do as he did, and she would do it, damn it!

With those reflections, Madame Plombart emerged from her corner, making her armchair and demi-table glide smoothly, and then, slowly, almost insensibly, as if obedient to an irresistible impulsion, she began gravitating around her husband.

Madame Plombart had been mechanized by influence.

Let the reader not lend to the word "mechanized" a vulgar sense that is far from my thinking. I am making use of it uniquely because its seems to me to characterize marvelously the phenomenon about which I want to talk, which does not yet have its place in pathological physiology, by virtue of its excessive rarity.

The case of morbid animal automatism, of neurotic mechanization that developed first in Monsieur Plombart as an effect of intense intellectual tension, and then in his wife by influence, I submit here to the physicians and philosophers who might one day corroborate these rudimentary data with personal observations, and enable science to take a further step forward on the path of enlightenment and progress.

The new phase into which we have seen the strange couple enter lasted for a week. Monsieur Plombart's mania had now attained its maximum intensity and confined madness. He imported even into his relations with society, and with external things, the irrefutable symptoms of his malady.

His gait had become more bizarre and eccentric than ever. It was a true torture for him to follow a straight line as he walked, and he avoided it as much as possible, taking roundabout routes everywhere, in no matter what circumstances. The broad streets of Paris, prolonged as far as the eye can see, with their tall houses, correctly aligned, got on his nerves. What he needed was tortuous little back streets describing curves and spirals from which one could no longer extricate oneself. He was particularly fond of the parabola, the ellipse, hemicyclical indentations, etc., and he could have wandered for entire days in a city combining those advantages. There was not a street corner that he did not have the desire to turn, not a public square of which he did not feel forced to make a tour; in brief, in every journey he made, whatever company he was in, always and everywhere, his invincible tendency to walk gyrostatically was manifest.

When he returned home in the evening he was always fatigued by virtue of having covered so much unnecessary ground, but that did not prevent him from propelling himself yet again around the room with his armchair and his fragment of table, and now that his wife was propelling herself too, in a more spacious orbit, the spectacle was no longer funny; it was pitiful; it was sickening.

Each retrenched behind a mahogany semi-circle, they glided solemnly around the room, drawing with them a confused retinue of objects, avoiding making contact, and ending up falling into a heavy slumber, provoked by the monotony of their glissades and the soft soporific effect of the lamp's radiance.

Meanwhile, Madame Plombart, finding that that kind of locomotion was not disagreeable, and that it did not prevent her from reading, had another of the sublime ideas that seemed to have sprouted within her since the study of mechanics had revealed her genius to her.

Now that we're in accord again, she said to herself, *why remain isolated like this? We could fit the two pieces of the table together again, and sit down facing one another as before. Our two forces would combine to form a rotatory movement, and everything would be even better.*

Having maturely weighed everything up, Madame Plombart thought the idea of that general reconciliation superb, and resolved to try it out on her husband that very evening.

As they both retired to the bedroom, she moved closer to him and, placing her plump little hand seductively on his shoulder, she said: "My darling."

"What can I do to be agreeable to you?" said Monsieur Plombart, in a perfectly natural tone.

"You're no longer annoyed, are you?"

"Me? Have I ever been, then?"

"Well..."

"Well what?"

"Well, what if we were to me reconciled? I mean, what if we were to fit the pieces of the table together again?"

Monsieur Plombart twitched an eyebrow in a fashion that indicated that the proposal did not cause him unlimited satisfaction.

Madame Plombart attempted to anticipate his objections.

"Oh, I can see what's stopping you. I thought as you did. But know that our reconciliation wouldn't prevent us at all from delivering ourselves to our little sentimental voyages. On the contrary—we'd have the pleasure of making them together, sitting facing one another. Our two equal forces, in combination, would transmit a rotatory movement to the table, which is the smoothest, the most delightful and the least fatiguing of movements."

"Ah!" said Monsieur Plombart, whose eyes widened at the prospect of a new kind of glissade. Anxiously, however, he added: "But what if you're mistaken? What if our two forces are no longer equal, and don't combine so easily?"

"I've thought of everything," replied Madame Plombino, triumphantly. "Listen carefully. Do you know what the parallelogram of rotation is?"

"No, do you?"

"Know, then, that rotations combine exactly like forces, following the law of the parallelogram—which is to say that if our table, by virtue of the inequality of our two forces, is solicited to rotate about two axes, it will rotate around an intermediate axis following the diagonal of the parallelogram constructed by the extrapolation of the two axes and proportional to the angular velocities of rotation. In sum, therefore, any inequality arising between our two forces will only tend to displace the axis of rotation, and in consequence, our table will not only be animated by a rotatory movement but also by a faint movement of translation that will fortunately break the monotony of the former, and will permit us, without making any effort, to explore successively all the corners of the room."

Monsieur Plombart remained open-mouthed before this sublime calculation. He had not understood a single word of it, but something told him that it must be marvelous, and he contemplated his wife while delivering his right arm to violent gyratory movements and tracing circles in the void in order better to penetrate what she was saying.

Seeing her success, Madame Plombart went on: "We would thus form a couple. Do you know what a couple is?"

"A couple? Yes, yes...who doesn't? A couple? Of course!"

"And we'll be able to measure our moment."

At this point a stupor mingled with alarm was painted in Monsieur Plombart's features. He could comprehend, strictly speaking, that the two of them formed a couple; he even recalled vaguely having learned something similar in grammar, but that they would be able to measure their moment surpassed his understanding. Couples measuring moments seemed to him to be something ferocious, thorny and monstrous.

Madame Plombart perceived the perplexity into which she had cast her husband, and wanted to enlighten him completely.

"You don't seem to grasp my meaning fully."

"Indeed...that is to say, I can see the couple but the moment escapes me somewhat, I must confess."

"Well, it simply means that if one takes the measure of couples as unity, the couple that has for force the unity of force, and for the arm of leverage the unity of length, the number that expresses the measure of any couple is equal to the product of the number that expresses the measure of the force, in units of force, multiplied by the number that expresses the measure of the arm of leverage, in units of length."

Monsieur Plombart tottered, as if seized by vertigo, stunned by the scientific volubility of his wife, who had just reeled all that off in a single breath.

"Only that!" he said, breathing noisily. And, fearing a further avalanche of the same caliber, he judged it prudent not to take his investigations any further.

He had just got undressed. An idea occurred to him suddenly. "I'd like to know who taught you all that!" he said.

"No one. I owe it entirely to myself. I've spent the last four months studying mechanics in depth."

Those words were like a revelation to Monsieur Plombart. He now had an explanation of the intelligent force that had been seeking surreptitiously during those four months to shackle his caprice.

But a malign and consoling idea immediately came to the fore: the efforts and perseverance of his wife had gone completely to waste, because she had now adopted his fantasy.

He had just placed his right foot on the edge of the bed.

The four months of his wife's study, the frightful difficulties that she had had to overcome, the patient persistence that she had had to deploy, and finally, the strange reversal that had taken place within her and had, so to speak, rendered all that labor and endeavor unnecessary, all passed through his mind like a flash of lightning, and provoked his good humor.

Then, one of those formidable burst of laughter that make the windows tremble seized him by the throat, and he writhed momentarily in a furious fit of nervous hilarity.

He was still laughing when a hideous contraction tugged at his facial muscles; the redness that had recently overtaken them turned successively to blue and green; the swollen veins designed gross protrusions on his skin.

Monsieur Plombart wanted to shout that he was choking.

He raised his two rigid arms in the air, and then fell face down on the bed, and nothing more could be heard than a stertorous respiration punctuated by convulsive coughs.

Madame Plombart launched herself toward him, crying: "My darling, my poor husband, in the name of Heaven, what's the matter?"

The next day, the concierge informed the whole neighborhood that Monsieur Plombart, the good Monsieur Plombart, had died of a devastating apoplexy.

SF & FANTASY

Adolphe Alhaiza. *Cybele*

Alphonse Allais. *The Adventures of Captain Cap*

Henri Allorge. *The Great Cataclysm*

Guy d'Armen. *Doc Ardan: The City of Gold and Lepers*

G.-J. Arnaud. *The Ice Company*

Charles Asselineau. *The Double Life*

Henri Austruy. *The Eupantophone; The Olotelepan; The Petitpaon Era*

Barillet-Lagargousse. *The Final War*

Cyprien Bérard. *The Vampire Lord Ruthwen*

S. Henry Berthoud. *Martyrs of Science*

Aloysius Bertrand. *Gaspard de la Nuit*

Richard Bessière. *The Gardens of the Apocalypse; The Masters of Silence*

Chevalier de Béthune. *The World of Mercury*

Albert Bleunard. *Ever Smaller*

Félix Bodin. *The Novel of the Future*

Louis Boussenard. *Monsieur Synthesis*

Alphonse Brown. *City of Glass; The Conquest of the Air*

Émile Calvet. *In a Thousand Years*

André Caroff. *The Terror of Madame Atomos; Miss Atomos; The Return of Madame Atomos; The Mistake of Madame Atomos; The Monsters of Madame Atomos; The Revenge of Madame Atomos; The Resurrection of Madame Atomos; The Mark of Madame Atomos; The Spheres of Madame Atomos; The Wrath of Madame Atomos* (w/M. & Sylvie Stéphan)

Félicien Champsaur. *The Human Arrow; Ouha, King of the Apes; Pharaoh's Wife; Homo-Deus; Nora, The Ape-Woman*

Didier de Chousy. *Ignis*

Jules Clarétie. *Obsession*

Michel Corday. *The Eternal Flame*

André Couvreur. *The Necessary Evil; Caresco, Superman; The Exploits of Professor Tornada* (3 vols.)

Captain Danrit. *Undersea Odyssey*

Camille Debans. *The Misfortunes of John Bull*

C. I. Defontenay. *Star (Psi Cassiopeia)*

Charles Derennes. *The People of the Pole*

Georges Dodds (anthologist). *The Missing Link*

Charles Dodeman. *The Silent Bomb*
Harry Dickson. *The Heir of Dracula; Harry Dickson vs. The Spider*
Jules Dornay. *Lord Ruthven Begins*
Alfred Driou. *The Adventures of a Parisian Aeronaut*
Sâr Dubnotal *vs. Jack the Ripper*
Odette Dulac. *The War of the Sexes*
Alexandre Dumas. *The Return of Lord Ruthven*
Renée Dunan. *Baal; The Ultimate Pleasure*
J.-C. Dunyach. *The Night Orchid; The Thieves of Silence*
Henri Duvernois. *The Man Who Found Himself*
Achille Eyraud. *Voyage to Venus*
Henri Falk. *The Age of Lead*
Paul Féval. *Anne of the Isles; Knightshade; Revenants; Vampire City; The Vampire Countess; The Wandering Jew's Daughter*
Paul Féval, *fils. Felifax, the Tiger-Man*
Charles de Fieux. *Lamékis*
Louis Forest. *Someone is Stealing Children in Paris*
Arnould Galopin. *Doctor Omega; Doctor Omega and the Shadowmen* (anthology)
Judith Gautier. *Isoline and the Serpent-Flower*
H. Gayar. *The Marvelous Adventures of Serge Myrandhal on Mars*
G.L. Gick. *Harry Dickson and the Werewolf of Rutherford Grange*
Delphine de Girardin. *Balzac's Cane*
Léon Gozlan. *The Vampire of the Val-de-Grâce*
Jules Gros. *The Fossil Man*
Edmond Haraucourt. *Illusions of Immortality; Daah, the First Human*
Nathalie Henneberg. *The Green Gods*
Eugène Hennebert. *The Enchanted City*
V. Hugo, P. Foucher & P. Meurice. *The Hunchback of Notre-Dame*
Romain d'Huissier. *Hexagon: Dark Matter*
Jules Janin. *The Magnetized Corpse*
Michel Jeury. *Chronolysis*
Gustave Kahn. *The Tale of Gold and Silence*
Gérard Klein. *The Mote in Time's Eye*
Fernand Kolney. *Love in 5000 Years*
Paul Lacroix. *Danse Macabre*
Louis-Guillaume de La Follie. *The Unpretentious Philosopher*
Jean de La Hire. *Enter the Nyctalope; The Nyctalope on Mars; The Nyctalope vs. Lucifer; The Nyctalope Steps In; Night of the Nyctalope; Return of the Nyctalope; The Fiery Wheel*
Etienne-Léon de Lamothe-Langon. *The Virgin Vampire*

André Laurie. *Spiridon*
Gabriel de Lautrec. *The Vengeance of the Oval Portrait*
Alain le Drimeur. *The Future City*
Georges Le Faure & Henri de Graffigny. *The Extraordinary Adventures of a Russian Scientist Across the Solar System* (2 vols.)
Gustave Le Rouge. *The Mysterious Doctor Cornelius* (3 vols.); *The Vampires of Mars; The Dominion of the World* (w/Gustave Guitton) (4 vols.)
Jules Lermina. *Mysteryville; Panic in Paris; To-Ho and the Gold Destroyers; The Secret of Zippelius; The Battle of Strasbourg*
André Lichtenberger. *The Centaurs; The Children of the Crab*
Listonai. *The Philosophical Voyager*
Jean-Marc & Randy Lofficier. *Edgar Allan Poe on Mars; The Katrina Protocol; Pacifica; Robonocchio; Return of the Nyctalope;* (anthologists) *Tales of the Shadowmen 1-11; The Vampire Almanac* (2 vols.)
Xavier Mauméjean. *The League of Heroes*
Joseph Méry. *The Tower of Destiny*
Hippolyte Mettais. *The Year 5865; Paris Before the Deluge*
Louise Michel. *The Human Microbes; The New World*
Tony Moilin. *Paris in the Year 2000*
José Moselli. *Illa's End*
John-Antoine Nau. *Enemy Force*
Marie Nizet. *Captain Vampire*
C. Nodier, A. Beraud & Toussaint-Merle. *Frankenstein*
Henri de Parville. *An Inhabitant of the Planet Mars*
Gaston de Pawlowski. *Journey to the Land of the 4th Dimension*
Georges Pellerin. *The World in 2000 Years*
Ernest Pérochon. *The Frenetic People*
Pierre Pelot. *The Child Who Walked on the Sky*
J. Polidori, C. Nodier, E. Scribe. *Lord Ruthven the Vampire*
P.-A. Ponson du Terrail. *The Vampire and the Devil's Son; The Immortal Woman*
Georges Price. *The Missing Men of the Sirius*
Edgar Quinet. *Ahasuerus; The Enchanter Merlin*
Henri de Régnier. *A Surfeit of Mirrors*
Maurice Renard. *The Blue Peril; Doctor Lerne; The Doctored Man; A Man Among the Microbes; The Master of Light*
Jean Richepin. *The Wing; The Crazy Corner*
Albert Robida. *The Adventures of Saturnin Farandoul; The Clock of the Centuries; Chalet in the Sky; The Electric Life*

J.-H. Rosny Aîné. *Helgvor of the Blue River; The Givreuse Enigma; The Mysterious Force; The Navigators of Space; Vamireh; The World of the Variants; The Young Vampire*
Marcel Rouff. *Journey to the Inverted World*
Léonie Rouzade. *The World Turned Upside Down*
Han Ryner. *The Superhumans; The Human Ant*
Pierre de Selenes: *An Unknown World*
Angelo de Sorr. *The Vampires of London*
Brian Stableford. *The New Faust at the Tragicomique;The Empire of the Necromancers (The Shadow of Frankenstein; Frankenstein and the Vampire Countess; Frankenstein in London); Sherlock Holmes & The Vampires of Eternity; The Stones of Camelot; The Wayward Muse.* (anthologist) *News from the Moon; The Germans on Venus; The Supreme Progress; The World Above the World; Nemoville; Investigations of the Future; The Conqueror of Death; The Revolt of the Machines; The Man With the Blue Face*
Jacques Spitz. *The Eye of Purgatory*
Kurt Steiner. *Ortog*
Eugène Thébault. *Radio-Terror*
C.-F. Tiphaigne de La Roche. *Amilec*
Simon Tyssot de Patot. *The Strange Voyages of Jacques Massé and Pierre de Mésange*
Louis Ulbach. *Prince Bonifacio*
Théo Varlet. *The Golden Rock. The Xenobiotic Invasion; The Castaways of Eros; Timeslip Troopers* (w/André Blandin); *The Martian Epic* (w/Octave Joncquel)
Pierre Véron. *The Merchants of Health*
Paul Vibert. *The Mysterious Fluid*
Villiers de l'Isle-Adam. *The Scaffold; The Vampire Soul*
Gaston de Wailly. *The Murderer of the World*
Philippe Ward. *Artahe ; The Song of Montségur* (w/Sylvie Miller) *Manhattan Ghost* (w/Mickael Laguerre)

MYSTERIES & THRILLERS

M. Allain & P. Souvestre. *The Daughter of Fantômas*
A. Anicet-Bourgeois, Lucien Dabril. *Rocambole*
A. Bernède. *Belphegor*; *Judex* (w/Louis Feuillade); *The Return of Judex* (w/Louis Feuillade); *The Shadow of Judex*
A. Bisson & G. Livet. *Nick Carter vs. Fantômas*

V. Darlay & H. de Gorsse. *Arsène Lupin vs. Sherlock Holmes: The Stage Play*

Séamas Duffy. *Sherlock Holmes in Paris*

Paul Féval. *Gentlemen of the Night; John Devil; The Black Coats ('Salem Street; The Invisible Weapon; The Parisian Jungle; The Companions of the Treasure; Heart of Steel; The Cadet Gang; The Sword-Swallower)*

Émile Gaboriau. *Monsieur Lecoq*

Goron & Émile Gautier. *Spawn of the Penitentiary*

Paul d'Ivoi. *Around the World on Five Sous* (w/Henri Chabrillat)

Rick Lai. *Shadows of the Opera: Retribution in Blood; Sisters of the Shadows: The Curse of Cagliostro*

Steve Leadley. *Sherlock Holmes: The Circle of Blood*

Maurice Leblanc. *Arsène Lupin vs. Countess Cagliostro; Arsène Lupin vs. Sherlock Holmes (The Blonde Phantom; The Hollow Needle); The Many Faces of Arsène Lupin; The Island of the Thirty Coffins; 813*

Gaston Leroux. *Chéri-Bibi; The Phantom of the Opera; Rouletabille & the Mystery of the Yellow Room; Rouletabille at Krupp's*

Richard Marsh. *The Complete Adventures of Judith Lee*

William Patrick Maynard. *The Terror of Fu Manchu; The Destiny of Fu Manchu*

Frank J. Morlock. *Sherlock Holmes: The Grand Horizontals; Sherlock Holmes vs Jack the Ripper*

Jean Petithuguenin. *The Adventures of Ethel King*

Antonin Reschal. *The Adventures of Miss Boston*

P. de Wattyne & Y. Walter. *Sherlock Holmes vs. Fantômas*

David White. *Fantômas in America*

Pierre Yrondy. *The Adventures of Thérèse Arnaud*

Victor Margueritte. *The Bacheloress; The Companion; The Couple*

www.ingramcontent.com/pod-product-compliance
Lightning Source LLC
Chambersburg PA
CBHW060346030726
47497CB00003B/620